The Trouble with Words

Suzie Tullett

Print ISBN 978-1-912175-43-7

A big thank you goes to Jeannette Prescott, a lovely lady who willingly relived her story to help me write mine. I'd also like to thank Linda Balis for advising me when it came to all things flora and fauna. If I didn't know anything about flowers before, I do now.
A massive thank you goes to everyone at Bombshell Books. It's been an absolute pleasure working with you all.
A very special thank you goes to Robert, my husband, whose unwavering support has made my writing journey possible. And to Adam and Ben, my reasons for writing to begin with.
Lastly, I'd like to say thank you to all you readers out there. When the going gets tough, you are the ones who keep me going.

ONE

Annabel checked her watch and groaned. She'd always had a problem with punctuality. No matter how hard she tried, how early she left the house, or even how fast she drove, she always seemed to be running late – a reality that had only gotten worse over the last couple of years. Despite any good intentions, it seemed even days like today weren't enough to get her act together. Then again, was it any wonder? Lost in her own thoughts most of the time, minutes often turned into hours without her even realising.

She dropped the car a gear as the brake lights in front turned red. 'Not that all this traffic seems to be helping any,' she said. 'Blooming Sunday drivers.'

Forced to come to a complete standstill, Annabel looked through her rear view mirror. With her car and theirs almost touching, she easily eyed the middle-aged couple sitting directly behind. Staring straight ahead, neither party exchanged a single word. Annabel assumed they were husband and wife, and thought it sad. She wondered if they'd always been that miserable together or if they'd simply woken up one morning and realised they had nothing left to say. Either way, she felt like going and banging their heads together. Some people didn't know they were born.

She couldn't bear to watch them any longer and diverting her attention, caught sight of a boy racer on the other side of the road. 'Now there's someone I'd definitely like to slap,' she said, her pulse quickening.

Annabel knew that under normal circumstances, he'd be beeping his horn and revving his engine by now. Drivers like him didn't care about anyone but themselves. This lad looked too shattered to create a fuss though and she guessed he was only just on his way home after a very heavy night out. He let out a long yawn and Annabel shuddered as he propped his elbow on the steering wheel so he could rest his head in his hand. She'd have put money on him still having alcohol in his system. *Selfish bastard!*

Refusing to let him get well and truly under her skin, Annabel began a more general look around, while telling herself it must be one of those days. No doubt most of it thanks to all this stopping and starting, but everyone in sight appeared as fed up as each other. Well not quite everyone, Annabel realised, her eyes happy to settle on one set of travellers in particular. Her heart began to melt. 'That's more like it.'

Continuing to watch them, she couldn't help but smile. Animatedly belting out a rendition of some song or other, the jolly family of three was certainly making the most out of their journey. Looking at the age of the tot strapped into the rear car seat, Annabel guessed it could only have been a nursery rhyme. Probably Eensy Weensy Spider, she thought, based on their accompanying actions, and with the tune instantly popping into her head, she felt tempted to join in.

She wondered if it was a sign, a message letting her know that despite the obvious concerns, she was still doing the right thing. She hoped so. At any rate, she couldn't help the warm glow settling in her tummy as she imagined the day in the not too distant future when she, too, would become a mother. She readily envisaged making a public show of herself in much the same way as the nearby trio. As far as Annabel was concerned, her little family was going to have as much fun as possible and at every available opportunity. Life was way too short for anything else.

The traffic began to move again, bringing Annabel back to the task at hand. 'Finally,' she said, at last shoving the car into gear and moving off. 'Maybe now I'll actually get there.'

Following the flow of vehicles, it never failed to surprise her how many people took themselves out and about at this time, as opposed to enjoying a Sunday morning lie in. Given a choice that's what she'd be doing. She and Tom would be propped up against their pillows right now, sipping on freshly brewed coffee while reading the papers. Something Annabel knew her husband would rather be doing too.

She pictured him pacing up and down as he awaited her arrival, telling herself he had to be used to her unfortunate time keeping by now. But, regardless of all the other road users, Annabel still couldn't excuse her lateness. She felt guilty and hated the thought of him simply hanging around on her account. Anxiously tapping her fingers on the steering wheel, she negotiated one road after another, and insisted that next time she really would do better.

At last, she spotted the church spire and, swinging her little car into the nearest parking space, she just as quickly hit the brakes, forcing her vehicle to a screeching halt. Emergency-stop complete, she took a second to compose herself. About to reveal the biggest news she'd had in a long time, the last thing she wanted to do was to make a hash of it.

She threw off her seat belt, and checked her watch again. 'Shit!' She jumped out of the car; even she hadn't realised she was that late. Unfortunately, this meant she now had to blooming well run and, sadly for any observers, her running had always been as bad as her being on time.

She grabbed a shopper and deckchair from the boot and hot-footed it along the path. However, struggling with the weight of her load, her foot seemed to catch and she almost fell. 'Jesus Christ!' she said. Tumbling forward, her heart leapt as she just about managed to keep her balance. 'Phew, that was close.'

Blushing, Annabel quickly glanced around. It would be just her luck to end up an unwitting participant on one of those TV mishap shows or worse still, an unsuspecting Internet sensation. Relieved to find that nobody or their camera had borne witness, she collected herself. She had enough to talk about this morning, without having to add a sprained ankle to the agenda. She pictured Tom's amused expression, had she been forced to limp towards him. He'd always said if anyone could trip over their own feet it was her. But it was alright for him, wasn't it? He'd never run behind schedule either.

Continuing on her way, she slowed her step a little so as not to stumble again and, for the first time in a while, took the opportunity to take in her surroundings. This was something she tended not to do these days. For one, she'd followed this route so often that she didn't need to. In fact, she could've done it blindfolded given the opportunity. But more importantly, it was such a uniform environment, man-made by its very nature, and in Annabel's experience, painful rather than peaceful.

She took in the array of organised flowers coming at her from all angles. But whereas some people could seek solace in a place like this, for her, it was still a cemetery; a place of death – no matter how well the grounds were tended and the graves lovingly cared for. Annabel knew paying it too much attention only put her in danger of feeling full of angst all over again. Tearful for the young and, dare she admit it, bitter for the old. She'd been there, done that and got the T-Shirt.

Picking up her pace, Annabel began to feel quite proud. For once, actually able to recognise how far she'd come. Thinking about it, it didn't seem all that long ago she'd have read more or less each and every one of these headstones, trying to gain comfort in the knowledge that, compared to some, her loved one had enjoyed a more reasonable stretch here on Earth. All in stark contrast to these days, she admitted. Now she knew reading dates on granite slabs made her just plain morbid and while the unfairness of it all still refused to leave her, at least that gut wrenching rawness had gone. Her heart had begun to feel broken rather than ripped out and she could finally think about the future as well as the past.

'Sorry, Tom,' she said, at last approaching his final resting place. 'I know, I know, I'd be late for my own funeral given half the chance.' She paused. That was another thing she'd noticed recently, her sense of humour making a return.

Chuckling, she leaned her chair against his head stone, at the same time wondering if her dearly departed considered such words bad taste. *Probably not.* Knowing him, he'd be laughing too; pleased she'd gotten to the point where she could actually joke about these things. No matter the subject, out of the two of them he always had been the one to see the funny side of life. Or in this case, she pondered, should that be death? She began to picture his smiling face. Tom, her eternal optimist.

She snapped herself back into the present, telling herself that anyway, if she didn't laugh, the only alternative was to cry and today of all days she certainly didn't want to do that. Having reached a sort of milestone she felt determined that nothing and no one was going to spoil things, not even herself. *Besides, haven't I shed enough tears already?*

She turned her attention to his grave, but couldn't bring herself to pull up the dandelions that had sprouted in the days since her last visit. They were yet another sign that spring was well underway and while most people considered them weeds, she quite liked the bright, abandoned cheeriness that came with them. Something that couldn't be said about the now wilting, blue violets, which she took out of their vase, and laid to one side, ready to replace them with her new offering. Carefully taking a posy of forget-me-nots out of her bag, she admired their simple beauty against the harshness of the stonework. 'That's better,' she said. 'Something new for you to enjoy, Tom.'

Opening out the deckchair, she plonked herself down in it. 'So how's your week been?' she asked. She paused, not that she really expected a reply, but it was nice to know he was listening if nothing else. 'Mine's not been too bad,' she continued. 'The shop's still doing okay. Oh, and your mum called round the other day.' Remembering the visit all too well, Annabel tried not to scowl. 'She said to say hello.'

She reached down and dipped her hand into her bag again, this time pulling out a flask of coffee. 'Caffeine, just what I need after the hassle of getting here,' she said. 'As usual the traffic was horrendous.'

Pouring herself a drink, she knew her ramblings were an attempt at stalling the inevitable; that she was worried about Tom's reaction once she'd told him what she was up to. While her plans for the future might be a positive move on her part, she certainly wasn't daft enough to think everyone would understand. If anything most people wouldn't, especially if his mother's reaction had been anything to go by.

She thought it strange how everyone and their dog insisted she move on, yet the second she did they created such a song and dance over it. Although if Tom did choose to join in with the dissenters, then just like them he'd only have to get used to the idea; particularly when this was entirely his fault to begin with. Annabel didn't want to play the blame game, but just like she'd said to his mother, she wouldn't be in this position if he hadn't upped and died in the first place. In her mind's eye, she could see Tom sitting opposite, his hands clasped as he patiently waited for her to tell him what was really on her mind. The man always could read her like a book.

'Okay, okay,' she said. 'Just give me a second.'

She took a couple of sips of coffee, determined to reveal all. But, in spite of practicing her speech all week, now that it came to it, those well-chosen words seemed to fail her. Resting her cup on her knee and refusing to let her conviction wane, she realised she was just going to have to come out and say it.

After three, *she told herself.* One, two, three …

She squeezed her eyes shut, in anticipation of the lightning bolt no doubt about to strike her down.

'I'm going to have a baby,' she said.

TWO

'Wow!' said Katy.

As Annabel entered the living room, she felt her cheeks start to redden. Was that wow in a good way? Or wow as in bad? It had been so long since she'd hit the town, she didn't have a clue what constituted the perfect Saturday night outfit these days. And while it felt good being all dressed up for a change, standing there in full make-up, a pair of high heels and tightly fitted black dress, she couldn't help but think she might have gone a bit over the top.

'You're sure you don't think it's too much?'

'Annabel,' Katy replied. 'You look amazing.'

Although reassuring to hear, Annabel still couldn't relax. Embarking on a new chapter in life felt way scarier than it did exciting. Moreover, she knew if she thought about the evening ahead too much, she was in danger of backing out.

Still, with her attire concerns out of the way, at least she could now have a proper go at tackling her nerves. The first glass of wine might not have done the trick on the anxiety front, but Annabel was sure as dammit that the second one would. She indicated to the open bottle of red sat on the coffee table. 'Drink?' she asked.

Katy shook her head. 'I'm driving remember. And besides, one of us has to make sure you don't make a complete fool of yourself.'

Any other time and Annabel would have appreciated the honesty. But while the two of them had been friends long enough for her to know that Katy didn't mean any malice, on this occasion a bit of support wouldn't have gone amiss. This was a huge step she was about to take, by far the biggest since Tom's death. And not only that, it wasn't as if she'd simply sprung this on her; Katy had known about her plans for ages, giving her more than ample time to get her head around them.

'Spoil sport,' said Annabel, reaching for the bottle. 'You don't mind if I do though, do you? Dutch courage and all that.' She poured herself one hell of a measure, managing to drink half of it down in one go.

'Annabel!'

'What?' she replied. Meeting her friend's horror with feigned innocence, the look on Katy's face told her she was having none of it.

'I really don't think you should be doing this,' she said.

'Drinking alcohol, you mean?' asked Annabel. 'Or going out on the pull?' She knew she sounded glib, but someone had to try and lift the atmosphere. A girls' night out was meant to be fun after all.

Katy rolled her eyes, clearly still not in the joking mood.

'Oh come on, lighten up. You're the one who kept saying I should move on.'

'Yes, but not like this.'

Feeling at a loss, Annabel took a seat on the sofa and poured herself another, more acceptably sized glass of wine. This time making sure to just sip it, she wished she was braver, that she had the guts to cut Katy loose for the night, absolving her best friend of her best friend duties. Regardless of any previous discussions, Katy obviously still thought she was losing the plot. But even with her bravado, Annabel couldn't quite bring herself to go it alone. Instead, she found herself yet again trying to explain herself. She needed her friend to know this wasn't some half-baked idea she'd come up with simply for the sake of it.

'We talked about having kids,' she said. 'Tom wanted to start trying from day one but I kept putting it off.'

'I remember,' said Katy, with a smile. 'What was it he used to say?'

Annabel began to smile too. 'Something about the world needing a few more little Annabels and Toms running around the place.'

She thought back to when they first married. At the time, she might not have agreed with Tom on the baby front, but that hadn't stopped them jumping into bed whenever they got the chance. Even now, she could hear the laughter in her husband's voice as he joked about there being a knack to this pregnancy malarkey. Trying to keep a straight face, he often suggested they could do with the practice for when Annabel did feel ready to take the plunge. As if either of them needed the excuse. The two of them never could get enough of each other.

'It wasn't that I didn't want children,' she carried on. 'I just thought we needed to be a bit more secure first. I mean, we had the mortgage on this place.'

Annabel looked around the room, recalling how happy they were at buying their first home together. In his excitement, Tom didn't just carry her over the threshold. He carried her over each and every doorway in the house, both downstairs and up, only listening to her pleas to be put down once they had gotten to the bedroom. What she'd give to be able to turn back the clock.

'Plus, we were trying to set up the business,' she continued. 'I kept insisting we had time on our side.' She drank another mouthful of wine. 'How wrong can a girl be, eh?'

'You weren't to know. No one was.'

'That doesn't stop me wishing I'd listened to him though, does it?'

'But why now?' asked Katy. 'Bringing up a family is difficult enough without doing it on your own.'

Annabel scoffed. 'And you'd know this how?' Katy had to be the most child averse individual she knew. 'Anyway, there are loads of single parents out there doing a fantastic job.'

'I agree,' said Katy. 'But how many of them started out that way? How many are actually doing it through choice?'

Annabel fell silent. She twisted her wine glass backwards and forwards between the palms of her hands, she couldn't deny that her friend had a point. Everyone knew someone who'd literally been left holding the baby. Either because, like hers, their husband had died, or he'd decided to be selfish and bugger off with the mistress. Women had left men to raise children on their own too. However, as much as Annabel felt for the difficulties these people faced, she couldn't let their experiences stop her from becoming a mother.

'I've been having this same dream for months now,' she suddenly began. 'Tom and I are at the park and we're pushing this little child on the swings. I can't see the child's face, or tell you if it's a boy or a girl. Everything's sort of hazy. I just know it's ours, mine and Tom's.' She felt herself automatically brighten as the dreamy images played out in her mind. 'It's such a beautiful day, I can feel the sun on my skin and the three of us are laughing and enjoying ourselves. And the child just wants to be pushed higher and higher.' She turned to Katy. 'When I'm in that dream it's just so real. You know?'

Her friend's face said it all. Of course she didn't. Having never been in a relationship that lasted more than a few months, let alone married and widowed, how could she?

'Then I wake up and I realise it isn't real at all, which hurts to the point that I just want to go back to sleep so I can re-live it over and over again. Stupid, eh? You'd think after all this time.'

Katy reached out with a comforting hand, but Annabel didn't want sympathy, she wanted understanding.

'So, you see, even though I know dreams like this don't come true, that I'll never have Tom's baby, at least by doing what I'm doing there's a chance a part of it might happen.' She stared at the photo of her husband sitting pride of place on the mantelpiece. 'He always said I'd make a great mum and I think this dream is meant to tell me I still can be.'

Another look at Katy and she could see she was convincing no one. Maybe it was time to give up trying to explain.

'You just don't like children,' said Annabel.

'I do,' said her friend. 'It's the responsibility that comes with them that I don't want. Honestly, Annabel, why would you put yourself through this? What if it's too big a step?'

Annabel understood the concern. When Tom died, she'd been barely able to function, and for someone who didn't see the point in carrying on anymore, it had been a long and hard road back. At one point, she'd been barely able to look after herself. There was no way she could have considered caring for someone else, let alone a baby, and having seen her at her worst, she supposed it no wonder her nearest and dearest were worried. Maybe to them she was still fragile? In their shoes, she'd probably feel the same. But that was all in the past and Annabel felt ready to embrace the future, just not in the way everyone seemed to expect.

'The doctor looked at me like that when I tried to talk to him about having a baby too,' she said.

'Really?' replied Katy. 'And that surprised you?'

Annabel recalled him trying to let her down gently. Lots of kind, amiable words were used, but the message was still the same—a big fat 'no-chance'.

'He said that, for all anyone knows, I'm perfectly able to conceive without medical intervention and that *NHS* treatment is for those who can't. He was very nice about it, of course. Although he did add that now might not be the right time to be making these kinds of decisions. He thinks I'm still grieving.'

'And are you?'

Annabel let out a burst of mock laughter. 'Yes, of course I am. A bit of me always will be. Tom was my soul mate, I think about him every day. But, that doesn't mean I can't raise a child.'

'Of course it doesn't,' said Katy.

At least they agreed on something.

'Surely there are other ways though?' she added. 'Other avenues you could try first?'

'I keep telling you there are,' Annabel replied. 'That's why I went to see the doctor to begin with. There's IUI, GIFT, IVF … but without the *NHS* and at thousands of pounds, where do you suggest I get that kind of money? Even if I donate a few eggs for some sort of discount I still couldn't afford the reduced rates; not with what these private clinics charge. And no one can guarantee any of them would work first time around anyway, so what then?'

'What about a sperm bank?'

Bless her, Annabel knew Katy was only trying to help, but she had done her research. On the other hand, she'd also done her sums and like most things in life, getting pregnant for a woman in her position came down to cold, hard cash.

'Katy, I just can't afford it. You've got to buy the stuff and get it shipped in these special containers and it still isn't cheap. Especially if one month turns into the next and then the next. It all adds up. And what with prams and cots and everything else I'd have to buy for the baby once I am pregnant, I'd rather keep my savings for then. Believe me, this is my best option.'

'Just not the safest.'

Of course, she was right, but having thought of that too, her friend didn't really have to point out the obvious. 'If you're talking about STDs, then I've got it covered,' she said. 'I'll just make sure any potential father gets tested before I even think about doing the deed.'

Her friend laughed. 'You really think some random bloke is going to go for that?'

In this day and age, Annabel wished she could say yes, a man would want to make sure he was clean. However, the realist in her knew it was a longshot. But as far as Annabel was concerned everything about this whole thing was a challenge. 'Maybe not,' she said. 'Time will tell, I suppose.'

Katy shook her head, clearly maintaining the view that Annabel was making a huge mistake and with the conversation going nowhere, it appeared they'd reached a stalemate.

Disappointed, Annabel couldn't tell if it was her decision to get pregnant that Katy disagreed with, or just the way she planned on going about it. But, whatever the case, she knew it would take a lot more than her friend's opinion to make her change her mind.

Annabel finished off her drink and rose to her feet. 'Ready?' she asked.

She watched Katy reluctantly reach for her handbag.

'No, not really,' she said. 'But, seeing as you're going to do this, with or without my blessing, it's not like I really have a choice, is it?'

THREE

Dan had no sooner opened the front door when some god awful smell attacked his nostrils. 'Bloody hell!' he said, unable to help but grimace. 'What is that?'

On second thought, he wasn't going to ask. His mum had undoubtedly been trawling the Internet for more weird, if not wonderful, dinners to cook up. Re-creating the culinary delights of her travels was her latest madcap endeavour and experience had taught him that whatever made up tonight's menu, he'd be better off not knowing. 'Just as long as she isn't having another go at the sea cucumber' he said. Dan recalled her last speciality dish with a shudder. He knew that an endangered species hadn't really been dumped on his plate. But, thanks to his mother's cooking skills, or rather the lack of them, the resemblance to one had been uncanny. There was no way that he could ever face that again.

'It's only me,' he called out.

Dan dropped his rucksack on the stairs; he heard his mother's voice, before realising she was too busy on the phone to respond. *Chatting to her partner in crime, as usual,* he thought. He wondered if he'd ever get the chance to meet his mother's accomplice.

'Don't you worry,' he heard his mum saying. 'With a bit of imagination I'm sure between us we can come up with something. It's probably just another flash in the pan, you'll see.'

He rolled his eyes; those two were always plotting something. Being old school friends, he could only imagine the trouble they'd brought to the Head Teacher's door. He thought it was a shame that, after college, Missy had moved away and they'd somehow lost touch. Still, having met up with each other again, they seemed to be more than making up for lost time. The pair of them had been in cahoots ever since. Talk about a second childhood.

'Anyway, I must dash,' his mum finally finished. 'Bye, Sweetie, bye.'

Dan slipped off his jacket and hung it on the bottom of the bannister before making his way into the kitchen. Expecting to find his mum as her usual flamboyant self, the way she'd sounded only moments before, he instead walked in to find her sitting at the table, now staring into space. It was as if she was lost in her own thoughts. He'd noticed her drifting off a lot lately, and wondered if he should be concerned. 'Everything okay?' he asked.

'Sorry?' she said.

He indicated to the phone and she immediately perked up.

'Oh, that was Missy. It would seem our young Maeve has only gone and got herself a Boyfriend.'

Dan smiled as he headed for the kettle. 'Really?'

'Yes, really. Although you don't have to look so pleased about it.'

'I do if it means you'll finally shut up about her,' said Dan. He filled the kettle with water and clicked the power on. 'Although to be fair, she's probably saying the exact same thing to her mother about me.'

He turned his attention to the cups and tea caddy; yet again he wished they could just use teabags like normal people. *Normal*, he thought, *in this house?* He supposed a guy could only dream.

His mum let out a wistful sigh which caused Dan to pause, his ears pricked ready for the inevitable.

'But the two of you would make such a lovely couple,' she said, right on cue.

Again, Dan smiled. 'So you've mentioned,' he said. 'Numerous times.'

He watched her get up from the table, pick up a wooden spoon, and begin stirring whatever concoction boiled on the stove. His stomach turned at the sight.

'I thought you were out tonight, anyway?' he said. 'At your dance class?'

'I'm not in the mood,' his mum replied. 'I'd much prefer to spend time with you. You're always so busy these days. We never seem to chat anymore.'

Dan couldn't deny it. When it came to needing extra space, more and more people seemed to be extending, rather than moving to larger properties these days. Which was great news for those like himself, who worked in construction; he'd been inundated with work lately and when he wasn't on site, he was out giving quotes.

'We're chatting now aren't we?' he said.

'Yes, but not like we used to.'

Maybe it was his imagination, but she seemed to disappear into her own head again for a moment, before shaking herself free.

'And anyway,' she said. 'Missy and I could do with your help in sorting out this Maeve business.'

Dan despaired. Did this woman ever give up?

'Mum,' he said. 'How many times do I have to tell you? I'm really not interested.'

'But how do you know when you've never even met her?'

He'd have been better off talking to the wall.

'Look,' she carried on. 'I know you think that what you do, and who you do it with, is none of my business, I just worry about you.'

Dan scoffed. 'You want grandchildren, you mean.'

'What woman my age doesn't?' she replied. 'But that's not what I'm talking about. I mean, who else is going to look after you when I'm gone? How will you manage on your own?'

Dan let out a laugh. As far as he was concerned, the chance to even try and look after himself would be cause for celebration.

His train of thought all at once made him feel guilty. He didn't wish any harm on his mother, let alone want her gone. He, of all people, knew it was simply her way. She could just be a bit full on at times. Although much to his annoyance, her interest in his love life did seem to be getting worse. Thinking about it, he was sure none of his mates had to put up with this from their mothers. Then again, most of them had siblings. Brothers and Sisters probably prevented them from being their parents' one, and only, focus.

'What're you talking about, when you're gone?' he said. 'You'll probably outlive all of us.' Despite not being superstitious, Dan made sure to touch the wooden kitchen cupboard, just in case.

'Which is exactly what I used to say to your father.'

Dan instantly stopped what he was doing and turned to look at his mother. The woman might be prone to a lot of things, but morbidity had never been one of them. 'Are you sure everything's okay?' he asked.

She gave him a reassuring smile. 'Of course I am. Why?'

'No, reason,' he said, even though he didn't quite believe her.

'Anyone would think there's something wrong with me for wanting to see you settled,' she said. 'Happy with that special someone.'

Dan automatically laughed. He couldn't believe what he was hearing. 'You could've fooled me,' he replied. His thoughts turned to his mother's past behaviour; even she had to see the contradiction here, surely?

She lifted the spoon again and put it to her lips, leaving Dan with no choice but to admire her bravery. His stomach turned again and needing to divert his attention, he resumed making the tea.

'Remember the first time I brought a girl home?' he said.

'How can I forget?' his mum replied, getting back to her stirring. 'She had dark hair.'

'And?'

'And nothing. I expected a blonde, that's all.'

Even now, Dan could hear the disappointment in her voice. The poor girl couldn't have gotten a worse reception had she had four legs and a tail.

'Like you used to be, you mean?' he said.

'Intelligent blondes are hard to come by. Believe you me, we're a rare species.'

Dan shook his head, knowing full well that his mum actually believed this. 'So why the dislike for Lisa then?' he asked. 'She was blonde.'

'Thanks to a bottle,' his mum corrected. 'Hardly the same thing.'

'Then there was Cara.'

'Tattoo girl! Don't remind me.'

She'd always given his girlfriends nicknames and none of them very complimentary. In fact, her approach to his relationships had been so infuriating over the years, Dan had long come to the conclusion that she simply couldn't help herself.

'Mum, she had a single tattoo and it was so tiny you could hardly see it. If she hadn't mentioned it in the first place, you'd never have known it was there.'

'But she did mention it, didn't she? And no matter the size, that's still one too many if you ask me.'

Dan knew he could've gone on, and on, if he'd wanted to. At thirty-three years old, his list of loved and lost seemed endless and most of the list was thanks to his mum. Every time he had gotten a new girlfriend she wouldn't stop nagging for an introduction, until he finally brought them round. Then she'd only find some reason to disapprove. Of course, if she didn't show her displeasure to the poor girls' faces, there'd be the onslaught of criticism after they'd gone; and to this day she stood by her every word.

'Every parent wants the best for their children, Dan,' she carried on. 'It's just that some of us want it more than others.'

'And you wonder why I'm still single.'

'Yes, well, that's the trouble with the youth of today. Regardless of the issue, it's always the parents who're to blame.'

She reached into the cupboard for a plate, Dan knew there was no way he could put tonight's dinner anywhere near his mouth. Thank goodness he already had plans. 'Don't worry about me, Mum,' he said. 'I'm off out later. I'll grab something to eat then.'

'You're going out? Again?' she asked. 'But I made this especially for you. It's based on an Aboriginal dish from my time in the Outback.'

He dreaded to think.

'Sorry, Mum, but I'm pricing a job up tonight.'

Her eyes narrowed.

'I did tell you about it. Remember? Mr Watson owns two shops in town and wants them knocking into one?'

She still didn't appear convinced, but even though Dan had definitely mentioned his plans, he'd rather suffer his mum's confusion than sample the food on offer.

'If I didn't know any better I'd be starting to think you don't like my cooking,' she said.

Dan looked at the single plate on the counter, enough to tell him she wasn't planning on tucking into it herself.

'Unless you've taken a leaf out of Maeve's book,' she continued. 'And have met someone else.'

Here we go again, *he thought.*

'I thought we were done with this subject,' he said.

She looked him directly in the eyes, waiting for the slightest hint of deception to reveal itself. Dan refused to look away. It was a game they'd been playing since he was a child, although back then, the challenge was usually over a biscuit he'd denied eating between meals.

As she continued to stare, a part of Dan understood the tight grip that his mother seemed to want to exert. After all, since his dad's death years ago, it had just been the two of them and they shared a pretty close bond because of it. At the same time, he hated the tabs she tried to keep on his love life, on his life in general. He wished she'd just let him get on with things for himself from time to time. Even when she was off on her travels, thanks to modern day technology, there was no escaping her, she knew her way around a smart phone better than he did.

'Now you're just being daft,' he said, although his denials did nothing to ease his mother's suspicions.

'You would tell me if you'd met someone though, wouldn't you?' she asked, scrutinising his face throughout.

His thoughts immediately transported back to the woman he'd met the other night. A woman he'd no intentions of telling his mother about. Introducing herself as Annabel, she'd managed to create quite an impression. After all, it's not every day a gorgeous lady asked him to father their child. Then again, she had been pretty drunk. And just like his mum, she was clearly as mad as a hatter. He smiled to himself, unable to help but think that she and the woman standing before him would probably get on quite well.

'How could I not tell you?' said Dan, maintaining his gaze. 'You interrogate me almost every week. Anyway, what about you?' Dan often wished his mum had another man in her life. If she had, then maybe she wouldn't focus quite so much on him. 'Who's to say you're not keeping something from me.'

'Rubbish!' said his mum, at last releasing her visual stranglehold. She turned her attention back to the stove. 'I mean, I've never been one to keep secrets, have I? So why would I start now?'

***

Dan stepped through the door, ready to dazzle with his building expertise. However, before he could even get his bearings, he found himself ushered back out into the street again.

'Sorry, mate,' said Mr Watson. 'Can we do this some other time?'

After having arrived to price the job up, getting a quote now seemed the last thing on his potential client's mind. This was something that Dan thought strange when he considered how keen the man had been when they'd first arranged the appointment. Mr. Watson's eagerness to get works underway was the sole reason Dan had agreed to an evening visit in the first place.

'Is everything okay?' he asked, trying to peer through the window.

'Oh it's nothing to do with the shop. I still want to go ahead and knock through,' the man explained. 'It's my son. He's had an injury at football practice. Nothing too serious, thank goodness. But I've got to get over there.' He began searching his pockets for his keys. 'Kids, eh? That boy will be the death of me.' He let out a little chuckle. 'That's if he doesn't kill himself first.'

Dan tried to raise a smile. His customer might have been joking, but he recognised genuine concern when he saw it. Injuries at various sporting events had elicited a similar response from his mother back in the day, even if, like this chap, she'd attempted to hide it.

'Maybe later in the week?'

'Yeah, sure,' said Dan. He stepped out of the way so the man could lock up. 'Give us a call and we'll sort something out.'

Dan watched him race off down the street, he hoped Mr Watson was right; that his son hadn't suffered too bad an injury. At the same time though, he couldn't help but wonder if serendipity was conspiring against him.

He seemed to be seeing fathers and their children everywhere at the moment, or in this case hearing about them. He recalled the chap at the park, playing ball with his little boy. The three-year-old having a tantrum in the supermarket when Dan had nipped in for some herb his mum had insisted she needed, which of course they didn't stock. Then there was that bloke who'd had to stop his kid from running out into the road, just as a motorbike zoomed by. Honestly, they were everywhere; something that Dan found disconcerting, to say the least.

He remembered it being the same when he got his new car. Nothing fancy, but he'd never noticed so many of that make and model on the road until he got his own. Still his pride and joy, they seemed to be all over the place. His mother had called it *Observational Selection Bias* when he'd mentioned it. Trust her to know. However, for Dan it was just plain spooky. Now he found fathers and their children coming at him from each and every angle. Again, something Dan found equally as strange and, no doubt, it was all because of that Annabel woman. Her proposition had obviously gotten to him.

Again, Dan's thoughts drifted back to the other night. Along with every other bloke present, he'd noticed her as soon as she entered the bar. He could see she was out of his league, the reason he spent the next hour or so trying and failing to pluck up the courage to go and introduce himself. In fact, he probably wouldn't have spoken to her at all had she not approached him.

He could still smell the sweetness of her perfume as she appeared at his side. Moreover, he still felt amazed that she'd picked him out of the crowd.

'Can I buy you a drink?' she asked.

He recalled the slight slur in her voice. Despite trying to hide it, she'd clearly had one too many. Then again, so had he.

She held out her hand, formalising her presence. 'I'm Annabel.'

'Dan,' he replied. 'Pleased to meet you.' Returning her gaze, she had the most beautiful, soulful eyes. They had a worldliness to them that he couldn't quite describe. He put his glass to his lips, still in shock because she was actually talking to him.

'Glad to hear it,' she said, simple as that. 'Because I have a proposition.'

Half way through a swig of his pint, Dan almost choked. For someone who looked all sweetness and light, this woman was certainly a fast mover. 'Excuse me?' he said. The part of him that liked to be wooed suddenly felt nervous, the other part couldn't believe its luck. 'A proposition?'

'Yes,' said Annabel.

Dan watched her down her drink. Her hands shook, telling him that she was as new to this situation as him. Composing herself, she took a deep breath, before looking him directly in the face. Imagining the night ahead, he waited for her to continue.

'I'd like to have your baby,' she said.

At the time, Dan thought her request ludicrous. Not that he admitted to this. Too busy thinking with his trousers rather than his brain, he'd have been back to her place like a shot if she hadn't insisted he take some time to mull it over- something he hadn't stopped doing since. To the point that the more he thought, the less absurd the idea seemed and all thanks to his over-protective mother.

He didn't know why, but he couldn't get Annabel out of his head. There was just something about her. He could be doing the most mundane of tasks and she'd simply appear in his mind's eye. Then again, he considered, she was bound to have had some sort of impact. Like he kept telling himself, it wasn't every day a gorgeous woman insisted he get her pregnant.

As for the so called *observational selection bias,* half of him wanted to accept his mother's explanation. However, the other half didn't feel quite so sure.

'Maybe the Gods are trying to tell me something,' he said, as he thought back to the earlier conversation he'd had at home. 'Maybe they're telling me I should take her up on her offer. That this could be my only chance.'

Dan had always wanted children, but thanks to his mum and her funny ways he couldn't see himself enjoying parenthood any time soon. In fact, the more he thought about it, the more the odds seemed against him when it came to having his own offspring in any conventional sense.

After all, in order for that to happen he'd have to be in a relationship and in order to be in a relationship, he'd have to get rid of his mother.

FOUR

Annabel put her pen to the corner of her mouth, repeatedly tapping it against her lip. She knew this bouquet had to be special, but in assessing what she'd come up with so far, it still didn't feel quite right. She began reading back her check list.

'*Avalanche Roses* for purity and innocence,' she said. '*Freesias*, delicate like the baby they've been praying for.'

'*Singapore Orchids* representing love and strength in the new Mum. And finally, *Gypsophila* – child's breath. All of them white.'

She stared at the piece of paper. As thoughtful as this creation might be, there was definitely something missing. Annabel recalled her conversation with the new Dad when he'd phoned to place the order. Maybe something he'd said could give her a clue? In his excitement, he rambled on, and on, about how he couldn't believe he'd finally become a father. He and his wife had been trying for years; in fact, nine months ago they'd just about given up hope.

'I know,' she said, at last, deciding the ensemble needed a bit of fun. 'A Hydrangea head, for their perseverance.'

Allowing her cheeky side to come to the fore, she giggled as she jotted this down; and while imagining the poor chap being summoned to the bedroom at all hours of the day, told herself that even florists were allowed the odd in-joke.

She knew the new Dad didn't really care what went into his bouquet. Her customers very rarely did. For most, having something that looked the part was all that mattered, but Annabel couldn't help herself. Every arrangement had to symbolise the event it was catering for and even though no one else knew the significance of each individual flower, at least she did. Choosing the right flowers for the right occasion was one of the things she most loved about her job. An aspect that had only come to the fore after Tom's death.

She thought back to that awful time. Making a wreath for him had been one of the most painful things she'd ever had to do. Yes, she could have asked another florist to step in. She could have even given them a list of all the flora and fauna she wanted to be included. But someone else wouldn't have put their heart and soul into it like Annabel had done. Not to mention their tears. Such was its impact, she still cried a little to this day when it came to making up arrangements for funerals. But from Tom's death onwards, she made sure that no matter what the event, all her creations had significance.

Finally, satisfied with her choices, Annabel put the pen down, ready to set about getting everything together. She grabbed the scissors and her belly began to rumble. 'It can't be lunchtime already,' she said. Annabel looked over at the wall clock, she noted that it was a quarter-past-twelve. 'Please, no. Not again.' Annabel pictured Katy sitting at their usual table, impatiently awaiting her late arrival. She sighed. 'Someone's not going to be a happy bunny.'

She dropped everything and quickly headed out back to collect her handbag. She silently insisted that if she was quick her friend would still be waiting. Annabel hastily flipped the closed sign as she made her exit and rushed off on her lunch date.

'Ouch!' she suddenly cried out.

In her haste, she hadn't noticed the individual about to pass by and bumped straight into them; it felt like she'd walked into a wall. 'Can't you watch where you're going?'

'Well excuse me,' said a male voice. 'Even if you are the one who knocked into me.'

Annabel dusted herself down, she couldn't believe the man's cheek and was ready to give him a piece of her mind. She looked him square in the face, and froze, recognising the human obstacle before her. Trying to speak, the words wouldn't come out.

She watched the man's face break into a smile. 'Hello again,' he said. 'Annabel, isn't it?'

Annabel cringed; she wanted the ground to swallow her whole. 'It's you,' she said. 'From last week.'

'Dan, yes.' The man replied.

Embarrassment welled as she recalled her drunken slurring that night; she'd taken the phrase 'Dutch Courage' to its limit. Seeing him grin back at her, he obviously remembered events too. Why, oh why, hadn't she limited herself to one or two glasses?

His amusement continued while he waited for her to say something, reminding Annabel why, out of the crowd, she'd ultimately chosen him as the one to father her child. He had one of those smiles that lit up his whole face, just like Tom had had. Of course, that still didn't excuse him not watching where he was going, she decided, at last pulling herself together. And what was he doing here anyway?

Her stomach did a little flip. Unless he'd come to take her up on her offer?

'I'd shake your hand,' said Dan. 'But I feel our relationship has already moved on.'

Annabel's heart sank. The man was clearly laughing at her and she felt her glimmer of hope fast disappear, along with the last of her dignity.

Not that she could blame him. Again, thinking back to her rather inebriated, yet very serious conversation about him being the one to help her procreate, he had every right to tease her. Talk about easy pickings. To him, she was probably just some drunken woman desperate for a shag.

However, if that really was his view, she supposed, under the circumstances, she should be glad he hadn't taken her speech all that seriously. On the down side though, this did mean she was going to have to go through the whole rigmarole again with someone else; except this time it would be minus the alcohol. But why the unexpected visit if it wasn't to talk about babies, she wondered and suddenly suspicious, she took a step back.

'So what can I do for you?' she asked. 'What are you doing here?'

It began to dawn on her just how stupid she'd been. Everyone knew there were lots of weirdoes out there, yet for some reason, stranger danger had been the one thing she hadn't banked on. In her search for a prospective father, the last thing she'd considered was the possibility of having a deranged stalker on her hands and she just hoped she wasn't about to pay the price.

She tried to remember if, apart from her mobile number, she'd given him any personal information that night. Her overriding feeling was that she was quite sure that she hadn't.

'I could say the same about you,' he replied, which, as far as Annabel was concerned, explained absolutely nothing.

Determined not to show any fear, she pointed to the sign emblazoned above the window. 'It's my shop,' she said.

Her heart sank even further as she suddenly realised what she'd just done. If the would-be maniac standing here didn't know exactly where to find her before, thanks to her and her big mouth, he certainly did now.

'Small world,' he said.

Annoyed with herself as much as she was him, Annabel gave him a stern look. 'If you could answer the question, please,' she said.

Finally, he relented. 'I'm doing some work around the corner, if you must know.'

'What kind of work?'

Dan laughed. 'What's with the twenty questions? Besides, shouldn't you have asked me these things before you gave me your number?'

She knew he had a point, but to be fair to herself, it wasn't his earning potential she'd been interested in. 'And what a fruitless exercise that turned out to be,' she said.

'Let's just say I'm still thinking about it,' he replied.

Great, more teasing, just what Annabel *didn't* need.

Annabel decided that she'd wasted enough time on this man already. 'Consider your decision made,' she said. 'Now if you'll excuse me, I have to go.'

She stuck her nose in the air and bustled off down the street. Without bothering to look back, she knew that he was staring after her.

'Make the most of it while you can, Danny boy,' she said, insisting that if he really was going to murder her he'd have done it by now. 'Because this is the last you'll be seeing of me.'

***

By the time she got to the coffee shop, Annabel was practically out of breath. Understandably so, she realised, checking her watch. In speed walking terms, she had just beaten her personal best. Upon entering, she spotted Katy at their usual table, and relieved to find she hadn't missed her, waved to catch her attention before racing over. 'Sorry I'm late,' she said, almost panting as she took a seat.

Her friend indicated to the latte on the table. 'It should still be warm. I guessed you'd be running behind, so it's not long been ordered.'

Grateful for the gesture, Annabel duly picked up the glass and took a sip. 'I had this arrangement to sort out,' she said. 'Some bloke wanting something special for his wife. They've just had a baby, the lucky so and soes. Anyway, I got waylaid deciding which flowers to include.' She took another drink of her coffee. At last able to relax, it was just what she needed. 'So,' she said, ready to give her friend her undivided attention. 'What's new?'

Katy didn't answer, but as far as Annabel was concerned she didn't have to. Her face said it all. She wore one of those expressions that didn't just say I thought you'd never ask, it said I have some really exciting news, but for some reason, I'm choosing to pretend it isn't. Annabel had seen that look on her friend's face enough times to know what it meant. 'Go on then,' she asked. 'Who is he?'

Katy grinned. 'Just some hunk of a man I met at the gym,' she coolly explained.

Annabel knew her friend's calm and collected exterior wouldn't last; that within seconds she'd be morphing into a rambling, excitable schoolgirl in front of her very eyes. She silently began counting down. *Three, Two, One.*

'His name's Oliver, but I call him sex on legs. Honestly, he's gorgeous. I can't wait for you to meet him. Well maybe not just yet, it's probably a bit early. Especially when it's nothing serious. You know me, I don't do serious.'

Annabel had never heard a truer statement. The men in her friend's life never lasted more than a few weeks. She was one of those women who liked variety. At least that's what she claimed. Annabel suspected it had more to do with issues around commitment, a suggestion that had always been met with denial.

'Anyway, enough about that,' said Katy. 'Just thinking about the man makes me come over all fuzzy. Tell me about your love life. How are things progressing with what's his name? Dan, isn't it?'

Annabel almost choked. 'You've changed your tune,' she said.

After spending weeks of showing nothing but concern over her plans, she found it amusing her friend now wanted a blow-by-blow account of what she'd been up to recently. In a way, she thought it was a shame that there was nothing to tell.

'Yes, well, if you're not going to take to my advice on the subject, I may as well keep up with events.'

Annabel shook her head. Katy always did like a good gossip.

'Has he called at all?'

'Firstly,' said Annabel. 'You know full well I don't have, and nor do I want, a love life. And secondly, no he hasn't.'

Her friend gave a look that fell somewhere between pity and 'I told you so', an expression Annabel couldn't quite bring herself to appreciate.

'If you ask me,' said Katy. 'The man's a player anyway. Out and about town with one woman and then a few months later it's some other poor girl. He's clearly a commitment-phobe.'

Annabel couldn't believe what she was hearing. 'Sounds like someone else I know,' she said, wondering if *commitment-phobe* was even a word.

'But that's my point,' she carried on. 'That's why he would've been so perfect. The second I fell pregnant, I'd be more than happy for him to go on his merry way, never to be seen again.' She picked up the menu and began scanning its contents. 'Besides, it's not his degree of loyalty that's worrying me.'

'What do you mean?' asked Katy. 'I thought you just said he hasn't been in touch?'

Annabel wondered if she'd said too much already. She didn't want to cause any unnecessary concern and for all she knew Dan could have been telling the truth when he'd said he was working nearby. Still, seeing him on her doorstep like that had freaked her out a bit, however, plausible his words might seem. 'I've just bumped into him,' she said. 'Literally, outside the shop.'

Katy straightened herself up. 'Again, what are you talking about?' she asked.

'Well I was just locking up to come here and there he was. To be honest, when I realised it was him I didn't know what to think. I mean he wouldn't be the first madman to get the wrong idea, would he? To take advantage of a woman's plight. You read about these cases all the time in the papers.'

'Shit, Annabel, that does sound dodgy. Maybe you should go to the police? Just in case.'

Annabel put the menu back down and scoffed. 'And say what? That first I ask a man to impregnate me and then I happen to see him in the street. I mean who's the real balm pot here?' She paused to drink another mouthful of coffee. 'I hate to say it, Katy, but I think you were right. Getting a complete stranger to father my child like this was a ridiculous idea.'

'Hallelujah!' said Katy, throwing herself back in her seat. 'And about time too.'

Annabel suddenly felt hurt. She knew how idiotic she'd been, that she should've thought to consider her own personal safety;

especially when she'd managed to analyse every other aspect of her plan. But while she understood her friend's relief, after all, the consequences of having a madman for a sperm donor didn't bear thinking about, did Katy really have to be this blunt?

Thankfully for Annabel, Katy seemed to realise how harsh she sounded.

'Look, I'm sorry. That was unnecessary,' she said. 'This plan of yours just seems so *out there*, I can't help but worry about it.'

'I know. I just wanted a baby so much,' Annabel replied. 'I still do.'

'But don't you think if it's meant to happen, it'll happen? With or without someone like Dan?'

After walking into him like that, Annabel didn't know what to think anymore.

She tried to hide her disappointment on the baby front. 'Short of having an immaculate conception,' she said. 'I can't see how.'

FIVE

With a take-away pizza box in hand, Annabel let herself into the house and dropping her keys down on the sideboard, headed straight for the kitchen. She didn't just feel hungry; her stomach insisted her throat had been cut. Unlike the lucky individuals who lost their appetite when they were stressed or worried about something, for her, life's trials and tribulations had the opposite effect. Turning to food for comfort was all well and good for those who could burn off the extra calories, which she couldn't. This was the very reason she'd gained a few extra pounds after Tom had died. She looked down at her mid-riff and frowned. Pounds which she doubted she'd ever shift.

Annabel grabbed a slice of pizza and knew that she should be laying the table instead of eating straight from the box. But it was so easy, with just one for dinner, to let civilities like that slide; and being honest, she simply couldn't be bothered. Savouring every mouthful of gooey melted cheese, juicy tomato, and spicy peperoni, she wondered if there was any point in cooking at all with just her to cater for, particularly when food like this tasted so good.

Annabel began to mull over the day's incident with Dan. She didn't really believe him to be a stalker. Even so, bumping into him like that had been enough to bring her to her senses. She supposed she'd just have to find another way to get pregnant, although, thanks to her finances, goodness knew how.

If all else failed, she knew she still had the adoption route to consider. Although, the reason she'd discarded it to start with was because she didn't hold out much hope. In her view, if her own doctor deemed her unsuitable when it came to motherhood, why would Social Services be any different? Naturally they had their checks to do, children couldn't be awarded to just anyone. However, jumping through every hoop imaginable felt a tad scary, especially when the odds were stacked against her. Annabel thought it sad; all those children out there, just as desperate for a home as she was to give them one.

She stuffed the last of her pizza slice into her mouth, ready to make herself a cup of coffee. With so much going on in her head, it was as if her brain began to hurt and she didn't want to think about it anymore.

Her ears pricked at the sound of her mobile ringing, giving her just the diversion she needed. She rummaged in her handbag in an attempt to find it. Pulling out her phone, she checked the number on display but didn't recognise who it belonged to. 'Probably a salesman,' she said. Talking to some stranger about double glazing or why she should change electricity companies wasn't quite the relief Annabel had been hoping for; putting the handset to one side, she decided to let it ring out.

Surprisingly, the phone bleeped indicating a voicemail. Her eyes narrowed as she took in the flashing light. In Annabel's experience, sales people never left messages and curious as to the caller's identity, she reached for her phone once more. As she clicked to listen, there seemed to be a slight pause in the recording before a male voice began to speak, and even then its owner sounded unsure. Annabel's eyes widened and her stomach lurched as, a few words in, it dawned on her who the voice actually belonged to. *Shit! What do I do now?* she thought, this being the last person she expected to hear from.

'Are you mad?' a woman suddenly called out.

Bugger! Much to her frustration, she recognised this voice too.

Footsteps marched down the hall and, cursing her sister's not so impeccable timing, she told herself there was nothing she could do about the message now; she'd have to deal with it later.

'What kind of question is that?' she replied, shutting her phone down just as Rebecca barged into the room.

'Well?' said Rebecca, adamantly awaiting a response.

Despite being caught off guard, Annabel was more than accustomed to Rebecca letting herself in. She often dropped by for a cuppa. Unfortunately, she was also acquainted with her occasional outbursts. However, taking in her sister's annoyed expression, Annabel had to admit they weren't usually as extreme as this. 'And I thought it customary to say hello when you entered someone else's house?' she said.

'Don't you play the innocent with me,' her sister carried on.

Having no clue as to what she was referring to, Annabel couldn't help but sigh. Out of the two of them, Rebecca had always been the more hot-blooded. Lately though, her moodiness had been taking over. Whatever was going on, Annabel wished she'd just sort it out; after the day she'd had, she felt way too tired to play these games.

'Tea? Coffee?' she asked, refusing to get drawn in. 'The kettle's just boiled.'

Annabel got on with making the drinks, giving her sister a minute to calm down. Coffee poured, she handed her a cup and indicated to the table, suggesting that they take a seat. Annabel could see from Rebecca's pursed lips that she still wasn't happy. Then again, she never did like being told what to do. Still, hanging her bag on the back of a chair, at least she did as instructed; even if it was reluctantly.

'So do you want to tell me what all this is about?' said Annabel, sitting opposite. 'Or am I to guess?'

'I saw Katy earlier,' she began. 'She told me about this ridiculous idea of yours.'

Annabel's shoulders slumped. She'd known all along what Rebecca's reaction would be, she'd purposefully kept her out of things. Something Katy should have realised, considering her friend knew the woman almost as well as she did.

'Really,' she said.

'Only because she's concerned, although I don't know why you didn't come to me in the first place. I am your sister, your *older* sister.'

Here we go again.

She'd never understood why being the oldest had always been so important to Rebecca. Why she seemed to think it made her wiser somehow, that she always knew best; a view that, at times like this, Annabel couldn't accept. It was one of the reasons their relationship often felt so strained. Rebecca seemed to think her position as the oldest meant she should be the first to have, or experience, anything. And although she knew deep down it wasn't really the case, Annabel's less charitable side often found itself wondering if her sister was just jealous; jealous because she hadn't been the one to be widowed first.

'How could you dream of doing something like this?'

Again, Annabel sighed. It was a question Rebecca shouldn't need to ask. Having enjoyed the honour of motherhood for quite some time now, she of all people knew what Annabel was missing out on. 'I'd have thought if anyone could understand it would be you,' she said. 'You're a mother yourself, of three at the last count.'

'Yes, but that's different.'

Annabel bristled. It was one thing her sister having an opinion, but quite another to be so righteous about it.

'Why?' she asked. 'Because your husband's alive to complete the perfect family unit, whereas mine isn't?' Annabel knew she sounded harsh, but she couldn't help it. As far as she was concerned, her sister had started this.

She watched Rebecca shift in her seat.

'That's not fair,' she replied.

Annabel almost laughed. The way her life had panned out, she couldn't have agreed more.

'Do you think I want to be in this position? Do you think if I had a choice, I'd want to raise a child on my own?'

She thought about how different things would be if Tom was still here. For one, she certainly wouldn't be getting a scolding like this. But he wasn't here, was he? And although Annabel wouldn't wish her pain on anyone, let alone her own sister, she'd never stopped wanting to know why, out of everyone on the planet, she'd been chosen to suffer like this. Why, out of everyone out there, her husband had to be the one to die? The two of them had made plans, they had a future. They were supposed to grow old together.

She looked her sister straight in the eye. 'Not everyone's as lucky as you are, Rebecca. And yes, you're right, it's not fair. Life isn't. Welcome to my world.'

'Annabel, please. The last thing I want to do is upset you.'

'Really? Then why come charging in here like this in the first place? It's not as if my reproductive system is any of your business.'

'Of course it's my business,' said Rebecca. 'You're my little sister. And if I think you're about to make some big mistake, it's my duty to say something. Having a child isn't a bed of roses, you know. It's hard enough when there are two parents involved.'

Annabel knew that they were never going to see eye to eye on the matter, and gave up. After all, what was the point? The way Rebecca was going on, anyone would think her brain cells had been buried alongside her husband. Having already gone over all the issues, not only once but numerous times, she could really do without the lecture. Besides, whatever Rebecca had to say, she knew she'd probably already heard it from Katy.

Refusing to discuss it any further, she got up from the table and put her cup in the sink. She knew Rebecca meant well, but the last thing she wanted was an argument. They were just so different and in so many ways. Admittedly, it was hard for either of them to understand the other at the best of times, let alone over something like this.

'Then you'll be pleased to know I've decided against getting pregnant,' she said, just wanting to move the conversation on. 'At least for the time being.'

'Yes, Katy mentioned that too,' replied Rebecca, the relief in her voice more than evident.

Annabel stiffened, wondering what the woman was playing at. If she already knew about her change of heart then why create all this fuss to begin with?

'You always were a bit impetuous,' Rebecca continued. 'At least on this occasion you're starting to see sense.'

Annabel spun round and told herself that some people just didn't know when to shut up. Her sister's words hung in the air between them, yet Rebecca still didn't seem to realise she'd gone too far.

'What do you mean, impetuous?' Annabel asked.

Annabel marched over to the cupboard, pulled out a hefty file and slammed it down on the table. 'Does this look like impetuous to you?' She opened the file and began turning one page after another, revealing print out after print out, each of them explaining all there was to know about *this* fertility treatment and *that* fertility treatment. Pulling out another big folder, she again turned page after page, this time on child rearing. 'Well does it?'

She watched her sister look from the files, to her and back again.

'Look, I'm sorry. I just …'

'What? See me as an imbecile?'

'No, it's …'

'Stop!' Annabel cut her off. 'I think you've said enough already, don't you?'

Finally, her sister fell silent and Annabel slammed the files shut. She took a second to calm herself down. 'I'd like you to leave now,' she eventually said. 'For both our sakes.'

Rebecca reluctantly rose to her feet and began gathering her belongings, but Annabel refused to feel bad. The woman had no right to come into her home and interfere like this. Her sister paused, as if yet again trying to say something, however, Annabel threw her a glare warning her not to. Thankfully, this time she got the message and, without uttering another word, left the room. Glad to see the back of her, Annabel just stood there, holding on to her annoyance.

She waited to hear the front door shut before allowing herself to relax. But even then, she knew it was only just, she still felt furious. 'How dare she come around here making such value judgements,' she said. 'Who does she think she is? My bloody keeper?'

She stared at the files on the table, and thought about the hours upon hours she'd put into her research. 'Impetuous, my arse!'

Annabel grabbed Rebecca's mug off the table and was ready to put it in the sink with her own, however she caught sight of her phone sitting on the side. She stopped in her tracks and realised she had the perfect opportunity to really give her sister what for. 'I'll show you,' she said, as she put the cup back down and headed straight for her mobile.

She clicked the button to listen to her voicemail and the more she heard the more her determination grew.

'You think I'm impetuous,' she said. 'Then I'll give you impetuous.'

She smiled and feeling very pleased with herself, indeed, clicked 'return call'.

SIX

Annabel's hands stung and, with her fingers glowing red from all the bleaching she'd done, she made a mental note to pick up a pair of marigolds the next time she went to the supermarket. Maybe a face mask as well, she considered, thanks to the ammonia gathering in her nostrils. She glanced around the room, and told herself it was worth the hardship. She could eat her dinner off the kitchen counter it was so clean. The floor shone and even the inside of her cupboards smelt fresh. And now they were organised to the point that anyone taking a peek would be forced to question her OCD status.

Finally, she picked up the shopping bag that leaned against the back door and left the room. As she made her way down the hall she paused to pop her head into the lounge, nipping in to straighten an already straight cushion. After a quick scan around, she breathed in the aroma and smiled. There was something quite satisfying about the smell of freshly polished furniture.

Annabel headed up to the bathroom and felt a spring in her step. When she entered the bathroom, she caught sight of herself in the mirror and finally took a moment to acknowledge the reason behind all her efforts. Her stomach did a little somersault and she let out a nervous giggle. If all went to plan, this evening could be the start of something big.

She stared at her reflection and tucked her hair behind her ears. Making a point of taking in every detail, Annabel wondered if she'd see a change in the face staring back at her once she'd achieved her goal. She turned side on and looking at her profile, tried to imagine herself with a heavily pregnant belly. Would she be one of those women who bloomed during pregnancy? She certainly hoped so.

'Tonight's the night,' she said.

Annabel felt a mix of excitement and anxiety; she took a long, deep breath, slowly exhaling in an attempt to calm down. She knew the odds were against her succeeding first time round and, in not wanting her donor to think she was bringing a baby into a pigsty, that she'd probably be scrubbing the house clean for the foreseeable future. Still, as far as anyone knew there was nothing to prevent her from having a baby. The doctor had said so himself. Annabel hadn't been on the pill for years, so there was no chemical reason to stop her getting pregnant. She just had to hope that all the chemicals in the numerous cleaning products she'd just immersed herself in weren't about to have their own adverse effect.

'That's something else I need to do,' she said, making another mental note; this time to research the dangers of household cleaning products when it came to a woman's reproductive system.

The evening ahead felt daunting; Annabel wished Tom would suddenly appear to offer some words of wisdom. He always knew exactly what to do, and say, when it came to difficult situations; when to hold her hand and when to tell her to simply get on with it. She wondered if he was looking down on her, full of support. Or if he felt betrayed somehow? She hoped not. But while her head insisted on the first, her heart didn't feel quite so sure.

'Why did you have to leave me?' she asked.

Her mind drifted back to that awful night, recalling how Tom had nipped out to collect their Chinese take-away, while she busied herself laying the table. A fifteen-minute return journey at best, she hadn't been surprised to find it taking longer. Tom had always been a people person. He had a habit of getting into conversation with complete strangers and was no doubt chatting to a fellow customer. As the minutes continued to tick by, Annabel decided to give him a call. However, the sound of his mobile filtered into the kitchen and following its direction, she headed out into the hallway only to find he'd forgotten to take it with him. *Typical*, she thought, abruptly ending the call. Annabel began to feel uneasy. Minutes had turned into hours, but insisting Tom was fine, she told herself she was worrying about nothing. The car must have broken down and he had no way of letting her know. Or, maybe someone else's vehicle had failed and he'd stopped to help them fix it ... . She felt relief when she finally heard a knock at the door, and realising Tom had obviously forgotten his key too, she raced out to let him in. 'Thank goodness,' she said, flinging the door open. 'I was starting to panic.'

'Mrs. Woods?' said the police officer, who was standing there.

Annabel quickly wiped the tears away. There was no point in crying. After all, if there was one thing she'd learned over the years it was that tears didn't bring him back. Besides, as much as she missed Tom, tonight was about moving forward, getting on with the future, not languishing in the past. 'A future you're meant to be embracing, remember.'

Annabel took another deep breath and, tried free her mind of all things sad.

Ready to get back to the task at hand, she pulled a pack of scented candles out of the shopping bag and opening up the packaging, began dotting them about the room. Of course, Dan might not want to use them, she considered; he might even find her mood inducing touches a bit silly under the circumstances. Yet, creating the right ambience felt important to her, even it is proved less so to him.

Annabel reached into the bag again and took out a little glass measuring jar. She hadn't paid it much attention when she'd bought it, but looking at it now, it reminded her of the ones she'd used way back when during Science class. Its technical appearance certainly contrasted with the candles, but she refused to see her baby as some scientific project, no matter how its conception occurred. She decided to dismiss the jar altogether and simply put it to one side before moving onto her next purchase.

Annabel emptied the bag of its final contents; she could still feel her embarrassment at having to buy a couple of porn magazines. While loitering in the aisle for at least twenty minutes, she thought the young chap browsing through *Biker's Weekly* would never move on. Eventually, plucking up the courage, she quickly reached up and grabbed the nearest two, hiding them in her trolley under the potatoes. With nobody able to see them, she quite happily got on with the rest of her shopping, adding a box of cereal, a cooked chicken, and a jar of coffee along the way.

But then she reached the till.

She began to cringe and realised that she had no choice but to place the magazines on the conveyor belt along with all of her other purchases. A conveyor belt, she noted, that seemed particularly slow on this occasion. Annabel tried not to put them too close to the glass jar, but could swear the giggling from behind meant that someone had made the connection. Despite flushing red, she did her best to ignore them.

The till operator smirked as she swiped the magazines over the bar code sensor and, while looking Annabel directly in the eyes, seemed to purposefully place them on top of the food mound for all to see. 'That will be forty-eight pounds and twenty,' she said.

Desperate to get out of there, the last thing Annabel wanted was to have to wait for change and, fumbling in her purse, she tried to come up with the right amount of cash. While counting it out to the last penny, she almost had to stop herself from throwing the money at the woman, doing her best to hold her head high. Finally, she could make her exit, and raced to the doors. At last, out in the fresh air, she just thanked goodness there were other supermarkets she could go to from now on.

Annabel couldn't help but feel a little disheartened as she took in her purchases. Not only did they look pitiful, but this certainly wasn't how she'd envisaged her inauguration into motherhood. Even so, she supposed needs must; after all, getting pregnant wasn't exactly something she could do on her own.

She let out a long, hard sigh and checked her watch. 'Thirty minutes and counting,' she said.

***

Dan shook the deodorant can, trying to get at the last dregs of spray. Despite almost covering himself in the stuff, he still felt hot and bothered. He'd never slept with a complete stranger before and the strain of knowing that's what he was about to do was clearly taking its toll. He felt nervous as hell, worried he wouldn't be able to perform. Yes, Annabel was gorgeous; he'd have to be blind not to see that. But stress could play cruel games when it came to a man's anatomy; especially when the pressure was on.

He wished he could be more like his mate Richard, a man who'd bed a different woman every night of the week given half the chance. Unlike him though, Dan more often than not preferred to get to know someone before sleeping with them. No wonder he felt nervous. Apart from their initial meeting in the pub and bumping into her in the street that day, he hadn't clapped eyes on Annabel since. They'd spoken on the phone, of course, and to be fair, Annabel had seemed just as nervy as him about the whole thing; as well as being surprised that he'd actually agreed to do this. Now he began to ask himself why?

He grabbed his jeans and while pulling them on, he suddenly paused, as an unwanted thought entered his head. 'What if she doesn't want to sleep with me?' he asked. Unwelcome images of being shown to the bathroom appeared in his mind; he being forced to do the business solo as while she watched TV in another room, turkey-baster at the ready. A situation he considered way more embarrassing than the both of them jumping into bed together. 'No,' he said. 'She wouldn't. Would she?' He shook the very idea away, telling himself he was just being daft. They might not have talked about the actual practicalities of getting Annabel pregnant, but he couldn't see her putting him through that.

He continued to dress, wondering what his baby might look like; whether he, or she, would inherit his pale blue eyes and unruly blonde hair. Annabel had made it clear that Dan would be the father in DNA terms only; that once the deed was done he'd be out of the picture. But that didn't stop him secretly hoping she'd change her mind once the baby was born. Or that there'd be something a bit more visual to indicate paternity, something obvious to back up the science. He almost laughed, forced to ask where this desire for a *mini me* had come from. He found it pathetic; he'd always viewed himself as more of a forward thinker.

Then again, he supposed becoming a donor was bound to raise issues. It could even explain why he'd been thinking about his own dad a lot more recently. Questioning how different his life would have been had his father lived?

My father, Dan thought. A man, who to all intents and purposes had taken good care of himself, yet had still only managed a relatively short innings. Thinking about it, his dad hadn't been much older than he was now when he'd passed away and surely if it could happen to him, it could happen to anyone.

Dan knew such a fear was irrational, but he had to wonder if his dad's mortality had somehow informed his decision to go ahead with Annabel's request. It would certainly explain his sudden need to let the world know his seed had what it takes. After all, without this opportunity, there might never be any living proof he'd ever personally existed. He thought about his dad's death again, knowing that if he remained childless there'd be no one left to continue the family name.

'That's a point,' he said. 'Will this baby even have my name?'

After acknowledging there was more to this agreement than he'd fully appreciated, Dan couldn't help but sigh. It was as if he had an angel sitting on each of his shoulders. One cheering him on, insisting he was doing the right thing, even if the finer details did still need ironing out; the other frowning and shaking its head, telling him that becoming a father was best left until he found the right woman.

'The right woman,' Dan scoffed. Picturing his mother with her long list of demands on the daughter-in-law front, he couldn't even be sure there was a strong enough candidate out there.

He checked his reflection in the mirror and, refusing to be swayed, once again told himself that he was just being silly. Going for casual yet smart, he wanted to create the right impression without being too formal. 'Not bad,' he said, liking what he saw. He turned his attention to the bedside cabinet and grabbed an envelope out of the drawer. Not the nicest of documents, he had to admit, but thanks to Annabel's insistence on a test at least he knew for certain that he was clean, that he wasn't carrying any STDs. He stuffed it into his pocket and took a deep breath in anticipation of the evening ahead. Now all he had to do was get past his over inquisitive mum without giving the game away, a task that could prove harder than having sex on demand.

Making his way downstairs, he found her at the kitchen table pawing over some fancy travel magazine. 'Planning on going somewhere?' he asked.

She looked up. 'No, not really, but a girl can dream.'

Her response surprised Dan. His mum was always organising a trip to somewhere or another. In fact, aside of himself, her travelling expeditions were what she lived for.

He clocked her taking in his attire and she suddenly perked up.

'Unlike you, by the looks of things. Anyone I know?'

'Yes, as a matter of fact,' said Dan. Obviously keen to know more, Dan saw her eyes widen and he couldn't help but smile. The woman could be so predictable. 'I'm meeting up with Richard, if you must know.'

'Oh,' she said.

Her eagerness turned to flat out disappointment, leaving Dan doing his best to hide his amusement. 'I'll pass on your regards, shall I?' he asked.

He knew he shouldn't tease, but lately she'd gone from being interested in his love life to bordering on obsessive, something he was sure nobody else's son had to put up with.

'Apparently Maeve and her new man have broken up,' she ventured. 'I could give Missy a call if you like?'

'No thanks,' he replied. 'A few beers with Richard will do me fine.'

Regardless of any entertainment value, Dan hated lying to her. Although, under the circumstances he didn't think he had a choice. Not that the baby issue on its own concerned him. His mum had always had a live and let live approach to life. However, this live and let live theory might be alright when it came to other people's children, but would she really extend the courtesy when it came to her own offspring? He took in her expression; the look of blighted hope was enough to answer the question in itself. Of course she wouldn't.

He decided to move the conversation on. 'What about you? No belly dancing, didgeridoo practice or whatever else it is you get up to tonight?'

His mum chuckled. 'You know full well I don't play the didgeridoo.'

Glad to see his mum smile, he leaned down and kissed her on the forehead ready to make his exit. 'Don't wait up,' he said, heading for the door.

'Maeve's a very nice girl, you know.' his mum suddenly called after him. 'You could do worse.'

Despite trying to hide it, the desperation in his mother's voice caused Dan to stop in his tracks. Feeling suspicious, she either had a good idea he was up to something and this was a last ditch attempt at stopping him; or, she was up to something herself. Whichever of the two, neither option boded well.

He quickly recalled his numerous phone calls with Annabel, mentally double checking that each and every one of them had taken place out of his mother's earshot. And knowing that, short of him talking in his sleep, there was no way she could be on to him, Dan realised this could only mean one thing. The woman had plans afoot of her own.

'Mum,' he said, turning to face her. 'What's going on?'

She didn't reply, her sudden silence on the matter increased his curiosity.

'Mum?' he repeated.

Whatever was on her mind, he could see she didn't want to tell him. Dan just hoped she hadn't taken her need to match-make one step further and organised some sort of blind date. Or worse still, booked the church for a wedding, something he wouldn't have put past her of late.

She patted the seat next to her, indicating he should sit down and wondering what this was all about, he accepted the invitation.

'Just promise me,' she said. 'That you'll be married, or at least settled, before I pop my clogs.'

Dan laughed. At least this meant she hadn't ordered a hat. But still, talk like this was way over the top, even for his mother.

His mum failed to share in his amusement and maintained her air of solemnity as she placed a hand on his. 'Promise me,' she said.

He decided to play along. The woman might be a tad eccentric, but they both knew she had years left in her; therefore, it was a vow he could easily make. 'Okay,' he said. 'I promise.'

He rose to his feet but she reached up to stop him.

'Come on, Dan. I'm being serious.'

The sincerity in her face began to worry him and he found himself sitting back down again. 'I know, Mum,' he said. 'And so am I.'

She took his hand once more and Dan felt her grip tighten. Confused, he watched her take a deep breath, as if gathering her thoughts.

'Mum, what's wrong?' he asked.

'There's something I need to tell you,' she replied. 'Something I should have told you before now, but every time I tried I couldn't find the right words.' She paused, bringing a hand up to her mouth. 'God, this is so hard.'

Dan suddenly felt frightened. 'What's so hard? You should have told me what?'

As his mother looked at him, he saw tears beginning to form in her eyes.

'I'm sick, Dan,' she said. 'Very sick.'

SEVEN

Elbows on the counter, Annabel sat by the till, propped her chin in her hand, and sighed. It was one of those days; one of those weeks, even. A few days ago, she'd had so much to look forward to. Becoming a mother had seemed a real possibility. Now, and through no fault of her own, parenthood was back to being a dream. She ached with disappointment. How could life be so cruel? How could *people* be so cruel?

She stared at the phone and willed it to ring. With all the births, deaths, and marriages taking place, let alone the engagements, the leaving-dos and the just-for-the-heck-of-its, someone somewhere must want a bunch of flowers. Of course they did. Just not from her it seemed. She gazed out of the window at all the passers-by, acknowledging there'd been a distinct lack of customers coming through the door. Annabel hated times like these. They weren't just bad for business, they gave her the headspace to think, whether she wanted to or not.

The one thing she most certainly didn't want to consider was her situation with Dan, a desire her brain adamantly refused to acknowledge. Images of the man popped into her head at every given opportunity. Pictures of him having a good laugh at her expense, while she just sat there waiting for him to turn up. She felt almost as annoyed with herself. From what Katy had said about him being a player, she should have known he'd pull a stunt like that. Not that any self-blame stopped her from wanting to throttle him.

While glancing around the room, she tried to conjure up another job to help keep her murderous thoughts at bay. It was a struggle. Having spent the last couple of days tidying the stock room, checking the inventory, and giving the shop a good old clean, there didn't seem to be any more chores left. She tried to look on the bright side and supposed that Dan had done her a favour. These were all jobs that had needed doing anyway and he had provided her with the required motivation to get stuck in. She frowned, wondering who she was trying to kid. The man hadn't done her a favour at all. He'd made a complete fool of her.

She reached over the counter and pulled a rose out of its container. After running her fingers along its velvety petals, she put it to her nose hoping its scent would be enough to soothe her. On this occasion, though, it seemed even her beloved flowers couldn't help and, she began to imagine what she was going to say, or better still *do*, to Dan the very next time she clapped eyes on him.

Annabel headed out back, telling herself a cup of tea would make her feel better. Not that she really believed in the power of the hot drink, her stash of teabags had failed to work their magic all week. She grabbed one from its box and simply tossed it into her cup before clicking the kettle on.

While waiting for the water to boil, the shop door opened and its bell sounded. 'At last,' she said. 'A customer.' With a bit of luck they'd want lots of fancy flower arrangements organising for some big event, a job detailed enough to give her mind another diversion.

She put on her best customer service smile before stepping out to greet them. Caught by surprise, both she, and her smile, froze. The last person Annabel expected to see standing there was Dan; and despite plotting his physical downfall all week, she found herself lost for words, let alone ready for action.

He looked exhausted, like he hadn't slept properly in days. But Annabel felt in no mood to sympathise, a lack of sleep was something she also knew all too well and recently, it was thanks to him.

'You've got some nerve,' she finally said.

'I wanted to explain,' he replied. 'And to apologise.'

Annabel scoffed. Folding her arms, she automatically pushed her hip out to one side. 'For what?' she asked. 'For agreeing to something you shouldn't have agreed to in the first place? Or for humiliating me after the fact?'

'That was never my intention,' said Dan.

His words sounded feeble. However, his expression told a different story. He actually had the decency to look like he meant it.

'I mean you could've told me you'd changed your mind,' said Annabel. 'I would have understood. But to just not turn up like that, how could you be so cruel?'

'You're right, I should've called you. I'm sorry.' He turned to leave.

Annabel couldn't believe it. How dare he turn his back on her, she deserved more than that. The man might not be begging her forgiveness, but an explanation wouldn't have gone amiss. And besides, just because he'd decided to be a man of few words, thanks to the way he'd treated her, she still had plenty to say.

'What? That's it?'

He stopped in his tracks. 'Like I said, I wanted to apologise.'

After seeing the man appear so defeated, Annabel suddenly found herself torn. Yes, a part of her wanted to stuff him, to let him walk out the door never to be seen again. Under the circumstances that would be the sensible thing to do. However, unlike the Dan she'd talked to on previous occasions, this Dan had no spark. He had no oomph. There was clearly something more going on here. Standing there looking at him, she just had to decide if she really wanted to know what.

Annabel felt herself relax and decided against her better judgement. 'Look, why don't we start again? Over a cuppa?'

Her question clearly needed some consideration.

'I was making one anyway,' she said.

He still didn't answer, but neither did he attempt to leave.

Annabel tried to hide her frustration, reminding herself that opening up didn't come easy for some. 'Here,' she said, dragging a stool from behind the counter so he could sit down, she refused to take no for an answer.

Despite his continued hesitation, she left him hovering while she went out back to re-boil the kettle and was surprised to find he hadn't moved an inch when she returned with two steaming mugs. 'You can sit down, you know,' she said, pointing to the pre-allocated seat.

Annabel watched him do as he was told; she wondered if inviting Dan to stay had been the right thing to do after all. Rather than engaging with her, he seemed to be on automatic pilot. Another feeling she knew all too well.

'Talking about it might help,' she said.

He responded with a smile, but it looked empty.

'Doesn't change anything, though, does it?' he replied.

Annabel handed him his drink and while wrapping both her hands around her own cup, she let the room descend into silence. If Dan was anything like her, he would speak when he was ready.

'So what happened?' he suddenly asked. 'To your husband, I mean?'

'But how did you …?'

As he nodded to the gold band that hung on a chain around her neck, Annabel immediately put a hand up to her chest, surprised to find her wedding ring on show. Quickly tucking it away, she made sure it stayed put where it belonged – resting against her heart. Unable to understand what Tom had to do with anything, Dan's question threw her a little; she wasn't used to talking about him with people he'd never known. 'He died,' she said, wondering where all this was going.

'Jeez.'

Annabel supposed there wasn't much else he could say. 'Tell me about it,' she replied.

'How?' asked Dan.

Annabel shifted in her seat, wishing he'd just move the conversation on. 'A hit and run. Some young lad, according to witnesses, although they never caught him.'

'I've only ever known one person die,' said Dan. 'My dad, when I was ten.'

Despite feeling uneasy with the subject matter, Annabel tried to look reassuring. 'I'm sorry to hear that,' she said.

As the room fell quiet once more, Annabel didn't just feel uncomfortable, she felt awkward. She knew Dan was working up to something but already felt out of her depth. Out of all her family and friends, she'd been the only one to suffer any real drama in life. And she'd gotten so used to receiving comfort it was as if she'd forgotten how to give it, a realisation made worse when tears began to well in Dan's eyes.

She'd never actually seen a grown man cry before. The men she knew weren't prone to demonstrating their emotions like this. Even at Tom's funeral, the attending males managed to keep their feelings in check. Unlike them though, Dan seemed to wear his heart on his sleeve. She considered his emotional honesty a refreshing change, at the same time knowing that if he went into a complete watery breakdown, she'd be useless. His tears would end up a horrible embarrassment to the both of them.

She reached out and placed a consoling hand on his, hoping it wouldn't come to that. However, he immediately withdrew from the gesture. An action that left her feeling a bit silly and with her palm now just resting on the counter, she too pulled back.

'And now my mum's dying too,' he said.

Jesus thought Annabel. No wonder the guy was a walking wreck.

She watched him take a deep breath and then slowly exhale.

'She told me the other night as I was about to leave for yours. That's why I didn't turn up.'

Annabel didn't know what to say. She'd realised whatever was going on had to be serious. His demeanour had told her that. However, she certainly hadn't anticipated hearing something like this.

'I know,' said Dan. 'What a kicker, eh?'

Annabel pictured herself stomping around these last few days and immediately felt ashamed. When he'd stood her up, she hadn't even considered the possibility he might have had good reason; that he'd have something more important to deal with. How could she be so selfish?

'How long does she have?' she asked.

'Let's just say we're talking months, not years,' Dan replied. 'She was diagnosed with oesophageal cancer, except now it has spread to her spine. I should've known something was wrong, I could see she was losing weight. I put it down to some stupid diet she'd gone on, low carb or something. First she was cutting the crusts off of her bread, then refusing to eat bread at all. Then she stopped eating potatoes.' He took a sip of his tea. 'Now I know why. Food like that can't get past the tumour.'

'I'm so sorry,' said Annabel. She of all people knew what it was like to lose someone.

Annabel gave him a moment; she couldn't help but think about the night Tom died. She could see herself pacing the length and breadth of the hospital family room. *Family room*, she silently scoffed. Such a title suggested a sense of comfort. Yet, with its plain, white washed walls, and hard, plastic chairs, let alone the reasons for its very existence, it didn't exactly live up to its name. The police officer who'd driven her there tried to do his job and offer support, but everything that came out of his mouth sounded hollow, and she just wanted to scream at him to shut up. She didn't, of course. She just stopped listening and instead, prayed like she'd never prayed before. She felt the all-consuming desperation as she willed Tom to live; he couldn't leave her. Not now, not ever. She pictured the doctor as he entered the room. No words were necessary, his face said it all, and as the room suddenly started to spin, Annabel felt her legs buckle.

Annabel saw the same kind of desperation in Dan's face. Experience told her the last thing he needed right now was a string of platitudes, knowledge that left her almost too scared to speak for fear of saying the wrong thing.

She wondered if she should feel relieved that Tom had been taken in an instant. There one minute and gone in the next. She hadn't been forced to watch him getting sicker and sicker, all the while knowing there wasn't a damn thing she could do about it. How on earth did anyone cope with that?

'I really am sorry,' she said.

She watched him take another deep breath and hastily wipe his eyes.

'Of course, it's just like her to refuse treatment,' he said, trying to raise a smile. 'She doesn't see the point in dragging things out an extra few weeks, especially if she's too ill to enjoy them.'

'What about you?' asked Annabel. 'What do you think?'

'It's not about me, is it?' said Dan. 'I have to respect her wishes.' He took a sip of his tea, the poor man's hands shaking as he struggled to keep it together. 'All I can do is be strong for her sake, which is really hard when she won't even talk about it. She's acting like there's nothing wrong.'

Annabel reached out once more; pleased to find that this time he didn't recoil.

'It's always the good ones, isn't it?' he said, a sentiment with which Annabel whole-heartedly agreed.

'What's your mum like?' she asked. During her own dark days, talking about Tom had a way of making her feel better and she assumed the opportunity to talk would benefit Dan too. 'Tell me about her.'

Just the mere thought of his mum made him smile, except now it wasn't just with his lips, Annabel saw his whole face light up.

'She's fun,' he said. 'You'd like her. Although she's completely mad with it, nothing at all like your typical mum.'

'In what way?'

'Well how many other women do you see wandering around the supermarket in an evening dress?'

Annabel had to admit that did seem a bit bizarre. Trying to picture the scene, she certainly couldn't imagine her own mother dressed to the nines while tottering up and down the freezer aisle.

'Don't get me wrong, she's not mentally ill or anything,' said Dan, as if reading her mind. 'Even if she does do the most random things going. She just doesn't believe in saving anything for best. It doesn't matter what it is, we could be talking about a silver coffee pot or a hat for all Mum cares. She says most of the stuff she owns wouldn't get used if it only came out for special occasions. She's the same about her wardrobe.'

Annabel thought about the rank and file of long forgotten clothes hanging in her own closet, she could see his mum had a point.

'Plus, she insists that looking nice makes a woman feel nice,' Dan added.

Annabel looked down at her own attire. Throwing on a pair of jeans, a t-shirt, and a pair of pumps every morning had become more of a routine than a fashion choice, and again, she could understand the woman's reasoning.

'Although she doesn't always make life easy,' he continued. 'Even now she's creating unnecessary challenges, can you believe?'

'Really,' said Annabel, intrigued. 'Like what?'

Dan nervously chuckled and shook his head. He seemed to be wondering if he should really be telling her this. 'Before she told me she was sick she made me make a promise.' He shifted in his seat. 'Oh, don't worry about it. It's just silly.'

'No, go on. Tell me,' said Annabel. Urging him to continue, this was the most relaxed he'd been since his arrival and not only did she think it important to keep his spirits up, he was right, his mum did seem fun and she wanted to know more.

'She conned me into giving my word that I'd find myself a wife before she dies.'

Annabel's jaw dropped. 'You're kidding me?' she said.

Dan shook his head. 'I wish I was.' He stared into his cup. 'It's only ever been the two of us, you see. I don't have any brothers or sisters and there's no other family to speak of. She probably thinks she's looking out for me. Of course, when I agreed, I didn't realise I'd be working to a time scale.'

Annabel could appreciate where his mum was coming from. Even with a family behind her, she knew first-hand what it was like to be left behind. Something she wouldn't wish on her worst enemy, let alone someone in Dan's shoes. She guessed his mother knew that too, being a widow herself. Dan was going to need all the support he could get. And if the support wasn't there, then where would that leave him?

'Oh, I don't know,' said Dan. 'I've been wondering if this is her way of keeping me busy so I don't have to think about what's really going on here. About what really matters.'

'That's one way of looking at it. Or she's just being a mum to the very end,' suggested Annabel. 'She's thinking about what's going to happen in *your* future rather than dwelling on her own.'

'Maybe,' said Dan. 'I hadn't quite thought about it like that.'

'So what now? Are you going to keep your promise?'

He shrugged. 'It's a big ask.'

Annabel had to agree. It took most people years before they found *The One* and this poor chap only had months. 'And I thought looking for a baby daddy was a challenge,' she said.

'About that,' said Dan.

Annabel felt herself redden. She hadn't meant to think out loud.

'Don't worry about it,' she quickly replied. Knowing what he was about to say, she understood why he'd want to back out. 'I'm sure I can find someone else. You need to concentrate on yourself and your mum right now.'

'But I want to do it,' he said.

Annabel looked at him surprised. With everything he had going on at the moment, she would've thought sperm donation to be the last thing on his mind. 'Sorry?' she said. Surely she must have misheard.

'Look, we both know the odds are against me. I'm never going to find someone I want to spend the rest of my life with in such a short time.'

Yet again, Annabel found herself wondering where all this was going.

'So to be able to tell mum she's going to be a grandma instead, at least that would be something.'

Annabel bit her lip. As sorry as she was for Dan, this was not part of the plan. She felt terrible. Having been the one to ask him for help in the first place, every fibre of her being screamed no, she couldn't return the favour. It was one thing giving him a listening ear, but to actually get involved in his mum's dying … after what happened to Tom, his request felt a bit too close for comfort.

'I know you said this arrangement was no strings attached,' he carried on. 'That I'm out of the picture once you're pregnant. I'll even admit to not being one hundred per cent sure about what I was doing when I agreed to become a donor. But things have changed now. If Mum knows I have a child on the way, she'll know I have a focus, a reason to keep going, just like she did with me when Dad died. You can see that, can't you?'

Lost for words, unfortunately Annabel could see it.

'Don't worry. You won't have to pretend we're in some sort of relationship. And telling her about the pregnancy would be a last resort. I just don't want her to go thinking she's deserting me. That she's leaving me completely on my own.'

Annabel still couldn't bring herself to speak. Yes, she fully understood his concerns. The prospect of leaving her son with more or less no one in the world must be devastating for his mother and she could appreciate why Dan would want to protect her from that. But his pleas didn't stop her wanting to run for the hills.

She looked into his desperate eyes.

'Annabel?' he said, clearly expecting an answer.

'Okay,' she found herself saying.

EIGHT

Standing at the sink in her finery, hands submerged in the washing up, Annabel giggled. She felt a bit silly being all dressed up with nowhere to go. At the same time, she had to admit Dan's mother was right. Having not stopped tittering since getting changed, looking good did go some way to making a woman feel good. *Breaking into fits of giggles probably wasn't quite what his mum had in mind though*, thought Annabel, laughing at herself regardless. And ignoring the splashes of water landing on her dress, she considered asking Dan whether there were any more tips in the offering.

'As long as he doesn't think the glitzy attire is for his benefit,' she said. Then again, with everything else he had going on at the moment, Annabel doubted he'd even notice.

She thought about their recent exchanges. Apart from a few cursory words about work and the weather, it wasn't as if they'd had any real conversation since that day in the shop. She always made a point of enquiring after his mum, of course, to which he continuously gave some standard reply. She was doing okay. A response that Annabel deemed strange in light of the emotional honesty he'd previously shown. Maybe he felt embarrassed at breaking down in front of her. Or, he could be burying his head in the sand, telling himself if he didn't talk about it, his mother's illness would just go away. Sad really, but whatever the reason, he hadn't confided in her since.

She stopped what she was doing for a moment, thinking how funny it was that a man could so easily donate his sperm, yet he refused to give his feelings away.

Annabel returned to the dishes and continued to ponder their actual interaction; she decided that it was a procedure more than anything else. A procedure whereby every Wednesday night Dan would arrive and more or less go straight up to the bathroom, then job done, simply leave her, and the turkey baster, to it. It all felt quite formal considering she hoped to carry his baby; Annabel couldn't help but think she should be getting to know at least a little bit about the man. In time, their child was bound to have questions regarding his or her father; questions that she wanted to be able to answer. As things stood, she didn't even know Dan's favourite colour.

On the other hand, she had to admit that their limited dialogue was hardly surprising. Even aside from his mother's illness; they hadn't exactly had the best start to their pregnancy journey.

Her stomach lurched as she recalled the first time he came around.

Annabel lead the way upstairs, her legs shook with nerves. Her palms felt sweaty as she sought the security of her wedding ring, sliding it across its chain, first one way and then the other, with each and every step. Finally, coming to a standstill, she indicated to the only open door on the landing, the entrance to the bathroom. Dan just stood there. Her heart raced as she stared at him, wondering what he was waiting for. He stared at her as if wondering what she was playing at. Then it dawned on her. This wasn't quite the stairway to heaven he'd been anticipating. Suddenly panicked, instinct took over and without thinking, she shoved him inside. The poor man almost toppled into the bath as she slammed the door shut. Left standing on her own, Annabel burned with embarrassment.

It was all her fault, of course. She should have made it clear from the beginning that they wouldn't actually be sleeping together. From then on, he'd been more than happy to just do the business and go. Although after a mix up like that, Annabel could hardly blame him. She sighed. If she was ever going to learn anything about Dan, it was obvious the effort would have to come from her.

As she placed the last of the washing up on the draining board, Annabel heard the front door open and close. She grabbed a tea towel to dry her hands, and questioned who it could be. It wouldn't be Dan. He always rang the bell and waited for her to let him in. Besides, he wasn't due just yet anyway, and unlike hers, his timing was impeccable.

'It's only me,' a voice called out.

'Of course,' said Annabel. 'Rebecca.'

Annabel could have kicked herself. While her sister had, inadvertently, been the one to spur her into action with regards to Dan, her annoyance had since calmed down and unfortunately, she still hadn't gotten around to mentioning anything.

Having already shown her disapproval on the family planning front, the last thing Annabel wanted was Rebecca causing another scene. Keeping quiet until a pregnancy test proved positive had seemed like the best thing to do. She realised her mistake and, knew she had to get rid of her. Why, oh why, hadn't she considered the possibility that both Rebecca's and Dan's paths might cross?

Annabel calculated that she still had about fifteen minutes before Dan got there, she told herself that with a bit of luck, Rebecca wouldn't be staying long. She never usually did. Her flying visits were more out of habit these days, a habit that stemmed from the time of Tom's death. Back then, her sister had all but moved in. She would sit for hours listening to Annabel cry, comforting her, making sure she ate, and showered even; acts that Annabel would be forever grateful for. However, despite that period having long since passed, she still popped in regularly to make sure all was well. This was something Annabel continued to appreciate, even if her visits could sometimes be a bit fraught, or, in this case badly timed.

'Oh,' said Rebecca. Making her entrance, she looked somewhat surprised. 'You're going out.'

Annabel had forgotten about her posh clothes and looking down at her attire, quickly realised they gave her just the excuse she needed. Knowing she always went red when she told a fib, she willed herself not to blush. 'Erm, yes,' she replied. 'I am.'

Annabel threw the tea towel to one side and tried to appear convincing. She hated lying, but at the same time, didn't think she had a choice. On the one hand, if she admitted she'd taken to dressing up for absolutely no reason, her sister was liable to get her committed. On the other, if she confessed to her weekly appointment with Dan, her sister was liable to commit murder.

She imagined the two different scenarios; one of them involving a strait jacket, the other a pair of hand cuffs. Neither of the pictures was pretty, and to save either of them from being locked up, she made a show of checking the time again. 'In fact, I should probably be leaving any time now.'

'Not to worry,' said Rebecca.

Annabel resisted shovelling her out the door as she waited for her to leave. But instead of moving, her sister just stood there.

'Was it anything important?' Annabel asked.

'Nothing that can't wait, I suppose,' she replied. She tried to raise a smile. 'I just wanted your advice on something, that's all.'

Annabel, unable to believe what she was hearing, momentarily forgot about Dan. As her sister finally turned to make her exit, she stopped her in her tracks. 'You want advice?' she asked. 'From me?'

Annabel wondered if she should be worried. Rebecca was usually the one giving counsel, not receiving it. She never asked for anyone's opinion on anything. Rebecca was one of those women who simply got on with things; who coped no matter what life threw at her. Annabel knew she must have swallowed a lot of pride to come here and ask for help like this; especially from her little sister.

'Really?' she added.

'Really,' said Rebecca.

Annabel looked at the woman and realised she'd never seen her quite so unhappy. Harassed, yes, but not dejected like this. After everything Rebecca had done for her over the years, Annabel couldn't just let her go. This was her chance to do something in return and she wasn't about to let the opportunity slide.

She checked the clock again and told herself that, if she was quick, she might be able to prevent Dan's arrival. 'Look, let me make a quick call and get changed,' she said, digging her mobile out of her bag. 'Then we can have a sit down and a proper chat.'

'No, don't worry about it,' said Rebecca. 'It can wait. I don't want to spoil your plans.'

Annabel ignored the protests and began dialling anyway. She didn't want to let her sister down. 'Honestly, I can re-arrange.'

'Annabel,' said Rebecca, stepping forward to stop her. 'It's not a problem. We can talk about it some other time.'

Disappointed, Annabel sighed and clicked her phone off; she could tell her sister meant what she said. Back to her usual controlled self, the moment had passed.

'But before I get off, you don't mind if I use your bathroom, do you? I've been dying for a wee all the way over here.'

With no choice but to admit defeat, Annabel nodded. 'Of course you can,' she said.

She watched Rebecca leave the room before taking a seat at the kitchen table. Her sister may have suggested they re-arrange, but she knew they wouldn't. That wasn't Rebecca's style. Asking for advice would've been hard enough in the first place and there was no way she'd allow herself to go through the stress of it again. Annabel felt at a loss. She supposed she'd just have to insist, regardless of any excuses the woman might try and come up with.

Annabel heard footsteps and she listened to Rebecca making her way back down stairs. She steeled herself, ready to assert some authority; Annabel wanted her sister to know that she was around day or night.

'Care to tell me what this is doing here,' said her sister, appearing in the doorway.

Annabel froze. Momentarily lost for words, Rebecca's problems suddenly vanished. *Fuck!* If ever she wanted the ground to swallow her whole, it was now. With its corner pinched between her finger and thumb, there was no escaping her sister's disgust as she held up one of the porn magazines. The poor woman would be washing her hands for weeks.

'Well?' said Rebecca.

Having completely forgotten about the candles, the glass jar and the magazines, Annabel cringed like never before. She felt her cheeks flushing red. 'I can explain.'

Annabel's blushing intensified as Rebecca slowly stepped forward and carefully placed the offending item on the table right in front of her. 'No need,' she said, gathering up her belongings. 'I should go.'

Annabel's embarrassment turned to confusion. The sister she knew would be ranting and raving by now, asking her what the hell she thought she was playing at. She certainly wouldn't just walk away.

She jumped up from her seat and hastily shoved the magazine into a drawer, before following Rebecca out into the hall. 'Please don't go,' she said. 'At least not like this.' She felt powerless. Marching straight for the front door, Rebecca was clearly having none of it. 'Rebecca,' she continued to plead.

While ignoring Annabel's plight, her sister simply grabbed the handle and pulled the front door wide open.

Annabel's eyes widened in horror as she saw Dan standing there, his finger poised over the doorbell, ready to signal his arrival.

Dan appeared as equally as surprised, he smiled. 'Oh, hello,' he said, friendly as anything.

As if things couldn't get any worse.

Annabel squirmed as her sister glared from him, to her, and back again; and without a single word simply continued on her way.

'Was it something I said?' asked Dan, clearly wondering what that was all about.

Annabel slumped against the hallway wall; she knew that she'd be lucky if her sister ever spoke to her again. 'Well that's really gone and done it,' she said. She took a moment before straightening herself up. 'You'd better come in.'

With nothing else for it, she headed straight to the kitchen leaving Dan no choice but to follow her down the hall. 'Cuppa?'

she asked. Offering him a drink was the least he deserved after that little scene.

He seemed to hesitate, then think better of it. 'Why not,' he replied.

She set about making some tea.

'Call it a silly question,' said Dan. 'But is everything okay?'

Annabel stopped what she was doing and turned to face him. After the way Rebecca had just behaved, she supposed she should explain. She pictured her sister holding up the offending material and suddenly realised it wasn't just any porn magazine on display, but *his* porn magazine. Again, she found herself lost for words. After deciding an explanation was no longer necessary, Annabel simply smiled. 'Everything's fine,' she said.

He furrowed his brow as if waiting for her to tell the truth.

She continued smiling, determined to maintain her silence. It was all to no avail.

'Okay, okay,' she said, holding her hands up in defeat. 'That was my sister, if you must know.'

'Ah,' said Dan. 'And?'

As far as Annabel was concerned, it was one thing sharing their favourite colours for the baby's sake, but quite another revealing family squabbles. 'And nothing.'

Dan clearly didn't believe her, which was hardly surprising.

'She just doesn't agree with what I'm doing, that's all. Or should I say, with what we're doing.'

'I can understand that,' Dan replied.

'You can?'

Dan laughed. 'Well it's not exactly the norm, is it?'

Annabel had to admit he had a point. She got back to making the tea.

'So how are things with you?' she asked. 'How are you bearing up?'

'As well as can be expected, I suppose,' he replied.

As he left it at that, Annabel turned to face him again. Fixing him with a knowing stare, Rebecca might have refused a listening ear, but she wasn't going to let him get away with it too. In any case, he started this sharing is caring malarky.

Her unwaveringness paid off and he seemed to relax.

'I'm fine,' he said. 'Thank- you for asking.'

'Mum's still being Mum, of course,' he added. 'Trying to pretend she isn't sick. Although, I have just left her writing out her Bucket List, like she hasn't packed enough in already.'

'A Bucket List? That's a great idea.'

'Yes, well, you don't know my mother. I dread to think what she's coming up with.'

Annabel laughed. She may not have met the woman, but she couldn't help but like her.

'It's not funny,' said Dan. 'You know, I actually thought she'd died the other day. I walked into the living room and there she was, flat out on the sofa with her arms crossed over her chest. I honestly froze. I didn't know what to do. Of course, I jumped out of my skin when she opened her eyes and smiled at me. Turns out she was practicing for when the time really comes.'

'Oh, Dan.' Annabel pictured the scenario and wondered if it was wrong of her to find it amusing. 'I don't know what to say.'

'Yes, well, a few choice words came out of my mouth, I can tell you. If I didn't know any better, I'd swear she's trying to take me with her.' He fell silent for a moment. 'So tell me, what would you put on your Bucket List?' he asked. 'If you were to write one.'

Annabel noted how smoothly he moved the conversation away from himself and put the onus on her. Still, at least he was talking and she supposed any exchange was better than none.

She thought for a moment. His question would've been easier to answer if he'd asked her what her list wouldn't include. She assumed most people would want to do a bungee jump or leap out of an aeroplane, things she most definitely wouldn't consider. 'Oh I don't know,' she said, trying to come up with something even remotely exciting. 'Maybe learning to skate board, something like that. There's a group of kids down the road who make it look so easy. And I suppose, like everyone else, I'd like to travel; although given the chance I haven't a clue where I'd go.'

Annabel listened to herself; she knew how dull she sounded. For someone who knew how short life can be, she certainly hadn't been making the most of her own. 'She's a smart lady, your mum,' said Annabel. 'Life is for living, no matter how much time we have left.' She couldn't help but laugh at the hypocrisy of her own words. For the last three years it had just been her and her memories; three years of existing, nothing more nothing less. 'Listen to me,' she said. 'Anyone would think I know what I'm talking about.'

'Oh come on,' said Dan. 'Things can't be that bad.'

'Let's just say I'm taking a leaf out of your mother's book.'

Dan smiled, taking in her attire. 'I noticed,' he said.

As she returned his gaze, butterflies suddenly fluttered in Annabel's tummy. It had been a long time since a man had looked at her like that and she wasn't sure if she liked it. She looked down at her dress. 'What this old thing,' she said.

He continued to stare and, desperate to break the spell, Annabel turned to the fridge to get the milk. She looked at the carton and wondered what was wrong with her. Most people liked an admiring compliment when they got one, they didn't flinch. Most people her age cracked open the alcohol when they had guests, yet here she was offering hers a cup of tea. She thought it no wonder people didn't see her as a suitable confidante, she was a fraudster. Too screwed up to help herself, yet she'd spent the last half an hour insisting she could help everyone else. 'Sod it,' she said, taking out a bottle of wine instead. 'Shall we?'

Annabel wondered what had gotten into her, she decided to go with it anyway; she grabbed a corkscrew from the cutlery drawer and set about trying to open the wine. No doubt, thanks to her sudden abandon, she seemed to be all fingers and thumbs and couldn't seem to manage.

'Here let me,' said Dan, getting up from his seat.

Annabel tried to relax. But his close proximity seemed to have the opposite effect.

They stood in silence as he reached out to take the bottle and, feeling his touch, her whole body tingled as his palms rested against hers. Looking at them, she'd never noticed his hands before. Used to hard work, they were strong and solid.

Without thinking, she let her gaze follow the line of his muscular arms, her heart was suddenly beating so fast she felt sure Dan could hear it. Pausing to take in his well-built chest, she breathed in the aroma of his aftershave. He smelt fresh and clean. A rush of heat seemed to course through her veins, a sensation that both scared and excited her. Finally, looking up into his eyes, Annabel could see from the intent way Dan now looked at her, he was experiencing it too. She took in the softness of his lips as they began slowly moving towards her own.

What are you doing? a voice in her head screamed.

Annabel relinquished the bottle and took a quick step back. 'I'm sorry,' she said. 'I can't do this.'

NINE

Dan looked forward to the evening ahead. He needed cheering up after the incident with Annabel. He hadn't imagined their connection that night, he was sure of that. And he certainly hadn't meant to act on it; it sort of just happened. Even so, trying to kiss Annabel was a line he should never have crossed. He'd apologised, of course, but words didn't seem enough. He supposed he'd just have to come up with another way to say *I'm sorry*.

'You okay?' asked his mum. She reached over from the passenger seat and gave his arm a comforting rub.

Dan smiled. 'Here with you, how could I not be?'

He loved surprises and couldn't wait to find out what his mum had planned for them. It seemed ages since they'd done something out of the ordinary together and arriving at their destination, he pulled the car over to the kerb, eager to check out the venue.

He looked at the building, with its huge glass dome, solid, greying stonework, and big, towering pillars it was certainly imposing. Victorian, he hazarded a guess; its architecture was reminiscent of an old Royal Bath House. These days it clearly played host to a bar or an exclusive club and Dan couldn't wait to get inside.

'So what's the plan?' he asked.

He gazed out of the window again, and clocked a poster advertising the evening's entertainment and, reading it, his heart immediately sank. He turned to look at his mother and told himself that even she couldn't be so cruel.

She grinned back at him, her excitement there for all to see. Enough to tell him that, yes, in the cruelty stakes, it seemed she could.

'You've got to be kidding me,' he said. 'No wonder you kept quiet. You knew I wouldn't have come.'

'Oh don't be so soft,' his mum replied. 'We'll have a great time. Where's your sense of fun?'

Dan looked at the poster again. When his mother had said tonight was about the two of them doing something special, this wasn't the kind of thing he'd had in mind. He'd envisaged some quality one on one time, something along the lines of a nice meal where they could sit and not just talk, but really talk – and to each other, not a bunch of strangers.

'Speed dating is not my idea of fun.'

'Don't worry, you won't be on your own,' said his mum. She pulled a compact out of her handbag and checked her make-up. 'You'll be pleased to know I've signed us both up.'

He inched round in his seat. 'You've done what?'

She laughed, as usual refusing to take his disapproval all that seriously.

'You of all people know I haven't been on a single date since I married your Father. This way I get twenty in one evening. See it as making up for lost time.' She pulled a pen and piece of paper out of her handbag and drew a tick next to one of her scribbles.

Dan recognised it as her Bucket List and rolled his eyes. 'I should have known that would have something to do with this,' he said.

'Don't worry. I'm not planning on replacing your Dad. We both know it's a bit late for that. Call it killing two birds with one stone.' She chuckled, as she stuffed the pen and paper away again. 'After all, this isn't just about me, is it? We still have your future to think about, remember, and what better place to start?'

He had secretly hoped that his mother would forget all about his promise to find a wife, but realised he'd only been kidding himself. She was never going to let up. As for her actual involvement, if she could do this, he dreaded to think what other delights his mother had in store.

'Now come on, let's get in there,' she said.

Dan reluctantly switched off the ignition and watched her get out of the car. He was more than happy to support her with her dying deeds, but surely she didn't really think he'd find his soul mate here of all places? She tapped on the window, excitedly urging him to get a move on. His shoulders slumped. Of course she did. In fact, it wouldn't have surprised him if this had nothing to do with her Bucket List at all, if her contribution to the evening was just a façade. She continued motioning for him to hurry up and he couldn't help but let out a hefty sigh. It was no use. He knew when he was beaten.

'Now let me have a look at you,' she said, as he climbed out of the vehicle.

She immediately began straightening his tie and stepping back to behold him in all his suited and booted glory, Dan felt like it was his first day at school all over again. Half expecting her to check behind his ears and make sure he'd brushed his teeth properly, experience told him he had no choice but to stand there until she was happy. Pride seemed to ooze out of his mother as she looked at him and he realised he couldn't begrudge her this moment. As his heart began to melt, nor could he begrudge it for himself. Thanks to her illness, this was one of the few mother and son moments they had left.

Inspection over, she gave him a satisfied smile. 'They're going to love you as much as I do,' she said.

'You think?' replied Dan.

Less than convinced, he looked up at the building once more, wondering what kind of people were in there, if any at all. Speed dating might have been the in thing once of a day, but to him, it now just seemed old hat.

He followed his mum inside and was pleasantly surprised by the smart interior. An ornately carved wooden bar spanned the whole length of the room; stylised framed posters of guitars, Che Guevara, and other iconic images hung in neat groupings against Olive green walls. Giant chandeliers also glistened across the ceiling. Everything in the room fit together perfectly. Dan would have loved to have had a proper look around, but within seconds it seemed that he and his mum had attracted attention.

A woman with a clipboard raced over to greet them. Assuming her to be the event organiser, she obviously ran a tight ship. As far as Dan was concerned, even her smile looked efficient.

'Thank goodness,' she said. 'As you can see we're ready to get started.' She checked her watch. 'A couple more minutes and you'd have missed out.'

'Really,' said Dan. Disappointed, he made a note to drive a little slower the next time his mother suggested an evening out.

He looked over at the hopeful participants and he was surprised to find how popular these events still were. Each one of them appeared to be as keen as the next to get proceedings underway; an eagerness that he could see also encompassed his mother. He took in the range of men she'd be chatting to, most of them geeks by the looks of things and the majority way too young. He just hoped there wasn't some stalking, serial killer sitting amongst them too. What with everything else they had to contend with at the moment.

'Now here's your name tag,' said the organiser. 'It is Dan, isn't it? I simply ask because that's the only guy's name I have left. We don't do walk-ins, you see. Registration only, I'm afraid.'

Tempted to seize the opportunity and deny his identity, a knowing flash in his mother's eyes warned him not to. Forced to appear keener than he felt, he found himself nodding. 'Yes, Dan,' he said. 'That's me.'

'Lovely. Now here's your sheet.' The organiser offered him an A4 piece of paper and a pen. 'Just to explain, your first date starts at the first whistle. After five minutes, you'll hear the whistle again and that's when you move on to your next date. It really is as simple as that. Just put a tick next to the names of all the ladies you'd like to meet up with again and only if there are any matches will we pass on your contact details.'

'If you could take that seat over there, please.' She indicated to an empty chair at the end table. 'And I'll show this lovely lady to her seat over there.'

His mum leaned into him. 'Let the fun commence,' she said.

She gave a little wink before sashaying off into the distance and, unable to help himself, Dan shook his head. How could she do this to herself, let alone him?

He headed over to his table and the first of his dates. A petite blonde with a friendly smile, she looked pleasant enough, although he didn't have a clue what he was supposed to say to her.

She got up from her seat, ready to shake his hand. 'I'm Sally,' she said.

'Dan,' he replied, accepting the gesture.

***

When the organiser signalled half time, Dan had never felt so relieved. The shrill of a long, drawn out whistle had never sounded so good. To say these mini dates were supposed to be a sharing of information, he'd certainly struggled to get a word in. On the plus side, however, he supposed he now knew about the need to grow his own veg, where to go for the most stylish of haircuts, and that as soon as he gets the chance he should visit the Big Apple. *Because NYC is definitely the best city on the planet.*

'That was quick,' said the woman before him. 'They say time flies when you're having fun, don't they?'

As she looked at her watch, Dan wondered what she was referring to. The evening so far? Or the last five minutes with him? Either way, he couldn't bring himself to agree. In his view, this event nowhere near lived up to its name on the speed front.

'Time for a drink, I think,' she said.

Her statement contained the hint of an invitation, but Dan chose to decline. 'You go ahead,' he said, preferring to wait for his mum. His lack of action seemed to confuse the woman, as if he should feel grateful for the extra few minutes in her company. But he pretended he hadn't noticed and, after an uncomfortably long pause, she finally got up from her seat, gathered up her belongings, and went on her way.

He looked down at his sheet of names. Yes, one or two of them had been interesting, but not enough to warrant a tick. As for another one or two, if he ever happened to see them in the street he wouldn't just cross the road, he'd cross the country. The things some people shared. As far as Dan was concerned, a couple of these women didn't need a partner, they needed help.

Dan watched most of the attendees head to the bar, he continued to sit there and looked over to his mother. Still chatting away, she seemed as bad as all the others. Her smile was bigger and brighter than everyone else's though and so infectious he felt his own lips curl. Seeing her so animated, it was hard to believe she was sick and wishing more than anything that she wasn't, Dan found himself asking how long before the tell-tale signs that she was dying would begin to show.

He didn't have a clue how he'd cope without her, a reality that obviously worried her more and more too. Why else would she bring him here of all places? He just wished she hadn't insisted he make that stupid promise to start with. But promise he did. He looked around the rest of the room and knew nights like tonight weren't the answer. Spotting marriage potential at the best of times, let alone in a simple five minutes, wasn't just difficult, it was nigh on impossible. Even Annabel had said so and she was trying to get pregnant via a turkey baster.

Annabel. As soon as her face popped into his head he wished it hadn't. Ever since they'd nearly kissed he'd been doing his best not to think about her. The last thing he needed right now was more complications and, as far as he was concerned, Annabel was one complicated lady. Of course, it didn't help that he liked the woman, the very reason he'd tried to keep things professional these last weeks. Maintaining a distance seemed safer somehow. Then she offered him a drink and one thing led to another – well almost. He knew if their lips had connected, he'd have been hooked. Yet further proof that he needed to find the real woman of his dreams and fast.

Dan willed his mother to hurry up, she at last ended her conversation and enthusiastically began making her way over.

'Isn't this fun?' she said.

Dan rose to his feet, doing his utmost to pretend he felt the same. 'That's one way of putting it,' he replied.

He showed his mother to a vacant table in the bar area and went off to get them a drink. Then he returned with two glasses of orange juice, he would have preferred something stiffer. Getting drunk might not solve his problems, but it would certainly get him through the rest of the evening. All in complete contrast to how his mum felt, he noted. Having a merry old time, she clearly needed no such assistance.

'You see that chap over there,' she said, indicating to a man in the crowd. 'The one in the grey suit?'

As he took a seat, Dan followed her eye line, identifying the man concerned.

'He's so lovely I can't believe he's still single. You'd think, as a doctor, he'd have no problem meeting the right woman, especially being surrounded by nurses every day. Unlike him over there.' She pointed to another man. 'It's no wonder he's on his own. He breeds rabbits. I tried to tell him a woman doesn't really want to know the difference between a Britannia Petite and a Dwarf Hotot, but he wasn't having any of it. The man's obsessed.'

'And that bloke there,' she continued.

Drawn into her chatter, Dan tried to keep up. 'The guy in the blue jumper?'

'That's the one. Well, his girlfriend's just dumped him. Come the end of our five minutes, I realised I knew more about her than I did him. Honestly, you have to wonder what some people are doing here. Men like that can't seriously be looking for a relationship.'

Dan laughed at the hypocrisy. 'And you're here because … ?'

'What choice do I have?' she asked. 'I have a son who won't grant his dying mother her one and only wish.'

Thanks to his mum's current vivaciousness Dan had almost forgotten she was sick. Why did she have to remind him?

'What's that supposed to mean?' he asked. According to her Bucket List she had lots of dying wishes.

'It means I have a son who doesn't know what's good for him. He refuses to settle down with the one beautiful, intelligent woman whom his mother knows is just perfect.'

Dan almost choked on his orange juice. She had to be kidding. 'Please tell me you're not talking about Missy's daughter again, Mum. Settle down with her, I haven't even met her.'

'And whose fault is that?' she asked. 'It's not like you haven't had the chance.' She took a sip of her drink. 'In some cultures you wouldn't have a choice in the matter, you know. In some cultures, it's the parents who decide these things.'

Dan couldn't believe what he was hearing. He'd guessed there'd be an agenda somewhere along the line, but he hadn't made a connection to Maeve. 'So all that stuff about us doing something fun together was just a ploy, was it? Tonight was meant to be so unbearable that I'd see the error of my ways? Are you sure you don't have cancer of the brain as well as the body?' he asked.

He froze, immediately horrified by what he'd just said. He couldn't believe such a thought would enter his head, let alone come out of his mouth. 'Mum, I'm so sorry, I take it back. I didn't mean that.'

Much to his surprise, rather than be upset by his words, his mother suddenly burst out laughing. 'Yes you did,' she said.

As she continued to howl, Dan stared at her incredulous. Try as he might, he still couldn't see the funny side.

'That's the first God's honest thing you've said to me in weeks,' she carried on. 'Thank you, Lord. A bit of normality.'

'Normality?' said Dan, wondering what the woman was talking about. Now he really, really needed a drink. 'Nothing about anything feels normal anymore.' He took in his surroundings. 'I mean look at us. You talk about mother and son. We're out speed-dating together, for goodness sake.'

Much to his frustration, this made his mum laugh even more. But despite not getting the joke, it felt good to see his mum like this. Her laughter became contagious and Dan found himself starting to titter as well.

'Oh, Dan, I have missed this,' she said. She pulled herself together and gave him a hug.

As he felt his mother's arms around him, Dan thought about the misery of the last few weeks and had to concede that he'd missed it too.

'Ditto,' he said.

Another long, drawn out whistle sounded signaling it was time to get back to it. However, rather than resume events, Dan wanted nothing more than to just stay put.

Dan's mum released her hold, ready for round two; it seemed that she had different ideas.

'Do we have to?' he asked, watching her rise to her feet.

'Well if you're not interested in Maeve,' she said, as she glanced around the room. 'Who's to say you won't be interested in one of these lovely ladies?' She looked him square in the eye. 'Although we do still have those profiles to go through.'

'Profiles?' said Dan. What on earth was his mum talking about now? 'What profiles?'

'Didn't I mention it?' she replied. 'I could have sworn I told you. I've signed you up with an Internet dating site.'

TEN

'Oh, Mum. What are you doing now?' asked Dan. As he entered the kitchen, he took in the sight before him. Worried for the woman's safety, if she carried on like this, she was going to be the death of him, never mind herself.

'Stop fussing, Sweetie. I'm not an invalid.'

Dan despaired. His mother could be so frustrating when she wanted to be, he wished that, for once, she'd listen to his advice.

'No, but keep going like this and you soon will be,' he said. 'What if you have a funny turn while you're up there and there's no one here to catch you?'

Seeing her part way up a step ladder, bottle of disinfectant in one hand, and a dishcloth in the other, it didn't matter how many times he insisted she start taking things easy, his words only fell on deaf ears. No matter how many times he offered to get on with things himself, according to her the place needed a good old spring clean; a job that apparently only she could do. Yesterday, it had been the utility. Today, it seemed the kitchen cupboards warranted her attention. It was as if she needed to put on a show most of the time, pretending the cancer wasn't taking its toll.

'And you are sick, remember,' he said. 'You could easily fall.' However, as usual she ignored him.

It wasn't that he hadn't tried to understand. He knew people dealt with the prospect of death in their own way, and in their own time. As for his mother, in her refusal to slow down, she seemed to be tidying up every loose end conceivable. Including jobs like this, so that when the inevitable came Dan would only have himself to think of. However, would he really care about a speck of dust loitering at the back of a cupboard upon her death? He very much doubted it.

As he watched her, Dan wanted nothing more than to be there for his mum. Not just emotionally, but through the physical pain she was clearly doing her utmost to hide. A difficult task when she refused to even acknowledge the *C* word, let alone talk about its impact on her body. Some rancid tumour was eating away at her insides, for God's sake, and as far as Dan was concerned, that was the immediate priority here, not the housework.

'We're going to have to talk about it at some point, Mum,' he said. 'You can't stay in denial forever. There are things we need to discuss. I need to know what's happening to you, what's going to happen. How else am I gonna be of any help?'

Finally, she began making her way down the step ladder. As tempted as he felt, Dan resisted the urge to jump in and assist. She'd remained as independent as ever these last few weeks and hated him making a fuss.

'I understand all that,' she replied. 'Just not yet. I'm not ready. Okay?'

He thought it strange how someone could accept the fact that death was looming, but at the same time failed to address its cause. He wondered where this inability to express what her body was going through came from. Did it stem from fear? Did she think an acknowledgement of what was happening to her physically would somehow speed up the dying process? Whatever her reasoning, Dan couldn't help but feel shut out.

'I understand you're scared, Mum. I'm scared too.'

Her eyes seemed to beg him to let it go, leaving Dan feeling guilty for pushing her on the matter. 'Okay,' he said. 'I'll shut up. But only for now.' He stepped forward to give her a hug. 'What are we going to do with you, eh?'

As he looked over at the kitchen table, he spotted a pile of Internet dating profiles next to his mother's laptop. He had hoped she'd been joking when she said she'd signed him up, but his mother was clearly on a mission, determined to get him on the road to marriage one way or another.

'What's going on?' he asked, suddenly noticing her passport too. Surely she wasn't planning a holiday as well as a bit of matchmaking.

His mother followed his gaze and suddenly perked up. 'Well you know that Bucket List I've been putting together?'

Considering the speed dating episode, how could he forget?

'Yes,' he cautiously replied.

'Well it made me realise there are still lots of wonderful places to see. I've been so busy taking myself off to the likes of Australia and Africa I've completely ignored what's on the doorstep.'

Dan dreaded what was coming next.

'Such as the Leaning Tower of Pisa and the Eiffel Tower.' She raced over to the table and picked up a travel guide, eager to show him the pages within.

His stomach sank. What was wrong with the woman? 'Please tell me you're not going to Paris?' he said.

'Nope,' replied his mum.

Thank God, thought Dan. At least that was something.

She giggled with excitement. 'I'm going to Amsterdam.'

Dan felt his shoulders slump. Thanks to the woman before him, he'd been experiencing one surprise after another as of late; none of them very nice. 'Mum, you're not well enough to get on a plane.'

She automatically dismissed his concern. 'You worry too much.'

'And you don't worry enough.'

It seemed they'd reached a stalemate. Not that his mother even tried to see things from his point of view. He could tell by the determination written all over her face that she was heading off to Europe with, or without, his blessing.

'Dan, I shall be absolutely fine,' she said. 'And I won't be on my own either. I'll have a travel companion.'

'Really? And who might that be?' Unable to condone her decision, he'd be damned if he was going to accompany her.

'If you must know, Missy has agreed to come with me.'

'Missy?' said Dan. 'And that's supposed to make me feel better, is it?' As bad influences went, this so-called friend of hers was turning out to be an expert.

His mum smiled, intuitive as ever. 'Am I detecting a little jealousy here?' she asked.

As much as he disagreed with her plan, Dan did have to admit he felt a little green -eyed. With precious little time left, he'd assumed she'd want *him* to experience these things with her. Not some woman that her son had never met. Plus his mother hadn't even attempted to humour him on the travelling front; regardless of them both already knowing his answer, it would have been nice to have been asked.

'I didn't suggest you come with me,' she said. 'Because, if we're honest, neither of us would enjoy ourselves. You'd fuss too much and insist we keep stopping for yet *another* rest. I'd want to keep going and we'd only end up getting annoyed with each other. I don't have time for that, Dan. Not anymore.'

Dan knew she was right; he constantly worried about her these days. He was forever telling her to put her feet up and rest. But, to not have him in the running from the start, his mum had to see why that would hurt.

'And if something happens to you?' he said. 'While I'm stuck here and you're over there? What then?'

'What can possibly go wrong in a few hours?' said his mum. 'You see that's the great thing about this continent of ours. No matter the city, I can be there and back in the same day.'

'And you're allowed to travel, are you?'

'Well I won't tell if you won't.'

Frustrated, Dan hated it when his mother had an answer for everything. He also realised there was no point in arguing. His mum had always been the same. Once she'd made up her mind over *anything* that was usually it. As for her trip, she'd clearly thought everything through. He'd just have to resign himself to the fact that she was never going to change. She'd probably be coming up with these balmy ideas of hers right up until her last breath.

'In that case,' he said. Seizing the opportunity, he took the dish cloth and disinfectant out of her hands. 'You can't have both. It's either Amsterdam *or* the cleaning. Your choice?'

She reached up and gently placed her right palm on his cheek. 'I do love you, you know.'

'I know,' he replied. 'And I love you too.'

A lump suddenly formed in his throat, Dan struggled to keep his tears at bay. Like she kept telling him, these next few months were about her enjoying the time she had left, not mourning any loss. He had to stay strong and, although she didn't always make it easy, allow his mum to do things her way. Dan put his arms around her and kissed her forehead. Then he let out a long lamenting sigh before pulling back again. 'Now sit down,' he said, painting a smile on his face. 'And let me get you a drink.'

His mum took a seat. 'Speaking of Missy,' she said.

Dan closed his eyes. Talk about a woman pushing her luck. 'Whatever it is you're about to say,' he said. 'The answer is still no.'

'But why, Dan? I wouldn't keep pushing if I didn't think Maeve was right for you. I don't understand what the problem is.'

Admittedly, Dan struggled to understand his reasons too. Until recently, his point blank refusal to meet Maeve had been because he hadn't wanted his mum organising his love life. Not anymore though, now it felt more complicated. Agreeing to a date simply because his mother was dying didn't just feel wrong it felt unfair—on Maeve as much as himself. The pressure on both of them to like each other would be unbearable. And, if it turned out there was some sort of spark, they'd only be going into a relationship for all the wrong reasons.

'Look, whatever it is, you know you can tell me,' said his mum. 'I just want you to be happy.'

'Happy with Maeve, you mean.'

She let out a laugh. 'Unless you have someone else in mind?'

Dan scoffed. The chance would be a fine thing. The only other woman he'd had any contact with lately was Annabel and, thanks to her issues, she seemed more unsuitable than his mother's friend's daughter. He couldn't deny they'd shared a connection, but she was still too wrapped up in her deceased husband for them to be anything more than just friends. Something, in an odd sort of way, he'd like to think they'd become over the last few weeks.

He thought back to the kindness she'd shown him when he'd first found out his mum was sick. Considering what she'd been through, it must have been difficult for her; yet, she still took the time to listen. *Friends*, he thought to himself, unable to completely deny his sense of disappointment. *Just two friends supporting each other and in the most bizarre way possible.* He pondered their arrangement. Sometimes it felt like total madness, but, in spite of that, he supposed they both had their reasons.

He looked at his mum, flicking through her travel guide. Dan thought about his own childhood, with all the love, care, and fun she'd provided over the years, he knew she'd make a fabulous grandparent. And, for a moment, he felt tempted to tell her what he and Annabel were up to. He quickly realised he couldn't, of course. He'd promised Annabel he'd keep schtum until absolutely necessary. Just like he'd promised his mum he'd find himself a wife. He sighed at the weight of his predicament and wondered where to go from here. Despite his reservations, he couldn't help but think that Maeve had been the answer all along. In giving things with her a chance, at least he'd be able to keep his word when it came to the other two.

As if feeling his stare, his mum looked up. 'What?' she asked.

'Alright, alright,' he said. 'Give Missy a call.'

'Really?' said his mother.

The look on her face was priceless.

'Really,' said Dan.

He watched her jump up from her seat and race towards him. She planted a great, big kiss on his cheek and then rushed to the phone, no doubt, to schedule a meeting before he could change his mind. He shook his head. Anyone would think Christmas had come early. He certainly seemed to have just given her the best present possible and, regardless of still feeling unsure on the Maeve front, he had to confess her response was worth it.

He left the room to get his coat after deciding to leave his mum to it. She was bound to completely embarrass him in one way or another and, as she could read him like a book, he didn't want her knowing that he wasn't going into this one hundred percent. Besides, there was something he wanted to do. Something he'd been meaning to do for days.

When Dan reappeared he signaled to his mother that he was going out, but she was already too deep in animated conversation to notice. He listened for a moment. Judging by the squeals on the other end of the phone line, it was clear she wasn't the only one getting all worked up. Her friend sounded equally as thrilled.

He wondered what Maeve would say when she found out that he'd agreed to meet her. If she'd feel just as daunted by this as he did? She might even flat out refuse to see him and who could blame her? The girl had to have the same concerns as him.

Dan continued to take in his mother's delight; he just had to hope that come any date, the two of them actually liked each other. After all, with both his mum and Missy involved in proceedings, this would be a bugger to get out of if they didn't.

ELEVEN

nnabel flicked through the TV channels, but couldn't find anything worth watching. Programme after programme; everything seemed to be either a repeat or the dullest of viewings imaginable. She wondered what was wrong with her. Normally, she'd be quite happy to lounge on the sofa, losing herself in some mind-numbing show whether she'd seen it before or not. Lately though, she just felt restless.

As much as she tried to deny it, Annabel knew she only had herself to blame. She'd been naïve to think that if she moved on in one aspect of her life, the rest of it could stay the same. She might not have anticipated it, but, even the most tentative step back out into the big, wide world was bound to have its impact, enough to show her there was more to life than these four walls and work. Why hadn't she listened to Katy and gone for an anonymous donor? If she had, her naivety might have stood a better chance. She sighed. It was just like her to be clever and go down the unconventional route.

Typical really, she thought. Out of all the men in the pub that night she had to pick the one going through the biggest crisis of his life. And who better to empathise than a woman who'd experienced the death of a loved one first hand? No wonder Dan didn't remain a mere sperm donor for very long; it would have been inhuman of Annabel not to see him as an individual with feelings and fears in his own right. Then he had to introduce her to things like Bucket Lists and posh frocks for no reason, reminders of how it felt to be living rather than existing. Under circumstances like that, was it any wonder things were getting complicated?

Of course, it wasn't enough that she felt for the guy, she had to make matters worse. Dan's and her lips might not have actually met, but for Annabel that wasn't really the point. They may as well have done. She shrank inside, yet again questioning what the hell had come over her. What had she been thinking, especially when she'd been the one to lay down all the ground rules. There was to be no physical contact between her and her donor, she wanted a baby and nothing more. Yet despite all this, she'd still seen fit to more or less throw herself at him. *Talk about being a tease. Dan must hate me right now.*

She hoped not. Although to be fair to him, it wouldn't have surprised her if she never clapped eyes on him again.

'Maybe it's for the best,' she said, particularly as Dan wasn't her only dilemma. She had her husband to think about in all of this as well, and if she were in his shoes, she had to admit she probably wouldn't be too pleased. Annabel had never forgotten their conversation and the promise she'd made. In fact, she could remember it verbatim. At the time, Tom had laughed and called her silly. But she'd meant every word of it. She still did. She looked up to the heavens, praying to God he hadn't been looking down to witness the whole event. 'I really am sorry, Tom,' she said, 'All I can tell you is it won't happen again.'

Frustrated, Annabel didn't want to think about it anymore and she tossed the remote to one side and glanced around the room. Her eyes settled on the book case and she considered losing herself in a good old yarn. It seemed ages since she'd done any reading; and getting engrossed in someone else's problems would certainly help her forget her own. One look at the titles on offer though and she knew her heart wasn't in it. Reading took too much concentration. Annabel turned her attention to the clock; she supposed that only left an early bath and bed. It might only be 7pm, but it wasn't as if she had anything better to do. Besides, she hadn't been sleeping properly as of late, so the extra few hours rest would do her good.

Annabel heard the doorbell ring. *Strange*, she thought. *I'm not expecting any visitors.* She trudged out into the hallway, curious as to whom it could be and knowing her luck, she'd be about to greet some religious group out to recruit new members. Then again, she scoffed, joining a convent-like sect might be just what she needed right now. After all, becoming a nun was one way of ensuring she kept to her marriage vows. She opened the door, ready to tell them she'd join whatever cult was on offer. Caught off guard, her heart skipped a beat.

'Oh,' she said, almost lost for words. 'Hello.'

Annabel felt awkward as well as surprised. Having not heard from Dan since that fateful night she wasn't prepared. She'd just been thinking she'd never see him again, yet here he was, large as life. Being a polite chap, doubtless, only to tell her the whole baby thing was off.

'Hello,' he replied.

Annabel braced herself for the inevitable; she took in his casual yet smart attire and looked down at her cosy sweatpants. If she'd known he was coming, she'd have at least tidied herself up a bit.

'For you,' said Dan.

Dan produced a gift from behind his back, Annabel felt confused. She'd always assumed men didn't like rejection, but this one had come bearing gifts.

'I was going to save it until Wednesday and then I thought what the heck. You don't mind me turning up like this, do you?'

'Not at all,' replied Annabel, although if truth be known she didn't know what to think. Things had been decidedly uncomfortable come the end of his last visit. 'But … 'She fell silent, not sure how to continue.

'Look,' said Dan. 'If you're worried about the other night, then don't be. We both have a lot going on and these things happen.'

Annabel shifted from one foot to the other. 'Not to me they don't,' she said.

He smiled. 'Annabel, we didn't do anything. Remember?'

She looked into his eyes, his sincerity making her blush.

'And our arrangement?' she tentatively asked.

He seemed to find her question unnecessary. 'Well I'm still game if you are?'

Annabel felt torn. Dan might be correct in his assertion that nothing had actually taken place between them, but that didn't mean she hadn't wanted it to—a *want* that continued to scare the hell out of her. On the other hand, she desperately wanted a child too and there was no way she could face having to go out and find another donor.

She told herself that she was being ridiculous, that surely she could pretend nothing had happened if he could.

'As long as you're sure,' she replied. 'Because …'

'I'm sure,' said Dan, before she could finish. He held out his gift. 'Call it a peace offering.'

Finally, Annabel allowed herself to relax. 'Thank you,' she said.

In spite of its wrapping, there was no disguising what the gift was. Annabel ripped open the paper, she couldn't help but laugh. 'And what am I supposed to do with this?' she asked. It had to be the scruffiest skateboard she'd ever seen.

'Sorry about the state of it,' said Dan. 'It's been in the shed for years.'

'You mean it's yours?'

'It certainly is. I got it when I was about eight. A birthday present from Mum.'

Annabel remembered what had been said during their Bucket List conversation and she felt touched that he'd remembered too.

'It's about time it came out of retirement,' said Dan. 'So …' He took a step back. 'When you're ready.'

'What? You want me to get on it now?'

Annabel stood there aghast. It was all very nice of him to think of her like this, but he couldn't really expect her to jump on it straight away, could he? Not only was she a complete novice, she wasn't prepared. She needed time to psych herself up.

'Unless you've got better things to do,' said Dan.

Annabel thought about the alternative, the choice between crap TV or an early night. If it was anybody else, she knew it would be a no brainer. Looking from the tatty, old skateboard to him and back again, she had to admit she felt tempted as she tried to remember the last time she'd done something so spur of the moment.

A little voice told her she was on dangerous ground, but looking him in the eye again, there seemed to be something about this man. He certainly had the ability to bring out the worst in her. Or could that be the best? Annabel wasn't sure anymore.

Bugger it, *she thought*. Why not?

Annabel kicked off her slippers and swapped them with a pair of trainers, she smiled. 'So where to?' she asked. After stepping outside, she shut the door behind her.

'We don't have to go anywhere,' said Dan. 'We have the perfect practice road here.'

Much to Annabel's horror, he indicated to her front street. 'You've got to be kidding me?'

'No, of course not. I mean look at it. It's sloping without being too severe, just right for someone who's never had the pleasure before.'

Annabel looked around at the surrounding houses, *pleasure* not being quite the word she'd have chosen. 'In front of the neighbours, you mean?' Knowing them, she'd have been surprised if the curtains weren't twitching already.

Dan ignored her concerns and just laughed. 'Do you want me to show you how it's done? Or would you prefer to dive straight in?'

She looked at the skateboard; the mere prospect of getting on that thing was enough to make her feel anxious. And thanks to their location, she knew she was about to show herself up; something she thought best delayed for as long as possible. 'After you,' she said, easily handing it over.

Annabel watched him head up the road and, ready for action, put one foot on the board before pushing off. She couldn't help but giggle as he slowly rolled towards her. Arms outstretched, he did nothing but wobble. Despite making it clear that he hadn't done this in a while, Annabel had still assumed he'd be a bit more capable than this. Compared to her, he was meant to be the expert.

'How cool is that?' said Dan, suddenly jumping off the board.

The man clearly didn't know what he looked like.

'Your turn,' he said.

Having just seen Dan's efforts, Annabel told herself that she couldn't be any worse and, took up her position in the road. With one foot on the skateboard she took a deep breath to steady her nerves. It reminded her of the first time she'd ridden a bike. Having never been a physical child that had filled her with fear too. Until she realised how easy it was. Using her other foot, she propelled herself forward, before instinctively placing it flat behind the other. Using her arms for balance, she seemed to get the hang of it and her face, at last, relaxed into a smile.

'I'm doing it! I'm doing it!' she excitedly called out.

While gradually making her way down the road, she dared to turn her head towards a cheering Dan as she passed him by. This had to be the most fun she'd had in years.

Annabel felt freer than she'd felt in a long time; even more so when the board began to pick up pace thanks to a sudden incline. A rush of adrenaline coursed through her veins and Annabel wondered if this was how those adrenaline junkies felt.

As she began to go even faster, Annabel thought she'd better slow down. 'What do I do now?' she shouted to Dan, after realising that she didn't know how to. Her adrenaline reverted to downright nervousness, as he shouted something back. But the noise of the wheels on the road's surface drowned him out, leaving Annabel no choice but to just keep going. The skateboard continued to gather momentum, she told herself not to panic. Advice she couldn't help but ignore when a car suddenly turned the corner, only to head in her direction. 'Shit!' she screamed. 'Dan! Dan!'

As the vehicle got nearer and nearer, everything seemed to move in slow motion and Annabel realised if she didn't want to hit it head on she had to jump. With her heart racing and no time to think, she spotted an up and coming garden hedge. 'That'll do,' she told herself. With one eye on the car and one on the greenery, she desperately held her nerve until just the right second and suddenly leapt off of the board, eyes tight shut. As she flew through the air, all she could hear was the sound of screeching brakes, then nothing as she suddenly landed face down in the foliage.

Confused and dazed, she felt someone suddenly upon her.

'Annabel! Annabel! Are you alright?' asked a frantic Dan. 'Annabel, talk to me.'

Flat out in the shrubbery, and with Dan's help, she managed to roll onto her back. Her eyes locked onto his for a moment, as it began to dawn on her what had just happened. She began to smile. 'That's the most fun I've had in years,' she said.

'Jesus,' said Dan, slumping down beside her. 'Thank God you're alright.'

A vehicle door opened and slammed shut. 'Of all the stupid things,' said the female car driver.

Annabel listened as footsteps angrily marched over.

'Do you want to get yourself killed?'

'Oh, fuck,' said Annabel. Now she was in for it.

'Annabel?' said Rebecca, the car driver.

TWELVE

'It's only me,' Dan called out as he let himself into the house. He took off his jacket and hung it on the bannister. 'Mum,' he called out again. Dan couldn't imagine where she'd got to. She hadn't mentioned going anywhere. In fact, apart from the necessary doctor and hospital appointments, she hadn't left the house since getting back from Amsterdam.

He recalled the morning's events. She had been acting pretty strange when he last saw her. Despite him paring jobs down to be around more, she'd certainly seemed keener than usual to pack him off to work, a sign that she could be up to something. Something she didn't want him knowing about. At the time, he'd simply put it down to his mum being Mum; after all, 'strange' could be her middle name. But that was at around eight- thirty and it was now almost two. He furrowed his brow. If she had planned on leaving the house soon after him, surely she should have been back before now.

Unless she hadn't gone out at all, he thought to himself. It would be just like her to want to get on with yet more cleaning. 'Shit!' he said, as he suddenly remembered the step ladder.

Dan pictured his ailing mother, unconscious and in need of medical attention, he raced down the hall to the kitchen, only to find she wasn't there. His panic levels rose; he re-traced his footsteps and ran upstairs to his mother's bedroom. 'Mum, are you in here?' he said. When he burst through the door there was still no sign of her. Back on the landing, he hastily checked the bathroom, his heart pounding as he wondered where she could be, if she was alright, and what he'd do if she wasn't. Dan quickly made his way down stairs again and re-entered the kitchen. There had to be a clue as to her whereabouts somewhere?

He scanned the room once more and spotted a note by the kettle. It simply read *Back Soon*. This didn't tell him when the note was actually written, he realised, and he cursed himself for not checking in with his mum at some point during the day. If he had, he'd have a better idea as to when she'd actually left the house and, therefore, whether 'soon' really did mean 'soon'. He usually called, but it was just his luck that today he'd had to deal with one crisis after another and hadn't found the time to. Not that he could excuse himself. Would it really have been so difficult to just pick up the phone?

He still felt uneasy, but insisted that if something serious had happened he'd have heard by now, somebody would have contacted him. Plus, for all he knew, the note could have been written in the last half an hour, rendering his panic completely unnecessary. 'Yes, that's it,' he said, in an attempt at self-reassurance. 'You're worrying over nothing.'

Rather than just wait for her return, Dan decided to try and calm down by making himself useful. He considered getting on with preparing dinner, but one look inside the fridge told him there wasn't much to choose from. A couple of eggs, some milk, and a ropey looking tomato clearly passed its best; he had to admit that he was hardly surprised. The household shopping had taken a back seat lately, neither he nor his mother having much of an appetite these days.

'Maybe she had the same idea,' said Dan. 'And she's nipped to the shop?'

He sighed. Who was he kidding, she could be anywhere.

He checked the water level in the kettle and clicked it on ready to make a cuppa. If she wasn't back by the time he'd drank it, he'd start to ring around. He felt glad of the noise as the water began to boil. Silence gave him the opportunity to think, something he tried not to do of late – about his mum, about what was happening to her.

He realised that they were as bad as each other on that score. She wasn't ready to discuss her actual cancer and he wasn't really ready to listen. Yes, he'd tried to push her on the matter, but he could have easily contacted the doctor, the nurse, or even a cancer charity for information, none of which he'd done. And, up until now, he fooled himself into thinking this was out of respect for his mother. In reality, he supposed they were *both* just burying their heads in the sand; a situation that Dan knew needed to change.

He headed over to the table, and his mother's laptop. Switching it on, he watched it fire up into life, determined to find out all he could about his mother's illness. He clicked onto the Internet and typed oesophageal cancer into the search bar, an endless list of sites from all sorts of organisations suddenly appeared in front of him. With articles from the *NHS, Cancer Research, Medicine.net,* and *Macmillan* staring back at him, he geared himself up ready to start reading, feeling almost irritated when his mobile began to ring, breaking his concentration.

Dan pulled his phone out of his pocket, he didn't recognise the number. *Oh God*, he thought. *Mum.*

He cautiously answered the call, dreading what he might be about to hear. 'Hello,' he said.

Dan listened to the voice on the other end, his eyes narrowed. He couldn't believe what he was hearing and told himself that this had to be a joke. 'What?' he asked. 'When? Why?'

Disbelief turned to horror as the caller continued to talk. 'Okay,' he said. 'I'll be right there.'

After he ended the call, Dan rushed out of the kitchen and down the hall. He grabbed his keys from his jacket and ran out the door, before quickly making his way to his car. Once inside, he couldn't seem to make the key fit the ignition. 'Come on! Come on!' he said, before finally managing to slot it into the keyhole. He started up the engine; he quickly shoved the gearstick into first and, with a hasty look over his shoulder, raced off down the street. His mind swirled in confusion. 'There must be some mistake,' he insisted. 'This can't be happening.'

Dan overtook one vehicle after another, every set of traffic lights he neared seemed against him. He thought he'd never reach his destination. Not that he could say he was relieved when he finally did. He knew he should find a space, but at first glance he couldn't see one and, rather than drive around in circles, he stopped his car on the spot. Dan didn't care if he'd blocked someone in, he got out and hurried towards the building, he told himself that a disgruntled motorist was the least of his problems. Dan charged up the steps and, once inside, headed straight for the reception.

'I'm here about my mother,' he said, trying to catch his breath.

'Name,' said the woman behind the desk.

Much to Dan's annoyance, she didn't even have the decency to look up.

'Gerry,' he said. 'Sorry, Geraldine. Geraldine Palmer.'

The woman slowly tapped the keys on her computer, while Dan impatiently willed her to get on with it. He absorbed his surroundings; the inside of a police station was the last place he expected to find himself.

'Oh yes, Geraldine Palmer,' the receptionist eventually said. At last giving him her full attention, she fixed him with a mocking stare. 'It says here she was arrested during a drug raid.'

'Yes, well,' said Dan. 'There's obviously been a misunderstanding.'

'They all say that, Sir,' she replied.

'No, you don't understand. My mum, she's sick.'

'Yes, that's something else they all say too.' Her condescending attitude continued as she indicated to the waiting area. 'Now if you could take a seat over there please. I'll go and find out what's happening.'

As she reluctantly rose to her feet and disappeared out back, Dan didn't know what to think. He began to pace up and down, desperate for someone to come and tell him what the hell was going on. His mother, a drug bust, there had to have been a mix up somewhere along the line. His mum was the most anti-drug individual he'd ever known. He imagined her stuck in some dank, dark police cell, insisting she must be terrified by now. In her condition, he dreaded to think what that was doing to any health she had left.

He finally took a seat and dropped his head in his hands for a moment. He looked up again and glanced around at his surroundings. With wanted posters showing video stills of shoplifters, burglars, and pickpockets, he knew his mum didn't belong here. Something these police officers had to have realised by now.

The sound of voices, at last, began to filter through from out back and Dan strained to hear. Convinced one of them belonged to his mother, he struggled to make out her words. Everything sounded cordial enough. Although in her shoes, he couldn't understand why she wasn't screaming and shouting. That's what he'd be doing after a wrongful arrest.

The door at the side of the reception desk suddenly opened. 'Mum,' he said. Relieved to see her, he jumped up from his seat. 'Are you okay?'

She smiled. 'I'm fine. Why wouldn't I be?'

As she turned to the big, burly officer accompanying her, Dan couldn't believe his mother's response. He couldn't believe her relaxed demeanour. This had to be a dream, or more to the point, a nightmare.

'Thank- you,' she said. 'You've been very kind.'

'Just doing my job, Madam,' the police officer replied.

'Kind,' said Dan, doing his utmost to keep calm. 'Mum, these people arrested you.'

'And it won't be happening again,' said the officer. 'Will it, Mrs. Palmer?'

'It certainly will not,' she replied.

'Now you take good care of yourself,' he added.

'I will,' said his mum. 'And it was lovely meeting you.'

Watching their exchange, it was all way too civilised for Dan's liking. He felt powerless, as if he was the only one who could see what was wrong with this scene.

'You ready, Dan?' she simply asked, moving towards the exit.

Dan looked from her, to the police officer and back again, waiting for someone to tell him what was going on. Surely he deserved an explanation as to why his mother had been rounded up with a bunch of drug-dealing, drug-taking thugs?

The police officer remained silent as he stared back at him.

Obviously not.

Lost for words, Dan realised he'd no choice but to follow his mum out.

'Well that was an adventure,' she said, once he'd caught her up.

'An adventure?' said Dan. 'An adventure? Is that all you can say? Do you know what you've just put me through? I've been worried sick in there. Not that anyone seems to care.'

His mum laughed. 'Oh, don't be such a drama queen.'

'A drama queen. Mum, this is serious stuff. You've just been locked up. I mean do you plan on telling me why?'

'Of course, I do. I just thought it would be nice to get home first. It's been a long day.'

She could say that again.

'Now where are we parked?'

Dan felt at a loss over the whole thing, he indicated to his car. As they began making their way over he told himself he was going mad, he'd inadvertently crossed over into the twilight zone. None of this was really happening and he just had to go with it.

'What's that?' his mum suddenly asked. She pointed to the windscreen.

Dan's stomach sank as he spotted the parking ticket. In hindsight, illegally parking on police property probably wasn't the wisest of decisions. He snatched the yellow packet from under the wiper and, without a word, turned back towards the police station.

'Where are you going?' his mum called out.

'To try and sort this,' he replied. 'One criminal in the family is enough, don't you think?'

***

Dan handed his mum a glass of whiskey before taking the seat opposite with a glass of his own. He knew alcohol wasn't really the answer, for either of them. But after the day's excitement he told himself one drink wouldn't hurt.

'So, about today?' he said.

He felt like this should be the other way round and waited for his mother to speak. He watched her twirl her glass backwards and forwards between the palms of her hands as she gathered her thoughts. She looked tired. In fact, more than that, she looked weary.

'There are over fifty museums in Amsterdam,' his mum began. 'Did you know that?'

'No,' Dan replied. 'I didn't.'

'It would take days to get around them. Then there are all the art galleries and historical sites like *Dam Square* and *Oude Kerk* to take in. That's a church in the Red Light District.' She paused for a second. 'You should go one day. It's interesting.'

Dan insisted she was advocating he visit the place of worship and not the brothels.

'I can imagine,' he said.

'That's where Missy and I were when we decided it was time for a break.' She sipped on her whiskey. 'We went into this coffee shop. You know the kind I mean. Brown cafes, I think they call them.'

'Excuse me?' said Dan.

'Well you can't go to Amsterdam without having a look, can you? And we fancied a sit down anyway, so we thought we'd kill two birds with one stone. That's when Missy told me about this research she'd come across.'

Dan threw himself back in his seat. 'Missy,' he said. 'Why am I not surprised?' He didn't want to think badly of his mother's friend, but the more he heard about this woman, the more he struggled to think anything but.

'She was trying to help.'

'Help?' said Dan. 'Really?'

He closed his eyes for a second, having an idea as to the kind of research his mother was talking about. The thought of two old ladies, high as kites, while puffing on a couple of dodgy roll ups wasn't an image he relished. He just prayed that he was wrong.

'Please tell me you didn't,' he said.

'What? Smoke a joint?' asked his mum.

Dan's eyes widened in anticipation of her answer.

'Of course not,' she said. 'I've never smoked in my life, why would I start now?'

Glad to hear it, the relief Dan felt was immeasurable.

'But we did sample some of their cake.'

Dan stared at his mother in disbelief. *Oh, God*, he thought. *My own mother, doing drugs*. He took a swig of alcohol, not sure he wanted to hear the rest of the story.

'It tasted much nicer than I thought it would,' his mum carried on regardless. 'And you wouldn't believe how relaxed it made me feel.'

Dan scoffed. 'I've heard that cannabis does that,' he said. 'Not that I've ever tried it, my law-abiding mother having taught me to say no when it comes to these things.' After all the warnings she'd given over the years, the lectures about drug-induced paranoia, personality disorders, depression, and goodness knew what other side effects, surely she had to see the irony here.

'More relaxed than I've felt in months,' she continued. 'And I got my appetite back, something I thought would never happen.'

Dan cringed. *For fuck's sake*, he thought to himself. Now he pictured his mother with the munchies, could things get any worse?

'Which is why we went back later for another slice.'

Yes, it seemed they could.

'Honestly, I almost felt normal.'

'Normal,' said Dan, not sure whether to laugh or cry. 'You're telling me that two pensioners stuffing their faces with a class B drug is normal?'

'Which brings me to today's events,' his mother continued.

Dan tried to calm himself. 'Go on,' he said. Although it didn't take a genius to work out what was coming next.

'I just thought if I could get my hands on some cannabis here, I could bake myself a cake.'

'Jesus, Mum, we're not talking about nipping down to the supermarket for a bag of flour. Even you must see that. Drug dealers are hardened criminals.' He sighed. How could she have put herself in harm's way like that?

'Of course, if I'd known the place was going to get raided, I wouldn't have gone.'

Dan told himself at least that was something. She hadn't completely lost her marbles.

'I'd have waited,' she carried on. 'Or found another dealer.'

'Another dealer!' Dan had heard it all now. 'Mum, do you know what you sound like? Not only that, you still haven't told me how you managed to find the first.'

'Oh, Dan, I'm not totally stupid.'

The way this conversation was going, Dan had to admit he found that debatable.

'I looked for a pair of trainers hanging over an electricity wire.'

He rolled his eyes. 'That's an urban myth.'

'Is it? Then I got lucky.'

'Lucky?' said Dan. He couldn't believe she'd just said that. 'Mum, you got arrested.'

'I know,' she replied. 'And I'm sorry, it won't happen again.'

As far as Dan was concerned, it shouldn't have happened in the first place.

'So did the police charge you with anything?' he asked.

'They gave me a caution. They said it wasn't in the public's interest to prosecute a dying woman.' His mum raised a smile. 'It's seems having cancer has its benefits after all.

Unable to see a positive side to any of this, Dan shook his head. It was a ridiculous situation from start to finish.

'You know if you'd asked,' he said. 'Explained it all to me, I'd have gone and bought the cannabis for you.'

His mum smiled. 'I know you would,' she said. 'Which is exactly why I kept everything to myself. I can afford to get a criminal record, you can't.'

Dan downed the last of his whiskey and wondered if life could get any worse. Not only was his mother dying, she was now trawling the streets attempting to buy drugs. He knew he couldn't stay mad at her forever though.

He got up from his seat to give her a hug, not sure which of them needed it the most. 'Why us, Mum?' he asked, putting his arms around her. 'Why do we have to go through this?'

'Hey,' his mother replied. She pulled back and looked him directly in the eye. 'Don't you be getting all morbid on me. I'm not done for just yet. We still have things to do, remember?'

'Like what?' said Dan. 'Because as far as that Bucket List is concerned you won't be going on any more trips, if that's what you're thinking. Especially if today's anything to go by.'

'Like making sure your love life is sorted,' she said. 'That's what.'

In all the excitement, Dan had forgotten about his up and coming date with Maeve. He tried not to show it, but his heart sank. It might have seemed like a good idea at the time, but thanks to Missy and her unwanted influence, he no longer felt sure he could go through with it.

THIRTEEN

Annabel sat at the counter chewing on the end of a pencil. She was trying to come up with new ideas for the shop's window display. While the display she already had was okay, she felt the time had come for a fresher, more exciting way to advertise her wares. Putting pencil to paper, she began to sketch, before changing her mind and scribbling all over it, ready to start again.

The doorbell rang and Annabel looked up to see Dan making an entrance. She wondered what he was doing here.

'Morning,' he said. 'I come bearing gifts.' He carried two take-away coffees and handed one out to Annabel as he approached.

'Thank you,' Annabel replied, still surprised to see him here at all.

He automatically dragged a stool over to the counter and sat himself down.

'Make yourself at home, why don't you?' she said.

Dan laughed. 'I was just passing and thought, if you're anything like me, you're probably ready for a brew by now.'

Annabel smiled. She pulled the lid off the polystyrene cup and peered inside. 'You know me too well,' she said.

A silence descended between them and Annabel found herself enjoying the quiet. It felt pleasant, companionable even.

'So, what's new?' Dan finally asked.

She tried and failed to come up with something. After all, when it came to anything out of the ordinary taking place, Dan had been around to witness events for himself. 'Nothing,' she replied. 'What about you?'

'Don't ask,' said Dan.

Intrigued, Annabel waited for him to continue.

'Well if you must know ...'

After listening to him recount the details of his mum's arrest, Annabel tried to keep a straight face. Dan clearly didn't see the funny side and the last thing she wanted to do was further upset him. She bit on her bottom lip in an attempt at quelling her giggles. But it was no good. She couldn't keep them in and her straight face automatically contorted as she suddenly burst out laughing.

'Trust you to see the funny side,' said Dan, still less than amused.

Annabel couldn't help it. His mother's antics never failed to bring a smile to her face.

'Next time you can get your own coffee,' said Dan. 'Which won't taste half as good as this one, by the way.'

'I'm sorry,' said Annabel, regaining her composure. 'You're right, I shouldn't laugh.' She picked up her cup, ready to take another drink. 'And thanks again for this,' she said, taking a sip of its contents. 'It's very nice of you to think of my caffeine intake.'

'Isn't that what friends are for?' asked Dan.

Annabel smiled again. *Friends*, she thought to herself. She liked the sound of that. She watched him drink his own coffee, knowing that a short time ago she'd have freaked out at him turning up unannounced in this way. Now, she realised, she actually welcomed his presence. Having him around somehow felt natural.

'Speaking of difficult relatives,' said Dan, interrupting her thoughts. 'How's Rebecca?'

'Are you trying to spoil my day?' she asked.

He raised an eyebrow, the man clearly expected a proper answer.

Annabel put her cup back down with a sigh. 'I haven't a clue,' she replied.

'You mean you haven't spoken to her?'

'Nope.' She recalled her sister's fury over the skateboarding incident. 'I thought it best to give her some time. You know, to calm down.'

'Coward,' said Dan, laughing.

Annabel didn't disagree.

'And the baby thing?' Dan carried on. 'Has she got her head around that yet?'

'Not as far as I know.'

'And what about you?'

'Me?' Annabel thought his question strange considering getting pregnant had been her idea in the first place.

'Any sudden cravings for broccoli or bacon sandwiches?'

Ah, thought Annabel. She immediately tensed up. 'No, no cravings.'

With her voice suddenly sounding strange even to her own ears, she thought it reasonable that Dan's face had turned quizzical. But she'd been determined to keep schtum until she was one hundred per cent sure. She hadn't wanted to needlessly get her own hopes up, let alone anyone else's.

Dan stared at her, as if waiting for her to continue and Annabel felt her whole body crumple as she realised she had no choice but to explain. She straightened herself up again, resolute in her desire to maintain that this was no big deal. 'I'm late,' she said.

Annabel tried to read his expression, but his face was suddenly blank. Understandable under the circumstances, she considered. No wonder he appeared to swallow, before speaking.

'You're what?' he finally asked.

'Late,' Annabel repeated. 'With my period.'

Again, Dan swallowed.

'But that doesn't necessarily mean anything,' Annabel continued.

'Like hell it doesn't,' said Dan.

'After all, these things do happen from time to time.'

Dan stared at her, in disbelief. 'When did you plan on telling me?' he asked. 'I mean, does anyone else know?'

She watched him jump up from his seat, not even bothering to wait for her to answer.

'Shit, Annabel,' he said. 'This could be it.' His mind seemed to race as he began pacing up and down, all the while fumbling in his pockets in search of something.

Annabel wondered what he was thinking. Was he regretting his decision to help her get pregnant? Was he simply overwhelmed with excitement? Was he thinking about his mother, relieved that he no longer had to keep his promise?

'We need to do a test,' he said. Eventually producing his car keys, he seemed to be talking to himself more than her. 'A chemist, yes, that's what we need.' He suddenly stopped still and turned to Annabel. 'Where's the nearest chemist?' he asked.

Glad to see he'd remembered she was, in fact, still in the room, Annabel stared back at him. She didn't know whether to find his reaction sweet or annoying. After all, this was exactly the kind of response that had prevented her from saying something in the first place. In trying to be sensible about the whole thing, she'd wanted to deal with her own emotions on the matter before having to deal with anyone else's. And as harsh as it might be, that *anyone else* had included Dan.

She silently got down off her stool and headed out back, before returning with her handbag. Plonking it down on the counter, it was her turn to rummage. She found what she was looking for and pulled out a slim, cardboard package. 'We don't need a chemist,' she said, holding up a pregnancy testing kit. 'I've already been.'

Dan looked from her, to the box. He appeared as nervous as she felt. 'What now?' he asked. He rubbed his down the side of his jeans in anticipation.

'What do *you* think?' she replied.

Annabel opened the packet and pulled out the instruction sheet. Reading it, she finally placed it down on the counter. She took a deep breath. 'I suppose there's no time like the present.'

She strode over to the shop door and flipped the open sign to closed, before making her way out to the back. Surprised to realise that Dan was following her she suddenly stopped and turned to face him. 'It's okay,' she said, preventing him from going any further. 'I think I can take it from here.'

Dan blushed red. 'Yes, sorry,' he replied. 'Inappropriate. I get it.' He crossed his arms and stuffed his hands under his armpits, before taking a step back. 'But I'm here if you need me.'

Annabel smiled. She found his embarrassed sincerity endearing and almost felt guilty at leaving him just standing there. 'I won't be long,' she said.

Taking the test with her, she continued on her way, this time heading to the loo. Following the instructions, she thought she'd never wee. The pressure to perform was obviously having an adverse effect on her body. 'Come on, come on,' she said, willing it to happen.

Job finally done, her hands shook as she placed the pregnancy test on the side of the sink. She turned on the tap and watched the warm water for a moment as it flowed over her fingers and palms, before slowly reaching for the hand soap. No matter what her increased heart rate seemed to say, she insisted she wasn't in any rush. After all, it would take a while for the results to show.

As the minutes ticked by, Annabel grabbed the towel and dried her hands, she began to feel her heart rate increase even more. She picked up the pregnancy test and took a deep breath, before daring to read its result. She looked at the image coming through on the display and gave herself a moment to absorb what it meant. She took another deep breath, calmly exhaling as she let herself out of the toilet.

Dan hastily stepped forward. Clearly eager for the result, his eyes widened in expectation. 'Well?' he asked.

Despite trying to keep it together, Annabel struggled to hide her disappointment. Slowly, she began to shake her head. 'It's negative,' she said. She tried to raise a smile. 'See, I told you these things happen.'

Dan sighed, appearing equally as saddened, which only made Annabel feel worse.

'Oh, come here,' he said, regardless.

As he pulled her towards him, Annabel suddenly felt Dan's arms wrap tightly around her. It was a gesture she readily accepted.

'I'm sorry,' he said. 'Maybe next time, eh?'

'Yep, maybe next time,' Annabel replied.

But that didn't stop it from hurting.

FOURTEEN

Dan let himself into the cubicle and closed the door behind him. He dropped the toilet lid and went to sit down. He let out a heavy sigh and wondered what was wrong with him. Yes, he felt disappointed that Annabel wasn't pregnant, a feeling that both surprised and confused him. But it was more than that. He almost laughed at himself. Most men he knew would be in their element in the company of a woman like Maeve.

Up to now, their time together had been pleasant enough and he had to admit that Maeve had lived up to her reputation, being every inch the lovely girl his mother had described. They'd chatted, albeit awkwardly at times, and had even managed to find a few things in common other than their mothers' friendship. Moreover, his own mum hadn't exaggerated when she'd said how stunning his date was. Of course, thanks to her view regarding blondes, he'd expected the long, fair hair, but with a name like Maeve he hadn't really anticipated the looks to go with it. As it turned out, she had to be one of the most gorgeous women he'd ever set eyes on and so far, seemed to have the personality to match. So why wasn't he feeling it? He asked himself. Why was there no spark?

He realised his predicament was all his own fault. He should have taken his mum's advice sooner. If he had, for all anyone knew he and Maeve could've been well on their way to wedded bliss by now. On the other hand, they could have learned about each other's insurmountable foibles and decided to call it a day. Either way, life would certainly have been simpler and he definitely wouldn't be sitting in a public toilet right now. He took in his enclosure, and, not for the first time, he wished he hadn't made that stupid promise.

Maybe the pressure of the situation had gotten to him. After all, if ever a man needed love at first sight Dan knew it was him. He could almost hear the ticking clock in the background, reminding him he didn't have to just like Maeve he had to fall in love with her. 'Cheers, Mum,' he said. The whole situation was insane.

He felt almost resentful and couldn't believe how easily his mother had conned him into giving her his word. He couldn't believe her determination to pretend all was well in the world – a condition that was obviously catching. Dan had spent the whole evening avoiding the subject of his mother's health, trying to deceive himself into thinking he was here through choice. The façade couldn't last though, he knew that; for his mother or for himself. Now he'd agreed to this date he had a decision to make and fast. He just felt scared that, if he did commit to Maeve, then that would be it. His mum's reason for living would be gone and, as a result, she'd simply give up.

Then again, he reassured himself, she could remain stoic to the very end. His mother never could stand sickness. Even when he had chicken pox as a child she refused to show any sympathy, the relentless itching apparently all in his mind. 'What's a few spots?' he remembered her saying, dragging him to school regardless. She even insisted the other parents would thank her for it; with him in the schoolyard they could get yet another childhood illness out of the way.

As far as his mother was concerned, it was what went on in the mind and not the body that mattered. A bit of positive thinking could get anyone through anything. 'Not this time though, eh, Mum,' he said, reality showing its face once more. That sparkle of hers was fading with each passing day whether she chose to openly admit it or not.

He recalled the bottles of *Oramorph* he'd found in the bathroom cupboard while he was looking for a fresh tube of toothpaste. They were the last thing he'd expected to come across. The bottles were unopened and stuck at the back, just reading the labels made him feel nauseous. His mum had obviously tried to hide them and, in respecting her wishes, he never let on to her that he knew they were there. Instead, they became a sort of comforter. Their daily presence allowed him to believe that his mum's condition wasn't worsening. Since her arrest though, the bottles had disappeared – along with his sense of security. If only she'd listened to him and not gone to Amsterdam that day. If she'd stayed home, her body's fighting spirit might have stayed too.

He thought about his promise again, about why his mum had made him make it. Yes, he understood her reasoning; she wanted to die safe in the knowledge that he wasn't alone. But did she really expect to be replaced so easily? Swapped for someone else? Because when he stripped everything back, that was what this all felt like.

Tears welled in his eyes and he quickly wiped them away. 'Why do you have to take her?' he asked. He looked up to the heavens. 'When there are so many absolute bastards out there to choose from?' He waited for an answer, it didn't arrive.

He took his phone out of his pocket and began scrolling through his contacts until Annabel's details appeared on the screen. With his thumb poised ready to hit call, just seeing her name felt reassuring, let alone the prospect of hearing her voice. Resisting the urge, he suddenly put the phone away again and taking a deep breath, he told himself he had to be strong.

He took a second to gather his composure and standing up, headed straight for the sink. Dan turned on the cold tap and began sloshing his face. He knew he should get a move on as Maeve would be wondering where he was by now. He imagined her checking her watch, and let out a burst of mock laughter. If he did want to get to know the woman better, the last thing he needed was for her to think he had toileting issues.

However, as he stared at his reflection Dan couldn't help but continue to just stand there. Rooted to the spot, it was as if his feet refused to move. Tears returned to his eyes and with his breath suddenly catching in his throat, he couldn't bring himself to stop them. He gripped the sink, his shoulders started to heave as he broke down completely and, finally succumbing to the agonising pain of his mother's dying, he let the tears and the sobs just keep coming.

***

'I'm ready for this,' said Katy.

'Me too,' replied Annabel, taking a seat. 'I've been saving myself all day.'

She glanced around the restaurant hoping the change of scenery would take her mind off recent events. Not that she'd told Katy about the pregnancy test. The last thing she wanted was pity.

She smiled at the waiter as he approached to hand over their menus; he returned the gesture with a wink before going on his way. She blushed, wondering what was going on. She seemed to be attracting a lot of male attention lately, although she couldn't think why.

'Did you see that?' asked a suddenly wide-eyed Katy, thankfully for Annabel at least having the decency to wait until he was out of earshot.

'What?'

'Him.' Katy indicated towards the waiter. 'Talk about fancying you.'

'Rubbish,' Annabel replied. As if she wasn't embarrassed enough. 'You're imagining things.'

'I am not,' said Katy. 'And you know I'm not. Why else would you sit there so red-faced? Although I shouldn't really be surprised, men have always looked at you like that. You've just never noticed before.'

Annabel laughed and shook her head. In her view, the menu deserved more attention than this ridiculous conversation. She began scanning its contents, trying to decide what to have. Being so hungry, it all sounded good. From the *Rabbit Rillette* to the *Wild Boar and Mushroom*, she'd have tried everything listed given half the chance. Unlike her friend, she noted, who hadn't even looked at her menu yet.

Annabel could feel her friend's eyes boring into her. 'What now?' she asked.

'Nothing,' Katy replied.

Deciding to take her at her word, Annabel hoped that, now, the conversation could move on.

'Anyway, speaking of who fancies who,' she said. 'How are things with Oliver?' Annabel watched her friend's whole face light up at the mere mention of his name.

'Absolutely wonderful,' she replied. 'I don't know what it is about that man, but he makes me so happy. Honestly, just the thought of him and I come over all tingly.'

'Sounds like he could be the one,' said Annabel, although going off her friend's track record she'd believe it when she saw it.

Now it was her friend's turn to blush.

'Oh my gosh, Katy, he isn't. Is he?'

'Maybe,' she replied. With a satisfied smile, Katy finally picked up her menu.

Her friend's sudden silence on the matter told Annabel that was all she was going to get on the Oliver front, for now. Not that she minded as such, Katy would reveal all when she was good and ready. On the plus side, it meant they might actually be able to eat at last.

'I saw Rebecca today,' said Katy.

Or maybe not, thought Annabel, as her stomach started to seriously rumble.

'She told me about the other day's incident.'

As much as her friend tried to sound matter of fact, Annabel felt a lecture coming on.

'I'm sure she did,' she said. She wondered if she should be good and order the beetroot salad or be greedy and go for a hearty rump steak. 'And how was she?'

'How do you think?'

Annabel stopped reading and recalled events She might have been too high on adrenaline at the time to take in Rebecca's words, but that hadn't stopped her seeing the fury written all over her sister's face. 'Still mad at me, no doubt?'

'Well what do you expect? She could have killed you. Imagine, her own flesh and blood.'

Annabel rolled her eyes. Talk about melodramatic. Although she should've known Katy would take Rebecca's side. She'd been doing that a lot lately. 'She's the one who came hurtling round the corner, when everyone knows pedestrians have right of way.'

'Pedestrians?' said Katy. 'Annabel, you weren't on foot. You were in the middle of the road on a skateboard.'

Annabel let out a child-like giggle. 'I know and you should have seen me, I was like the wind. Honestly, it was so much fun.'

'Your poor sister didn't think so. And what if it had turned out for the worse?'

Annabel still didn't see what all the fuss was about. As far as she was concerned, everyone was so serious these days. Anyone would think she had no right to enjoy herself. 'But it didn't, did it?' she said, refusing to see anything but the funny side.

'I don't know what's so amusing,' said Katy. 'There's a reason they build skate parks, you know. Anyway, Rebecca thinks you've changed lately and after hearing about what you've been up to, I'm starting to agree.'

Annabel began to lose her appetite. 'I've changed? Have you noticed what's happened to her? She seems so worked up all the time, definitely more than usual and as much as she blames me for whatever's going on, there has to be more to it.'

'Then you should talk to her,' said Katy. 'Find out what's going on.'

'You think I haven't tried?'

'Then try again.'

Annabel knew she was right. Things were getting so strained between the two of them, someone had to do something. 'I will,' she said, although she didn't exactly look forward to the prospect. Rebecca had been so furious on that skateboarding night that she'd stormed off in yet another huff. The likelihood of which meant she still had plenty to say on the subject. And as well as trying to get to the bottom of her sister's problems, the porn magazine issue still hadn't been resolved. It was safe to say that when the two of them did finally sit down together, they were going to have one hell of a conversation.

The waiter began to hover and Annabel signalled that they weren't yet ready to order. She returned her attention to the menu.

'You're sleeping with him, aren't you?' said Katy.

Annabel stopped reading again. What on earth was her friend talking about now? 'Excuse me?' she said.

'Dan. You're sleeping with him.'

Annabel stared at her friend incredulous. 'I most certainly am not,' she said. Fed up with having to defend her actions when it came to her sister, she shouldn't have to do the same with her best friend.

'I just can't believe you didn't tell me,' said Katy.

Annabel bristled. 'I didn't tell you, because there's nothing to tell.' To say she thought tonight was going to be fun, things weren't quite panning out that way.

'But that doesn't mean you don't want to though, does it?'

The evening of their almost kiss popped into Annabel's head; his strong hands, firm chest and tempting lips. She tried to re-focus on what to have for dinner but felt herself flush red.

'I knew it!' said Katy. 'I knew there was something going on the minute you suggested we come here.'

Annabel looked around the restaurant. 'What's this place got to do with anything?' As far as she could recall, this was the first time she'd ever stepped foot through the door.

'Not the place itself,' said Katy. 'The fact that we're here at all.'

Annabel still couldn't follow.

'Yes, we might meet for lunch, but when was the last time we did anything of an evening?'

Now her friend really was talking rubbish. 'A few weeks ago, actually,' said Annabel. 'When I first met Dan, remember?'

'Oh, you know what I mean. That was for a specific reason.'

'What, so the two of us catching up over a nice meal isn't reason enough?' Annabel made a mental note to never invite her friend out to dinner again. Especially if this is what she got for her trouble.

'No, as a matter of fact,' said Katy. 'It isn't. I mean, can you even remember when we last did something like this? Because I can, it was before Tom died.'

Annabel set her menu down. Was her friend trying to spoil the night? This might be the first time in a while that they'd visited a restaurant of an evening, but that didn't mean she could come over all *psychologist* on her. As for Dan, he really was just a sperm donor, nothing more, nothing less. Granted, a sperm donor who happened to be introducing a bit of fun into her life and yes, there'd been a bit of confusion along the way. But what she and Dan got up to was no one else's business. As far as Annabel was concerned, business separate to the rest of her life; it was everyone else trying to merge the two.

'I'm not saying you shouldn't have a relationship with Dan,' Katy carried on.

'Which we're not,' said Annabel.

'God knows it's about time you got back into the dating game.'

'We're not dating.'

'And it's obvious that you like the man.'

Annabel gave up. Her friend was clearly away with the fairies. Yes, she liked Dan. He brought out a side of her she'd long since forgotten about. In the silliest of ways imaginable she was enjoying herself again and it felt good, like she was re-joining the land of the living. Admittedly, there was no denying Dan was easy on the eye, but that didn't mean she was ready to betray her husband. Surely her inability to even kiss him proved that?

Her mind began to wander as she thought about the kindness Dan had shown. He had so much to deal with at the moment, yet he still found time to think of her. As soon as it was over she'd forgotten about their Bucket List conversation, but he hadn't. She wondered what man did that. What man put his own worries to one side to think of someone like her? Annabel smiled. *Dan, that's who.*

'I just want you to be careful,' said Katy. 'I don't want you getting hurt.'

'Hurt?' she replied. 'Katy, you don't know what you're talking about.' If anything, Annabel felt confident of the complete opposite. Dan didn't just turn up with his skateboard that night, he re-affirmed his commitment to her pregnancy plan. Something he did again a few days later, when they'd gone through the rigmarole of a pregnancy test. 'In fact, you're concerns are so misplaced,' she said. 'I'm even planning a shopping trip.'

'A shopping trip?'

'Yes. Obviously not for anything extravagant like a pram or a cot just yet.'

Katy looked horrified. 'I should think not,' she said.

The expression on her friends face was priceless, but Annabel didn't care. She knew baby shopping was supposed to be a no, no until after she was pregnant, but how else could she prove to Katy that she was worrying over nothing.

'But a few baby grows and scratch mittens, wouldn't go amiss,' she carried on. 'You know the kind of things I mean, all the stuff that's too cute to resist.' While Katy continued to look at her like she'd lost the plot, Annabel began to imagine the rows and rows of teensie-weensie baby clothes to choose from. Now she'd given herself permission to buy, she actually felt quite excited at the prospect. 'You're welcome to come with me,' she added. 'It'll be great fun.'

'Annabel, I think you need to back up a bit,' said Katy. Rather than being put at ease, her fears were clearly growing.

'Why?' she asked. 'I'm going to need these things sooner or later, so I may as well get them now.'

Katy indicated to something over Annabel's shoulder and Annabel turned, wondering what she was looking at. She spotted

Dan, she felt her spirits lift. Now her friend could find out for herself what a great guy he was.

She waved in an attempt to catch his attention, but he didn't see her and, disappointed, she had no choice but to watch him continue on his way, completely oblivious to her presence. Tempted to call out his name, she suddenly felt her heart sink. No wonder he hadn't noticed her, taking a seat at another table he already had company. *Not just any company though*, thought Annabel. She noticed his dinner date, a long haired and, by the looks of it, a long legged, blonde, she suddenly found herself lost for words.

'That's why,' said Katy.

FIFTEEN

Annabel heaved her shopping onto the kitchen counter, to say she felt tired was an understatement. She didn't know why seeing Dan with that woman had affected her so much, but she'd struggled to sleep properly since. On top of that, she now had an abundance of this flower and that flower crowding her head. She sighed. With a last minute wedding to provide for, she certainly had her work cut out.

She thought back to the young couple concerned, knowing her job would be a lot easier if they'd had the slightest idea as to the kind of design they wanted. Then again, she supposed their indecision was understandable. From what they'd said, their wedding did seem very last minute. And to be fair to the bride, she had given her a starting point. She'd said her favourite colour was red.

Annabel's heart sank. *Red.* Usually such an exciting and vibrant colour, moody even depending on the shade; today, however, it symbolised failure.

Up until now, she'd managed to keep a lid on her disappointment and, doing her best to quell it once again, told herself not to be silly. She'd known all along that getting pregnant wouldn't be easy, her pragmatic side insisting only a fool would think otherwise. No, this morning's bathroom visit didn't really bring any great surprise. Her time of the month had arrived as it always did – even if it was a bit late on this occasion. Trying to be positive, Annabel told herself that thanks to today's young couple, it was probably a good job anyway. With her current work load she didn't have the time to deal with morning sickness, let alone to feel sorry for herself.

She scoffed. Maybe she should thank them for the welcome diversion.

Annabel forced all thoughts of pregnancy to the back of her mind. She refused to feel down and was determined to do the young couple proud; she let her mind drift back to the run up to her own wedding. She'd been so looking forward to their good old-fashioned elopement, followed by a weekend in bed. At least that had been the plan until Tom let slip what they were up to. She laughed. She should've known he wouldn't be able to keep his excitement to himself. On the other hand, her soon-to-be husband should have known not to tell his mother.

The woman had always been one for great displays of emotion, especially when it came to getting her own way. 'I want to sit at the top table,' she'd said. 'I want a bunch of flowers.' Annabel recalled her frustration as, before she knew it, the date had been postponed and her mother-in-law had elected herself wedding planner, ensuring every man and his dog made up the invitation list. *It's funny how things turn out,* she considered. Now Tom had gone, it was a day Annabel would be forever thankful for.

She waited for the wave of loss that usually accompanied thoughts of her wedding, but this time it didn't come. Yes, the sadness was still there, but she didn't feel bowled over by it. Confused, half of her wondered if this was a good thing, a sign that, finally, she really was moving on. The other half felt like a traitor to her marriage. Something else Annabel didn't want to think about.

She turned her attention to the bag of shopping and the evening ahead. An evening that would no doubt finish the day in the same way it had started – miserably. Tempted to rearrange, she knew that would only be delaying the inevitable. She and Rebecca had to sort things out at some point and she supposed tonight was as good a night as any.

Annabel emptied the bag's contents, her purchases looked pitiful and she wished she'd made more of an effort. Not that there was anything she could do about it now. A bottle of wine and a couple of ready meals might not be up to her sister's exacting standards, but, on this occasion, the woman would just have to like it or lump it. She imagined Rebecca going all out to produce some fabulous gourmet meal were she the host and not the guest. But trying not to be too hard on herself, it wasn't as if Annabel hadn't intended on delighting her sister's taste buds. Wandering around the supermarket, her heart just hadn't been in it. 'You'll have to do,' she'd said, picking up a couple of lasagnes. However, looking at them now, sitting there waiting to be pierced and popped into the microwave, she couldn't help but sigh. There was no way they were going to look as good on the plate as they did on the packaging.

She put the bottle of white in the fridge and hoped it would cool sufficiently before Rebecca arrived. The food on offer might not be up to much but at least they could enjoy that. With a bit of luck, it would also help her sister loosen up enough to divulge whatever had been on her mind lately; a problem shared was a problem halved and all that. At any rate, that was the plan. After all, talking about Rebecca's issues would keep them off the whole *Dan* subject. Annabel paused and realised that, compared to him, she'd spent the day feeling sorry for herself over nothing. Having to deal with his mother's illness and find himself a wife. Now that was someone with a real problem.

Annabel began to puncture the cellophane covering tonight's dinners with a knife. At the same time, she recalled the other evening when she'd seen Dan with his mystery woman. For some reason it had made her feel uneasy, a strange reaction considering she'd known about his promise all along. Under the circumstances, of course he'd be out and about meeting people. She guessed she just hadn't expected to witness this for herself.

She insisted that she was adult enough to know things could get messy, especially if he met someone he was interested in. Messy not just for herself, but for everyone concerned and standing there, Annabel had to wonder if the best, in fact, the only solution was to try and get another donor. She didn't relish the prospect. Finding Dan in the first place had been embarrassing enough. More importantly, she had to admit that she didn't *want* to find someone else. It was as if Dan wasn't only helping her on the pregnancy front, he was helping her along in other ways too. Something in her had changed since she first met him and, despite everyone else's views, it felt like a change for the better.

If only she had someone to talk things through with. Not only did Rebecca fail to understand, she obviously had her own stuff going on. Katy hadn't agreed with her actions from the start. She also seemed to spend all her time with Oliver lately; Annabel had never seen her so loved up. That only left Tom and even though she could talk to him about anything, going into detail with regards to Dan no longer seemed right.

She suddenly felt guilty. She and Tom had always told each other everything, be it good or bad. Yet here she was wondering whether or not to keep secrets.

'Penny for them,' a voice suddenly said.

Knife in hand, Annabel spun round to spot Rebecca in the doorway.

'I think they're dead now, don't you?'

Annabel looked down at the food containers, realising she hadn't just perforated the two lots of packaging, she'd completely obliterated them.

'Doesn't hurt to make sure,' she said, pulling herself together.

'Is it anything you want to talk about,' asked Rebecca, hanging her coat on the back of a chair.

'Not really,' said Annabel. As far as she was concerned, the two of them had enough to discuss already. 'But you can open this.' She took the bottle of wine back out of the fridge and handed it over, before grabbing a couple of glasses from the cupboard ready for her sister to pour. Surprisingly, Rebecca set the bottle down after filling just one. 'Aren't you having any?' she asked.

'No, just water for me thanks.'

Annabel headed for the sink and filled the empty glass with tap water. Disappointed, she hated drinking on her own. It also meant her sister was intent on keeping a clear head throughout the evening, a sure sign that Rebecca also meant business. 'So,' she said, handing it over and taking a seat.

'So,' said her sister. She followed suit and sat at the table.

Sipping on her wine, the atmosphere felt awkward. While Annabel wanted to bring up Rebecca's recent behaviour, she could tell her sister wanted a similar discussion about hers. It was simply a case of who was going to get in there first.

Keeping things casual, Annabel decided to bite the bullet.

'How's things?' she asked.

'Fine,' Rebecca replied.

'It's just that the last time you popped in you said you wanted my advice.'

'Did I? I don't remember.'

Annabel knew she was lying. With a memory like an elephant, she no doubt remembered every single word that had come out of both their mouths. The situation made her feel sad. Rebecca had had something that needed sharing on her mind for a while, yet remained intent on keeping it to herself. Not only that, she also looked tired; like she was carrying the weight of the world on her shoulders. Usually preferring the Dunkirk Spirit approach to life, it was an image Annabel wasn't used to. She wished that, for once, her sister would let her in. 'You do know I'm here for you, don't you?' she said. 'That whatever's going on you can talk to me about it?'

Rebecca put on one of those annoying, brave smiles of hers. 'I've told you,' she replied. 'There's nothing to tell.'

With their conversation over before it had begun, Annabel gave up. 'Whatever you say,' she said, rising from the table. 'Just remember, I'm here when you're ready.'

Disheartened, she put one of the lasagnes in the microwave, pressed a couple of buttons, and clicked start. Watching the plate go round and round, the timer beeped with every passing second. The countdown had begun in readiness for yet another argument. After all, if Rebecca wasn't here to talk about her own problems, it could only be because she wanted to address what she saw as Annabel's.

'I'm pregnant!' her sister suddenly said.

Annabel froze. She needed a second to absorb what she'd just heard; she tried and failed to respond. Out of all the statements that could have left her sisters lips that was the last thing she'd expected to hear. Considering the irony of the situation, she didn't know whether to laugh or cry. Annabel thought back to the morning's bathroom visit, she told herself that Rebecca couldn't be having a baby. That just wouldn't be fair. And, knowing full well what her sister could be like, she found herself silently asking why now? Why would Rebecca and Gavin choose now to get pregnant? She hoped to God it had nothing to do with her own pregnancy plans.

'Really,' she finally said. Not sure what else she could say, it was her turn to put on a brave face. She turned. 'I didn't know you were even trying.'

'That's the thing,' said Rebecca. 'We weren't.'

Annabel told herself at least that was something; there'd been no competition to get in there first. However, despite doing her best not to show it, her sister's admission still stung. It seemed that Rebecca only had to blink and she got pregnant. Annabel, on the other hand, had spent weeks tracking her menstrual cycle, learning all about the follicular and luteal phases in readiness of finding a donor. Then there were the hours, upon hours, she'd spent lying on her back, legs and bum in the air once her donor had come along to do the business. And she still had nothing to show for it.

'But you being pregnant is a good thing, right?' she asked.

Annabel ignored the fact that life could be cruel sometimes and tried to sound positive. Unlike Rebecca, she noted, who refused to play along.

'Is it?' she simply replied.

Her sister's tone sounded flat and emotionless, making it hard for Annabel to tell what she was getting at. Was she being sarcastic? Expecting Annabel to be so upset she'd create a scene? Or was she simply playing the news down because she thought that was the right thing to do? After all, Rebecca had to know how much this would hurt. She searched her sister's face for a clue, but even that failed to give anything away. One thing was clear though, tonight's announcement certainly didn't compare to those of her other three pregnancies. With each of them Rebecca had been overflowing with joy. Then again, realised Annabel, on those occasions, so had she.

Annabel felt ashamed. She told herself this baby deserved better, that, regardless of their differences, her sister deserved better. Annabel put her personal woes to one side and insisted Rebecca's family planning issues had nothing to do with her own. As hard as it felt right now, she knew that she should celebrate this pregnancy; particularly when she expected others to celebrate hers when the time came.

'Well you've always said you wanted a big family,' said Annabel, re-taking her seat at the table. 'You're just having baby number four a bit sooner than we all thought, that's all.'

Much to her surprise, Rebecca's bottom lip began to quiver, leaving Annabel feeling guiltier than she already did. Not that she fully understood why. Given the nature of Rebecca's news, a part of her still thought any consoling should be the other way round.

'Please don't get upset on my behalf,' she said, tentatively reaching out with a comforting hand. 'It'll happen for me too. I just have to be patient.' Unfortunately, her understanding on the matter seemed to fail in its desired outcome. If anything, rather than feel reassured by it, her sister appeared confused. *Okay*, thought Annabel, now forced to acknowledge any tears weren't for her benefit. Something she supposed she could live with, even if she shouldn't have to. As long as the woman pulled herself together, that is, and told her what the hell was going on.

She watched her sister throw her arms, and then her head, down on the table. 'What am I going to do?' she cried.

Hormonal or not, Annabel had never seen her like this. As for the question, she couldn't believe what she was hearing.

'What do you mean, what're you going to do?' she asked.

Annabel thought back to previous discussions, she couldn't seriously be thinking about an abortion? From where Annabel stood, having four children couldn't be much different to having three. Besides, this baby had two parents not one. Surely the next move was a decision mum and dad should be making, not mum and mum's sister.

'What does Gavin think you should do?' she asked.

Rebecca suddenly looked up. 'I don't know. I haven't told him.'

Annabel stared at the woman before her. 'You haven't told him?' she asked.

Rebecca slowly shook her head.

'Why not?'

An unwanted thought suddenly began to form in Annabel's mind; a thought that would certainly explain her sister's unusual behaviour. 'Tell me to mind my own business if you want to, but he is the father, isn't he?'

'Of course he's the father,' Rebecca replied. 'How could you think he's not?'

By now, Annabel didn't have a clue what to think.

'So what's the problem then?' she asked.

'I'll tell you what the problem is. I'm going to get fat. I'll be waddling down the street like some overgrown penguin. Suffering back pain and developing a taste for gherkins.'

'And having mood swings,' said Annabel, unable to quite help herself.

'Exactly!' said Rebecca.

Annabel wondered if her sister knew how selfish she sounded. She'd have traded places with her in an instant given half a chance, waddle or no waddle. There had to be more to this than she was admitting. Everyone knew her sister bloomed during pregnancy.

'What's all this really about?' she asked. 'You've always loved being pregnant.'

Her sister reached into her bag and pulled out a tissue.

'Well?' said Annabel. Waiting for an answer, she was determined to get to the bottom of this if it killed her.

'It's about Gavin,' Rebecca finally replied.

At last, maybe now they were actually getting somewhere.

'What about him?'

Rebecca's lip began to quiver again.

Another unwanted thought suddenly entered Annabel's head, this one worse than the first. 'He's not sick is he?' she asked. She felt her whole body tense up in anticipation. 'Please tell me hasn't got some god-awful disease.' Having lost her own husband, the thought of her sister losing hers felt equally unbearable; and not just on behalf of Rebecca, but for the children as well.

'No, it's nothing like that,' she replied, wiping her eyes.

Thank God, thought Annabel, relaxing.

'So what is it then?' she asked. 'What's the matter?' In her view, if Gavin wasn't dying, nothing could be so bad as to warrant all this.

'He's bored with me,' said Rebecca. 'After nearly ten years together, he's finally got fed up.'

'What are you talking about now? Of course he's not fed up.' As far as Annabel was concerned, life with her sister as of late was anything but boring. 'I think the fact that you're pregnant proves he's still interested, don't you?'

Feeling a mixture of frustration and helplessness, she watched Rebecca burst into full blown tears.

'Then why is he having an affair?' she said.

SIXTEEN

'At last,' said Dan. Relieved to hear voices filtering up from the hallway, he tossed his book to one side. Reading had been a fruitless exercise from the start, but he'd had to find something to take his mind off what was taking place in the kitchen. Try as he might though, he hadn't absorbed a single word, and all courtesy of that vulture downstairs.

He listened as the front door finally opened and closed, he imagined his mum's visitor making his way down the path. All the while rubbing his greasy hands together thanks to the sale he'd just clinched. Dan sneered. Not that he'd had to work for it. Not in his game.

Glad he no longer had to hide away; he swung his legs off the bed and stood up. He stretched his back out and could only guess at the amount of money his mother had just spent. He felt cowardly for not offering his support, especially when she'd made it clear she valued his opinion. However, it was bad enough Dan knew that his mother was going to die, without listening to her organise her own funeral. Funeral arrangements signified the end, something he wasn't yet ready to face.

Dan headed downstairs and told himself that today was no different to when the nurses came. Apart from the fact that in those instances, rather than let him be present, his mother actually ordered him out of the room. Heaven forbid he should glean the slightest bit of information on her condition. So much so, she'd instructed her medical staff to keep schtum when it came to him.

He recalled how he'd tried to discretely accost, Jill, one of the nurses, in the hope of having a little chat; except, just like today's reading, that turned out to be a pointless exercise too. She was very nice about it, even if she did politely and sympathetically tell him that patient confidentiality kept her from divulging anything. *Thank God for the Internet*, thought Dan. If it weren't for modern day technology he'd still know absolutely nothing.

He entered the kitchen and caught sight of the various coffin brochures littering the dining table. They seemed to mock him as he put the kettle on. 'Everything sorted?' he asked.

His mother failed to look up and continued to scribble in her notepad, her concentration was there for all to see. No doubt, making notes on what she'd decided upon, getting everything down before she forgot most of it.

She'd been doing that a lot lately, thought Dan. She could be half way through a sentence and suddenly not know what it was she'd wanted to say. Partly because of her illness, he realised, cancer pain was enough to stop even the greatest minds in their tracks. And partly because of the side effects of all the drugs she was now taking. *Oramorph* for the pain, *Stemetil* for the nausea, *Midazolam* for the anxiety … the list went on.

Anxiety, Dan scoffed to himself, *such a funny word under the circumstances.* As far as he was concerned, anxiety was something you felt when you didn't want to go to the dentist. Surely the excruciating agony his mum experienced, and the fact that she faced certain death, deserved something more fitting? In Dan's opinion, *Midazolam for pain-induced suicidal thoughts and being shit-scared of dying* might not have the same ring to it, but it certainly seemed more appropriate.

He observed his mum for a moment, there was no denying the woman was sick. She'd all but lost her rosy glow and as for those loose-fitting dresses, she might think they hid her drastic weight loss, but they didn't. Not really. She'd been turning to skin and bone in front of his very eyes for weeks now, and no amount of fancy clothing could disguise the fact.

She had managed to hold on to one thing though, thought Dan, which was her dignity. The respect he felt was immeasurable as he wondered how she managed to handle everything with such grace and composure. He swelled with a mixture of both pride and admiration; he doubted he could do it. He'd be lucky to have even an ounce of her emotional strength.

'Cup of tea?' he asked.

He watched his mum put her pen down and reach into her pocket for her pills.

'Just a glass of water for me, please,' she said.

As he grabbed a glass from the cupboard, Dan heard his mum struggling with the blister pack and, as she began to mutter, he could hear her patience decreasing by the second. Her annoyance surprised him; it was the first time she'd shown anything other than a *carpe diem* attitude since breaking the news. Then again, if anyone was entitled to a fit of frustration he knew it was her.

'No,' said his mum. 'Stupid, stupid, stupid.'

Dan turned just as the pack hit the ground, one of the much needed pills disappeared off and out of sight. His mum dropped to her knees in a pitiful attempt to find it and he immediately raced over to help. 'Here, let me,' he said. 'You sit down. I'll get it.'

As he took her by the arm and helped her back onto her feet she felt so light it shocked him. Her body was clearly losing the battle even if her brain continued to fight. It struck him just how close to the end they could be; Dan suddenly found himself enveloped with fear. He couldn't lose her, not yet.

He crouched down in an attempt to locate his mother's medication; his emotions flittered between anger and sadness. He felt angry that she was being taken away from him; angry at her for not accepting treatment and for shutting him out all these weeks, choices he didn't think he'd ever fully understand. When it came to his sadness, it wasn't fair that he was losing the one person who mattered more to him than anyone else. And why did she have to go like this? Why now? His mum's death shouldn't be for years yet and even then she should be allowed to pass away peacefully in her sleep. No one should have to go through this.

Dan fought his tears; he didn't want to imagine life without his mother. He didn't want to think about the gaping hole she'd leave behind. Something he wouldn't just have to endure on a day-to-day basis, there were all the events and celebrations he'd have to experience without her. Like his wedding and the birth of his children. His mum should be around to see her grandchildren grown up. For God's sake, being a big kid himself at times, she should be around to see him finally grow up.

He tried to pull himself together while insisting to himself that he was being selfish. She was the one who was dying for goodness sake, not him. Dan discreetly wiped his eyes and focused on his search efforts, she didn't need to see him like this. He spotted the little white pill and reached under the dresser before rising to his feet. 'Found it,' he said, handing it over.

His mum gave him a grateful smile. 'I feel like a drug addict,' she said. 'No, strike that.' She indicated to the tablet resting on her palm. 'Thanks to these, the morphine, and all the other stuff, I am a drug addict. Me, who'd have thought it, eh?'

Dan leaned down and kissed his mother's forehead. 'So what?' he said. Everyone knew about the addictive qualities in cancer medication, but he'd rather that than the alternative suffering. 'Does it matter?'

His mum smiled again. 'You're a good son,' she said. 'I shall miss you more than you know.'

He fetched a glass of water and after a few sips she managed to swallow her pill. 'Better?' he asked.

His mum nodded. 'Ooh,' she said, suddenly springing to life. 'Before I forget, I have something I want to show you.'

Dan wondered where this burst of energy had come from, but he realised that he should have known his mother wouldn't stay defeated for long. She'd never been one to feel sorry for herself and, whatever the circumstances, she always tried to find something positive amidst any problems.

'Pass me my bag will you?' she carried on.

She pointed to the shopper by the door and Dan duly went to get it. He handed it over and watched his mum pull out an, as of yet, unopened pack of photos. He rolled his eyes. Her camera may be digital but as easy as it might be downloading her snapshots onto the PC, she still preferred the hassle of getting physical copies. For her, scanning through pictures on a screen didn't give her memories the respect that they deserved. Only a proper photo album did that.

He watched her rip open the pack.

'My visit to Amsterdam,' she said.

His mother was clearly excited to show him what she and Missy had gotten up to, Dan tried to summon up the degree of enthusiasm his mother expected. He struggled; as far as he was concerned, it was her daytrip to The Netherlands that had quickened her down turn. He'd known all along it would be too much for her body to cope with, but would she listen? As usual, the answer was no.

'Now this is outside the *Van Gogh Museum*,' she said. 'A lovely Dutch gentleman took the photo for us.'

Dan looked down at the two women who stood, arms linked, in front of a big glass and concrete building. Missy wasn't what he'd imagined. Compared to his mum, in her tweed suit and with her pinned back hair, she looked quite the conservative. And healthy, he noted, taking in her voluptuous frame, a frame that contrasted, a little too much for his liking, when next to his mother's.

'The paintings in that place,' said his mum. 'Such talent. And not just by the man himself, there are also works by Guaguin, Monet, Toulouse-Lautrec and Bernard. All of them wonderful.'

She continued to chat away as she moved on to the next picture and then the next. His mum seemed to see the wonder in anything and everything and Dan couldn't help but question how she found the stamina, both physical and emotional, to keep going. Yet again, he had to admire her. The woman lived on a diet of scrambled egg and soup as nothing else would go down properly; and she often winced when she thought no one was looking. Plus, she swigged morphine and popped pills like there was no tomorrow, yet she still managed to get through each day and usually without a single complaint. He paused in his thinking and told himself that that was the whole point. For his mum, there really was no tomorrow.

She gave him a playful nudge. 'You should take Maeve to Amsterdam one day,' she said. 'Or better still, to Paris. They don't call it the City of Lovers for nothing.'

Her suggestion caught him off guard. However, despite his discomfort, Dan did his best to raise a convincing smile. 'Maybe I will,' he said, a statement that seemed to please his mother no end.

As she continued to chatter, he wished he could be honest and tell her that deep down, he knew Maeve wasn't the one for him; that he didn't really have the desire to take the woman anywhere, let alone somewhere as romantic as Paris. He wanted to admit that he was scared; scared that if he continued to play this game, he'd end up stuck in a relationship that never had a chance from the beginning. But as she carried on animatedly explaining each photo, he knew he couldn't do that to her. He couldn't let his mum think that she was deserting him, leaving him all alone in the world. What kind of son did that?

He felt his mother's eyes boring into him, suddenly aware that she'd stopped talking.

'I know you're worried,' she said, as if reading his mind. 'That there are things you're not telling me.'

'You do?' said Dan.

He wondered if this was his chance to come clean. After all, he hated deceiving his mother, pretending all was well on the Maeve front when really it was anything but. He hated keeping secrets in relation to Annabel too.

Annabel. He felt himself brighten at the mere thought of the woman. In a strange way, it was their time together that had kept him sane throughout all of this. Their Wednesday nights gave him something to look forward to; a diversion from reality which he had to admit had nothing to do with babies. Annabel was funny and smart and quirky. She made him laugh. In fact, in many ways she was just like his mother and he knew the two of them would fast become friends were they ever to meet.

'Of course I do,' his mum replied.

He almost laughed. In reality she didn't know the half of it.

'If I had to watch my mother waste away like this I'd be worried too. There'd be lots of things I'd want to say, but for whatever reason couldn't. That's natural. But know that I'm here for you.' She patted the seat next to her, encouraging him to sit down. 'I haven't meant to push you away, Dan. I just think why let you get upset over what's physically happening to me if I don't have to. I want us to make the most of the time we have left. That's what matters, not what's going on inside this clapped out body of mine. You do understand, don't you?'

Dan put all thoughts of honesty to one side and nodded. He might not necessarily agree, but putting it like that, of course he understood. Besides, whatever information his mother had chosen to keep to herself, *Google* had been more than happy to share.

'You know I've never been one to pity myself,' she carried on. 'In my book, we just have to make the best of the cards that we're dealt.'

As he looked his mum in the eye, she seemed so accepting of everything. Why couldn't he feel the same?

'Of course, it helps that when the inevitable does happen, I know you won't be on your own, you'll be in good hands. Missy has assured me that she and Maeve will give you all the support you need.'

Dan felt like a part of him was dying along with his mother. Why couldn't she see he didn't care about Maeve? He didn't care if she was there for him or not. He wanted her in his life, not some substitute, which is what Maeve seemed to represent.

'I don't want you to go, Mum,' he said. 'Not now, not ever.'

'I know, Son. And goodness knows I don't want to leave you. But we've had a good life together, haven't we? Better than most.' She put a hand up and touched his cheek. 'If truth be known, Dan, I'm almost ready. I'm tired and every day seems to be getting harder.'

Unable to help himself, Dan began to cry. 'Please don't say that,' he said. 'Please don't die, Mum.' But he could see in her face that she meant it.

'When it's our time, it's our time,' she simply said. She smiled. 'And it'll be wonderful to see your father again. I can't tell you how much I've missed him.'

As his mother wrapped her arms around him, Dan felt like his heart was being ripped out. He told himself that she wasn't really choosing his father over him, no matter what the little boy inside said. His tears turned to sobs as she began rocking him back and forth, stroking his head in the same way she used to when he was a child.

'So you see in the middle of all this sadness, it's not all bad. We both have a future to look forward to. Your dad's up there somewhere waiting for me, just like Maeve's going to be down here for you.'

Dan began to sob even more.

SEVENTEEN

Dan searched the kitchen counter for his car keys. 'Where are you?' he asked. As he moved this canister and that canister, he felt sure he'd left them here somewhere.

'They're hung up,' said his mother. As she entered the room, she indicated to the key hook.

He rolled his eyes. The one place he should've thought to look but didn't. 'Cheers, Mum,' he said. She was forever tidying up after him, at least one of them had the sense to put things where they belonged.

He gave her a kiss on the cheek, ready to leave.

'Let me have a look at you,' she said. Giving him a quick once over, she smiled proudly as she straightened his tie. 'Very smart. Very smart, indeed.'

Dan looked down at his clothing. Aside of any big event where protocol dictated, he tended not to wear a suit. This evening though, he'd decided to make more of an effort and admittedly not just on the clothing front. He'd done a lot of soul searching since yesterday's heart-to-heart with his mother. Their talk had made him realise it was time to get real – about everything, and starting tonight.

'Thanks, Mum,' he said. 'Now are you sure you're going to be okay?'

'I'm sure.'

'And you've got everything you need?' he asked.

'I have.'

'Because I can always re-arrange if you'd prefer.'

His mum laughed. 'Go!' she said.

Dan gave her another kiss, then left the room, and headed out to the car. With one hand on the vehicle door handle, he looked back at the house, half tempted not to go out at all. He felt guilty about leaving his mum at home alone. What if something happened? Not that he really had a choice. Thanks to his track record, it wouldn't matter if it was for her benefit or not. She'd only accuse him of making yet more excuses.

Dan reassured himself in the knowledge that he'd promised to be back in a couple of hours and readied himself for the night ahead. He took a deep breath and finally let himself into the car. After settling into the driving seat, he turned the key in the ignition, repeatedly insisting to himself that he didn't have to do this, he wanted to do it. He put the vehicle into gear, at the same time, he recalled what his mother had said. He let out a little laugh. The woman always did make a lot of sense. This time, it was her words about making the best of the cards they'd been dealt that had struck a chord; and feeling determined, that's exactly what Dan planned to do.

As he set off down the road, he thought about what lay ahead. Life might still feel daunting, but at least he'd come to a decision. In a funny sort of way, getting to this point had been the difficult bit. Now he had clarity and could focus.

He wondered if Maeve would notice a difference in him now he felt ready to commit. He hoped so. After all, in the time they'd spent together she'd made it more than clear that she saw they had a future. Yes, she understood his concerns and yes, she'd have liked to have met him under different circumstances, but who wouldn't? He, himself, had wished the same thing. He, again, insisted he'd come to the right conclusion and while his heart might not have embraced Maeve just yet, he felt sure given a bit more time that would change.

He tried to picture the two of them a few years into the future. Would they be genuinely happy? Would they have the perfect two-point-four family unit? He obviously hadn't had enough sleep as his brain began playing tricks. In his mind's eye, Maeve kept morphing into Annabel, an image he didn't want. 'Like that's ever going to happen,' he said.

Forced to shake himself free, Dan knew there was no point going there. Thanks to his soul searching, he may have realised that's what he secretly hoped, but in reality Annabel could never be the woman for him. In the last twenty-four hours, she'd gone from being *just* like his mum to *too much* like his mum and, even if he'd wanted to, there was no way he could compete with a ghost.

He'd always wondered why there'd never been another man in his mother's life. However, thanks to their heart-to-heart, he finally understood. His mum had remained so emotionally connected to his dad for all of these years that she simply hadn't been able to move on. So much so, she now seemed to be giving up on life for him. Just like Annabel couldn't move on from her deceased husband, he acknowledged, although to be fair to her, she had made it clear from the start she was only after one thing – a baby.

He thought about the night the two of them had almost kissed and, despite his better judgement, he couldn't help but question whether things would have been different had their lips actually met. Would he be on his way to see her now instead of Maeve? He doubted it and again told himself it would be silly to think otherwise. If they had kissed, she'd have probably refused to see him again, putting paid to their agreement, which in the long run he supposed would have been for the best. Even an idiot could see that, if he and Maeve were to have any real chance, he had to stop all contact with Annabel. He sighed at his own stupidity. Even an idiot could see he should never have agreed to father Annabel's child to begin with.

'No, you've made the right decision,' he insisted. 'It's time to move on.'

He might not have relished the prospect of letting Annabel down, but it had to be done; and sooner rather than later, he realised, for both their sakes. He checked his watch and calculated how much time he had before his date with Maeve. With enough to spare, he told himself there was no point delaying the inevitable. He turned the steering wheel and began making a U-turn in the road. If he was quick, he could get it over and done with, ready to move on with the rest of his life.

***

Annabel turned on the taps, and looking forward to a good, long soak, added a measure of bubble bath to the water. She felt tired and her body ached. After an early start, she'd spent most of the day on her feet, putting together the arrangements for the young couple's wedding. Thankfully, the bride loved them, especially her bouquet, a mix of raspberry red *Darcy Roses, Red Gerberas* and *Burgundy Calla Lilies*. All of them symbolising love and loyalty in one way or another, perfect for their big day. She smiled, as she recalled the young woman's appreciative, verging on tearful response; a job well done in anyone's book.

Annabel grabbed a hair band and secured her hair in place. With the bath tub almost full, she turned off the taps and slipped out of her dressing gown. The water felt hot against her skin as she climbed in and bubbles frothed and fizzed around her ears when she leaned back. She could feel the day's physical stresses and strains immediately start to leave her body. 'Heavenly,' she said. Lying there, she closed her eyes. Now she just had to wait for her brain to relax as much as her muscles.

With everything that had been happening lately, switching off mentally seemed easier said than done. Of course, being worried about her sister didn't help; if only she could get a hold of her. She hadn't heard from Rebecca since the night that she had disclosed the news of Gavin's infidelity; and she wondered if she should try calling again. Or she could ring the man himself? He'd definitely know what was going on.

Annabel felt a bit out of her depth and didn't know what to do for the best. Contacting Gavin might create more harm than good, particularly if her sister hadn't confronted him yet. Having left her numerous messages already, she supposed one more wouldn't hurt. She just hoped Rebecca didn't do anything stupid in the meantime. Annabel shook the thought from her head. Her sister was far too sensible a woman for that. She probably just needed time on her own to consider her next move. Plus, her sister would never do anything to hurt the baby she was carrying.

Annabel sighed, wishing more than anything that she could be pregnant too.

Laid there amongst the bubbles, she considered whether or not to ask Dan if he minded upping their weekly appointment. But with the man having so much on his plate already she decided she couldn't be that selfish. It would mean taking him away from his mum and time with her had to be getting more and more precious. *Poor Dan,* she thought. It must be unbearable to watch someone fade away like that while knowing there isn't a thing anyone can do about it.

She pulled herself up into a seated position and picked up the soap, simultaneously wondering how his search for a wife was getting on. When she pictured him on his dinner date at the restaurant, she recalled the woman's appearance – perfect make up, hair to die for, and legs up to her armpits. As she slowly spun the soap around in her hands, Annabel found herself curious. Was this woman *The One* Dan had been looking for? Probably not, she decided. The woman was clearly all window dressing and no substance.

She paused and asked herself where this resentment for a total stranger had come from. Anyone would think she was jealous. 'Now you're just being stupid,' she said. She began lathering faster and faster. 'Jealous, my arse.'

Annabel dismissed the very idea and began to scrub herself clean. However, the sound of the doorbell ringing stopped her in her tracks. She realised it could only be Rebecca and hastily ducked her body under the water in a quick rinse, before climbing out of the bath. She put on her dressing gown, but didn't even bother drying herself first. Instead, she simply paddled out of the room and quickly made her way down the stairs, ready to find out why her sister had been so elusive these last few days. 'Thank

God,' she said, unlocking the front door and swinging it open. 'I was beginning to … .'

Annabel fell silent, surprised to find Dan standing there instead. Obviously on his way out for the evening, the man looked very dapper indeed. She cringed, unable to say the same about herself. *Does this man ever think to ring ahead?* she silently asked.

After telling herself the little somersaults in her tummy were the result of embarrassment, she watched his eyes widen at the sight of her and, realising that's how bad she looked, she blushed. She pulled her dressing gown tight over her chest, at the same time wishing its hemline sat below the knee and not over.

'It's not a bad time, is it?' asked Dan.

Annabel gingerly put a hand up to the messy pile of hair on her head, conscious of the bathwater still running down her legs. 'Erm, no,' she replied. 'I wouldn't say that exactly.'

He seemed to be waiting for her to say something else.

'Oh, sorry,' she said. All at once remembering herself she stood aside. 'Please, come in. Just let me go and throw some clothes on.'

Annabel raced back up the stairs and into her bedroom and grabbed the first clean items to hand. 'There's no point worrying about what you look like now,' she said. She donned a set of fleecy pyjamas and a pair of fluffy bunny slippers. *The man has just seen you half-naked.* She caught sight of her reflection in the dressing table mirror and stopped to look at herself. 'I bet his lady friend couldn't carry this off,' she insisted. Her shoulders slumped. 'Then again, would she want to?'

She left the room and headed back down stairs, surprised to find Dan still standing in the hallway. 'You could have gone through, you know.' She gestured the way to the kitchen.

As she followed him in, she could tell by the aroma trailing behind that his aftershave was expensive. 'Lucky lady,' she said.

'Sorry?' he replied.

Annabel squirmed, mortified at having just thought that, let alone said it. 'What? I didn't say anything.' It was a lie he thankfully seemed to accept and she quickly moved the conversation on. 'Can I get you a drink?' she asked. 'Cup of tea or a glass of wine?' She looked down at her attire. 'A mug of hot chocolate?'

He didn't appear to get the joke. Then again, looking at him he didn't seem his usual self at all. In Annabel's experience, there should have been at least one wise crack from him by now, but instead he had this serious air about him. As if he had something important to say.

He shook his head, declining her offer. 'I can't stay long,' he said.

Oh God, thought Annabel. Try as she might, she couldn't understand his demeanour. *What if it's his mother? What if she's dead?* She felt terrible at the thought of her trying to be funny when he could be on his way to the Chapel of Rest, a visit that would certainly explain the attire.

'Is everything okay, Dan?' she tentatively asked. 'It's not your mum, is it?'

Strangely, her question seemed enough for him to relax a little. He smiled. 'No, it's not Mum. But thank you for asking.'

'That's a relief,' said Annabel. Although why he'd be thanking her for thinking the poor woman was dead was anyone's guess. 'So what can I do for you then?' she asked.

Her mobile phone suddenly beeped, a text had come through. She decided that it could wait and she ignored it.

'Well?' she said. 'You're here because?'

She watched him nervously run a hand through his hair. Whatever he had on his mind it must be important.

'I've been thinking. About our arrangement.'

Annabel's heart skipped a beat. Glad not to be the one to have to broach the subject, he'd obviously come to the same conclusion as her, that once a week wasn't getting them anywhere.

'Don't worry,' she said. 'I know what you're going to say and, to be honest, I've been thinking the same thing.'

'You have?' asked Dan. He seemed relieved to hear it.

'Of course. It's not as if these Wednesday nights have been working, is it? If they had, I'd be pregnant by now.' She let out a little laugh.

'There is that, I suppose,' he replied.

'So it's only sensible we up our chances. Now, it's understandable you might want to keep your weekends free, but that still gives us five other days to choose from.' She knew she was rabbiting on, but she couldn't help herself. 'In fact, how about we forget the middle of the week altogether, and go for Mondays and Thursdays?'

Judging by his silence, she could see Dan hadn't expected her to be one step ahead of him.

'Well,' she said. Annabel smiled as she waited for his answer. 'What do you think?'

He seemed to pause for a second, but just as he was about to speak, her mobile began to ring. Irritated, she picked it up and looked at the screen. 'Sorry,' she said. Annabel recognised the caller and knew she had to answer. 'It's my sister.'

As he indicated for her to go ahead, she clicked to take the call. 'Rebecca, thank goodness. You do know I've been trying to get a hold of you, don't you? Is everything alright?'

She turned to Dan and mouthed another apology.

'What?' she suddenly said, her attention immediately back to her sister. 'Just stay where you are. I'll be right over. I mean it, Rebecca, don't do anything silly.'

Annabel frantically ended the call. 'Sorry, Dan, but this will have to wait.' She began searching for her handbag. 'I've got to go out.'

EIGHTEEN

As she and Dan stepped outside, Annabel slammed the door behind them. She fumbled in her bag for her keys as she hastily made her way to the car.

'What's happened?' asked Dan, hot on her heels. 'Is everything okay?'

'Let's just say I've got my fingers crossed,' said Annabel.

Frustrated, she crouched down, almost tripping over her bunny slippers as she tipped the contents of her handbag out onto the roadside. 'I know they're in here somewhere' she said. While sifting through the pile of crumpled receipts, her purse, and even a tatty old address book, Annabel sighed. She still couldn't find what she was looking for.

'Look, wherever you need to be, I'll take you,' said Dan.

Annabel paused. 'And spoil your plans, I don't think so.' She got back to her search, this time tossing a pack of headache pills to one side. 'Honestly, you go. We'll talk soon, yeah?'

She felt Dan's hand on her arm as he lowered himself down to her level. 'I don't mind and this is obviously important.'

Annabel momentarily relaxed when she saw the concern on Dan's face. It was good of him to think of her like this, but there was no way she could ruin his evening. 'I'm fine. It's just a family issue and believe me, you'll have a lot more fun doing whatever it is you're supposed to be doing.'

With one last grope around, she finally had to concede. Her keys weren't there. 'They must be inside,' she said. She looked towards the house as she scooped everything back up. 'Shit!' Annabel rose to her feet and realised that the keys to her home were on the same ring as those to her car. 'What the hell am I going to do now?' She put one hand to her forehead and the other on her hip as she tried to think. With only the bathroom window left open, the prospect of shimmying up the drainpipe did not feel like fun.

She watched Dan stand up. He pulled the keys to his vehicle out of his pocket and dangled them in front of her.

With no time to argue, Annabel zipped her bag shut. 'Okay,' she said, deciding it couldn't hurt to have a bit of back up in a situation like this. As she quickly headed for his car, she expected him to be right behind her. 'Well what are you waiting for?' she asked.

He pressed the button on his key fob and released the central locking. Dan shook his head and indicated to her clothing as they climbed inside. 'I can't believe you didn't get changed,' he said.

Annabel looked down at her attire. 'Who's going to see me?' She put on her seatbelt. 'And like you said, this is an emergency.'

As Dan turned the ignition, she took in the interior of the car. *Very nice*, she thought. Annabel compared it to her clapped out and rather basic little number; this one seemed to have a display for everything. It was obviously built for speed, something Annabel felt comfortable with. Her lack of punctuality had given her lots of experience on the speeding front, something Dan clearly didn't realise.

Having expected him to just pull out and hit the accelerator, Annabel waited for them to move. Forced to watch Dan double check for other traffic before slowly pulling away from the kerb, the last thing she'd had him down as was a Sunday driver. He seemed to carefully and methodically move through the gears, from first, to second, to third. She found it painful viewing; especially as they'd already established this to be a life or death situation. Even in her old car, she could have done nought to sixty in no time at all and, as they carried on down the street, Annabel itched for him to put his foot down. 'You can go a bit faster,' she said. Her impatience grew. She glanced at the speedometer; surely he was going to go above thirty at some point?

'Where is it we're off to?' he asked.

'Nowhere by the looks of things.' Annabel silently insisted she could walk quicker than this.

'I've already had one ticket recently,' said Dan. 'I don't want another.'

'Really?' She'd have put money on it not being for speeding.

'Really.'

Annabel realised no amount of complaining would make him go any faster, so she decided to just go with the flow. 'You need to take the next right and then a left,' she said.

She continued to give him directions, all the while thinking they were never going to get there. At this rate her sister had to think she'd been deserted in her hour of need, or worse, gotten herself into trouble. *Finally,* she thought, at last spotting their journey's end. 'You see that car park over there,' she said. 'That's where we're heading.'

Although still in no rush, Dan pulled in, while Annabel scanned the area for her sister's vehicle. 'There she is,' she said, as she pointed out a blue car so Dan could draw up alongside.

'A pub?' he replied. 'We've come to a pub? I thought you said this was an emergency.'

Annabel rolled her eyes. The drive had taken so long, no one would have guessed.

She decided to ignore his questions and hastily unclipped her seatbelt; but paused to look her driver directly in the eye before getting out. 'You're not to say a single word,' she warned him. 'You're here for your brawn should anything go wrong and not your brains.'

'Excuse me,' said Dan.

Annabel could see that he was wondering what he'd gotten himself into.

'Plus, I could do with the moral support,' she added. 'Silent moral support, that is.' After opening the car door, she paused for a second time. Annabel knew that Dan's presence wouldn't exactly be welcome, but thought it better to excuse her sister's impending behaviour prior to the fact. 'Rebecca can be a bit difficult, you see,' she said.

Dan smiled. 'I remember,' he replied, obviously recalling the couple of times their paths had crossed.

She finally disembarked and, with Dan following suit, climbed straight into the back of Rebecca's vehicle. She could see her sister had been crying, something Annabel thought understandable under the circumstances.

'Two questions,' said Rebecca. 'One, what on earth are you wearing?'

Annabel looked from her sister to her pyjamas and fluffy bunny slippers, no longer quite sure how to respond. Yes, she might be inappropriately dressed considering their venue, but with mascara and eye liner smeared all over her face, she had to ask if Rebecca was really in a position to comment.

'And two, what's he doing here?'

Annabel saw that Dan was about to reply, but quickly put her hand up to silence him. Rebecca had long made her mind up with regards to her dislike for the man and, no matter the explanation, she'd still want rid of him. Besides, having already made it clear Dan's role here was non-verbal, she felt more concerned about her sister's well-being. She'd never seen such an emotional wreck.

'Never mind him,' she replied. 'What are you doing here?'

'I've been asking myself that for the last two hours,' said Rebecca.

Annabel peered out at the building before her. With a boarded-up window and half its neon signage refusing to light up, the pub couldn't be more of a dive if it tried. Considering their surroundings, her sister was lucky she hadn't been robbed at knifepoint or car jacked. And goodness only knew what kind of woman her brother-in-law had got himself mixed up with.

'Earlier,' her sister carried on. 'When he rang to say he was working late again, something just snapped. I got in the car and waited outside the office for him to finish. That's when I followed him here.' Tears began to well in her eyes. 'He's in there, Annabel, with his other woman.'

'Oh, Rebecca,' she said, her sister's pain almost tangible. 'You shouldn't be doing this to yourself, not in your condition.'

Out of the corner of her eye, Annabel saw Dan move, as if about to speak. Anticipating his question, she decided to get in with the answer first. 'She's pregnant,' she said.

Dan's whole body seemed to slump. 'Jesus, Annabel,' he replied.

His reaction surprised her. Dan appeared as shocked by the news as she'd been, he didn't seem able to say anything else. Instead, he just sat there. Then again, Annabel supposed there wasn't much he could say. All the platitudes in the world wouldn't change things. Her sister would still be having a baby and she still wouldn't. She could see a tenderness in his eyes as he leaned over with a comforting hand, a gesture that left her, like him, lost for words. As she was taking in his gaze, the moment seemed to go on a little too long and, suddenly uncomfortable, Annabel snapped herself out of it. 'Now is not the time for sympathy,' she said, trying to re-focus.

'I just needed to see it for myself,' said Rebecca, as her lip began to quiver.

'And if he is with another woman,' said Annabel. 'What then?'

Her lip quivered some more. 'I don't know. I haven't thought that far ahead.'

'I take it you still haven't spoken to Gavin about any of this then?' asked Annabel. She again took in their dodgy environment. 'I'm guessing we wouldn't be here if you had.'

Rebecca shook her head. 'So he can tell me I'm imagining things? That it's my hormones playing up?'

As her sister broke down in tears, Annabel didn't know what to say for the best. She turned to Dan, hoping he'd have some words of wisdom, before quickly changing her mind again. After all, this was the last person Rebecca would take advice from. With no other options, she simply dug into her handbag and pulled out a clean tissue before silently handing it over.

Annabel watched her sister wipe her eyes and couldn't help but question why life had to be so complicated. If Gavin no longer felt happy in his marriage he should have come clean about his feelings, not turned to another woman. And once Rebecca had suspicions, she should have confronted her husband, not taken to sneaking around after him like this. Why couldn't people just be more honest with each other? She suddenly felt the warmth of Dan's leg against hers, forced to ignore the little voice inside of her that was suggesting that she might want to take her own advice. *Great*, she thought. Now she was hearing things. Maybe her sister had been right of late; maybe she was losing the plot.

Annabel insisted all of this sitting around wasn't getting anyone anywhere, and decided to take charge of the matter at hand. 'Just to get things straight,' she said. 'You haven't actually been inside the pub yet?'

Again, her sister shook her head. 'I've tried to pluck up the courage,' she said. 'But that's why I rang you. I was hoping you'd go in for me.'

Annabel looked into her sister's rather smudged, yet pleading, eyes. Then she once more turned her attention to her pyjamas and bunny slippers and wondered why these things always happened to her. She wished she'd listened to Dan and got changed before setting out.

'Annabel, you can't,' he said.

She threw him a look. 'What choice do I have?' she asked.

He held his hands up and, gesticulating his surrender, leaned back in his seat as if retreating to a safe distance.

Okay, *she thought*. You've been in worse situations. You can do this.

She took a deep breath. 'Right, any idea as to whereabouts in the building he might be?' she asked. With a bit of luck she could just march in, grab him, and march straight back out again.

'None at all,' replied Rebecca.

'Bugger!' said Annabel.

Dan tried to say something, but again, she refused to let him. She opened the car door, ready to get out.

'You're going in like that?' asked her sister.

Annabel scoffed. 'Not without trying to locate him first, I'm not. I'm hoping I'll be able to see him through the window.'

'I'm coming with you,' said Rebecca. She opened her car door too.

'So am I,' said Dan, doing the same.

Fantastic, thought Annabel. With her rocking her PJs, her sister doing a great panda impression, and Dan all suited and booted, they had to look like the weirdest search party on the planet.

Once out of the vehicle, Annabel scanned the car park, just hoping no one was watching. She led the way as the three of them headed towards the building and approached one of the pub windows. 'Can either of you see him?' she asked, peering inside. 'Because I can't.'

'It's too busy,' said Rebecca. 'He could be anywhere amongst that lot.'

Annabel turned to Dan, who simply shrugged. 'I wouldn't know him if I bumped into him,' he said.

Understandably so, she supposed, considering he'd never actually met her brother-in-law.

She turned and slouched against the wall. 'Blast,' she said. Annabel pictured herself having to go from room to room until she found Gavin, she could only imagine the comments about to come her way. She closed her eyes, cringing at the very idea. 'This is going to be so embarrassing,' she said.

'It doesn't have to be,' replied Dan.

Annabel opened her eyes again. 'What are you talking about?'

'I can go in for you,' he said.

'But you've just admitted you haven't a clue who he is.'

'I haven't. But one of you must have a photo. Everyone carries pictures of their nearest and dearest, don't they? Look.' He reached into his back pocket and pulled out his wallet. 'Even me.'

He offered it to Annabel who took in the picture of him and his mother. Seeing him at such a tender age she couldn't help but giggle. 'Wow,' she said, causing him to suddenly snatch the wallet back.

'That's enough of that,' he said, tucking it safely away again. 'It was the nineties. Every young boy had hair like that.'

Rebecca's coughing interrupted the banter. Purse in one hand and photo in the other, Annabel took the snapshot from her and, after a quick peek, handed it to Dan. She watched him smile as he took in the photographic scene – Rebecca, Gavin, and their three children in happier times.

'Good looking family,' he said, ready to go.

'Thank you,' her sister curtly replied.

'We'll wait in the car,' Annabel informed him. 'Come and get us the minute you spot him.'

'I will,' he said. 'I better take this with me though, if you don't mind.'

Rebecca nodded her consent and, as Dan headed inside, Annabel took her sister's arm and led her back to their vehicle. 'Everything's going to be okay,' she said. 'You'll see.'

After getting into the car, they seemed to sit there for ages; and as time ticked on Annabel's confidence began to wane. She wondered if she should be worried. After all, if the pub's exterior was anything to go by, its clientele had to be equally as suspect. In an environment like that, she knew poor Dan wouldn't stand a chance and, continuing to clock watch, she couldn't help but think they were going to have to send in a search party to locate the search party.

'What do you think's happening?' asked Rebecca. The woman was obviously thinking the same thing. 'Surely he should be back by now.'

'Maybe, but we both saw how packed it is in there.' Annabel tried to reassure herself as much as anyone else. 'It's probably just taking a while to get through the crowds.'

Dan finally re-appeared. 'Thank God,' said Annabel as she and Rebecca jumped out of the car. 'And he's still in one piece.'

She tried to read Dan's face as he approached, hoping for some sort of clue as to what he'd found, but there was nothing.

'Well?' said Rebecca.

He looked her sister directly in the eye. 'I think you need to come with me,' he said.

NINETEEN

Annabel finished keying in her text and pressed the send button. She might have thanked Dan for all his help already, but she wanted him to know just how appreciative of his assistance she'd been. Going into that place fully dressed, let alone in her pyjamas, would have been bad enough, a message she'd tried, and somehow failed, to convey.

She thought back to the drive home. Despite her grateful wittering, he'd seemed unusually quiet. Almost as if he wasn't listening. Of course, it had been an unusual night and come the end of it, he had to think she and her family were balm pots. Not that he actually said this out loud. In Annabel's view, Dan was far too much of a gentleman for that. Most men would probably run a mile rather than get involved in someone else's marital issues, and they definitely wouldn't partake in a spot of breaking and entering. Her lips curled as she once again recalled his chivalry. When he handed her his jacket and rolled his shirt sleeves up, he'd made climbing that drainpipe look so easy. And he'd been right, there's no way she could have managed it herself, with or without the pair of fluffy bunny slippers.

'What are you smiling at?' asked Rebecca.

'I'm not,' said Annabel. She put her phone down to one side. 'Unlike you, I see.' She took in her sister's features, the woman didn't just appear happy, she glowed. 'You haven't stopped grinning since getting here.'

'I know. It's like a great, big weight has been lifted off my shoulders.' She let out a long sigh. 'How could I have been so silly as to think Gavin would do something like that?'

'Tell me about it,' said Annabel. 'I've never been one to say I told you so, but everyone knows how much that man loves you.'

She joined her sister at the table. 'I suppose that's what happens when people keep things from each other. They get the wrong end of the stick.'

'It's very romantic though, don't you think?'

Annabel laughed. 'What? Having to take a second job in some grotty old pub to make ends meet? If you say so.'

'It's not to make ends meet,' said Rebecca. 'He's earning the extra cash for something special.'

'For your up-and-coming wedding anniversary? You've said, numerous times.'

Her sister frowned. 'You don't have to be like that about it,' she said. 'I've also made it clear how sorry I am for dragging you into this. And all for nothing as it turns out.'

Annabel looked up to the heavens. 'Rebecca, I'm teasing,' she said. 'And I don't remember you dragging me into anything. We're sisters, if you have a problem, it's my problem too. I'm just glad you're back to your old self.' As she looked at her sister again, she noted it was good to see her so relaxed, to see her smiling for a change. 'Better than your old self, in fact.'

'I could say the same about you,' said Rebecca.

Annabel narrowed her eyes. 'Meaning?'

'Meaning nothing.'

Frustratingly, her sister she refused to say anymore. She simply raised a knowing eyebrow before moving the conversation on.

'I told Gavin about the baby,' she said.

'And?'

'And he's as ecstatic over this pregnancy as he was all the others.'

'I'm pleased to hear it,' said Annabel. She felt torn. On the one hand, she couldn't be happier for Rebecca, on the other, she couldn't be more disappointed for herself.

'Are you? Because I'm not sure I could be quite so gracious in your shoes.'

Annabel appreciated her sister's concern, but it was completely unnecessary. Despite her mixed feelings, she planned on supporting this pregnancy along with everyone else. 'What kind of question is that?' she replied. 'Of course I am. I admit, I wasn't as excited as I should have been in the beginning, but what would be the point in feeling resentful? If anyone knows life doesn't always go according to plan, it's me and so what if you've gotten in there first? It just means I get plenty of practice on your baby before I have one of my own.'

Thankfully, her reassurances appeared to have the desired effect and Rebecca seemed to relax.

'Anyway, that's enough about me,' said Annabel, ready to talk about something else. 'Tell me about this surprise gift Gavin's saving for? What do you think it is?'

'Oh I don't know,' said Rebecca. 'I'm hoping it's a holiday, to somewhere exotic, like the Caribbean. We always said we'd mark the Big Ten with something really special. Although if it is.' She looked down at her stomach. 'I'm going to look a right treat in a bikini.'

Annabel began to picture a clear blue sea, gently lapping the shore of a white sandy beach. She could almost feel the heat of the sun as she imagined herself, cocktail in hand, soaking up its rays. It had been years since she'd had a holiday. Her last break being her honeymoon and, although she and Tom had had a great time, it hadn't been what anyone could call glamorous. The cost of the wedding itself, and the fact that she'd been setting up the Florist, hadn't left enough money for anything fancy; a few days in Torquay was all that they could manage. Annabel sighed wistfully. Maybe the time had come to treat herself?

'Speaking of special,' she said. 'Any idea what this is all about?'

'I haven't a clue,' replied Rebecca. 'Katy just said she had something important to tell us, and to get myself round here. All very cloak and dagger if you ask me.'

'She's probably about to announce she's also with child.'

'Annabel!' said a shocked Rebecca. 'How can you say that?'

She laughed. 'Well, it would be just my bloody luck!'

'I was thinking more along the lines of an engagement,' said Rebecca. 'This Oliver chap could have popped the question?'

'No,' said Annabel. 'Surely not? We haven't even had the pleasure of meeting him yet. And I wouldn't have thought they'd been seeing each other long enough, would you?' She thought for a moment. By Katy's standards, this relationship did seem different to all the others and, in light of that, Rebecca's suggestion definitely provided food for thought.

'It would certainly explain all this palaver,' added her sister. 'And she does seem more committed.'

'I know what you mean,' said Annabel. 'Before she was all *love 'em and leave 'em.*'

'Whereas now ...'

Annabel couldn't help the grin spreading across her face. 'You know, I think you might be right.' Her ears pricked at the sound of the front door opening and closing; she made sure to lower her voice. 'Talk of the Devil,' she said. 'At least now we'll find out for sure.'

'It's only me,' Katy called out. She exuded excitement as she burst into the room. 'Thank goodness you're both here,' she said. 'Have I got news for you?'

Annabel looked to Rebecca full of anticipation. She noted that her friend was carrying two bottles of champagne, it was clear that whatever the news Katy had, it was big. She discretely checked out Katy's ring finger, but disappointingly couldn't see any jewellery. Not that this necessarily meant anything, Annabel told herself. After all, to walk in with a diamond on show would only spoil the surprise.

'So, what's all this about?' she asked. Annabel tried to sound casual, she didn't want to ruin her friend's moment.

'First thing's first,' said Katy, with a giggle. 'Glasses, please.'

As Rebecca began to protest that she, and the baby, would be fine without the alcohol, Annabel wasted no time in doing as instructed. In her mind, the quicker they got this bit over with, the quicker her friend could make her announcement.

'One little mouthful isn't going to hurt,' said Katy to Rebecca, expertly popping the first of her champagne corks.

Annabel produced three champagne flutes and couldn't fail to be impressed as her friend proceeded to fill them. Left to her, the stuff would have been everywhere and she wasn't about to reveal her engagement.

'Right, now we're all ready,' said Katy. She handed everyone a glass.

Here we go, thought Annabel.

Annabel was already imagining herself as Maid of Honour, she never dreamed she'd see the day. Totally against the whole boy meets girl and lives happily ever after scenario, Oliver must be one special guy for Katy to do such an about turn.

'So,' said Katy. 'You know how Oliver and I have been getting pretty close of late.'

'Yes,' said Annabel.

'Yes,' said Rebecca.

'And that our relationship has gotten quite serious?'

'Yes,' said Annabel.

'Yes,' said Rebecca.

'Well last night, we decided to take things to the next level.'

Annabel could hardly contain herself. She willed Katy to get on with it, this build-up was killing her.

'So much so, that last night he got down on one knee and gave me this.'

'Oh my goodness,' Annabel whispered to Rebecca. 'We were right.'

She watched as her friend reached into her bag. Holding her breath, her eyes widened.

'Ta daaa!' said Katy, revealing all.

Looking from Katy's hand to her face, Annabel froze, speechless.

'It's a key,' said Rebecca.

'I know,' said Katy. 'To his apartment. Of course, we're not moving in together. That would be taking things a bit too far. But isn't it exciting?'

Annabel watched on as Katy lovingly looked down at the shiny piece of metal in her hand, sighing at the heart shaped ring it was attached to.

'So, Ladies,' she said, back to giving them her full attention. 'What do you think?'

Annabel knew she should say something. This might not be much of a step as far as she, herself, was concerned, but for Katy it was clearly something else. 'I think it's wonderful,' she said. 'Don't you, Rebecca?'

'Wonderful,' her sister replied. She continued to stare at the key. 'That's one word for it.'

Katy narrowed her eyes, suspicious. 'I'm getting the sense you're both a little underwhelmed here,' she said.

'No, not at all,' replied Annabel, images of this bridesmaid dress and that bridesmaid dress fast disappearing. 'I wouldn't say that, would you, Rebecca? It's just come as a bit of a surprise.' She could see her friend didn't believe her. 'I mean it's such a big step,' she carried on regardless. 'You and Oliver haven't been together very long, have you?'

'You expected a ring, didn't you?'

'No,' said Annabel. 'Of course not. We didn't expect anything of the sort, did we?' She turned to her sister, willing her to play along.

'Yes,' said Rebecca, her tone as blunt as ever. 'We did.'

Having just been dropped in it, Annabel fell silent. With the game up, she just hoped her friend wasn't too offended.

Much to her relief, Katy suddenly burst out laughing.

'Guys, it's me we're talking about,' she said. 'Sorry to be a drag, but this is as big as it gets, I'm afraid. You'll be down the aisle long before me, Annabel, that's for sure.'

Pleased to see her friend see the funny side, Annabel stepped forward to give her a hug. 'No, we're the ones who are sorry, Katy. We didn't mean to spoil it for you.'

Annabel realised what her friend had just said and she suddenly pulled away again. 'What are you talking about? I'll be down the aisle long before you?'

She looked from Katy to Rebecca. It was clear the two of them had been gossip mongering and she waited for an explanation. They obviously knew something she didn't.

'Oh come on,' said Katy.

'I told you she'd deny it,' said Rebecca.

'Deny what?' asked Annabel.

'That there's more to you and Dan than you're admitting,' said her friend.

Annabel almost spluttered.

'Even a blind man can see he's besotted with you,' said her sister.

'And don't think we haven't noticed the twinkle in your eyes too,' Katy carried on.

'Rubbish,' said Annabel. 'The two of you don't know what you're talking about.'

'Is it me?' asked Katy. 'Or does the lady protesteth too much?'

'You know what,' replied Rebecca. 'I think she does.'

'You don't even like the man,' said Annabel, to her sister. 'And how did we go from your anniversary?' She turned to Katy. 'And your non-engagement, to me anyway?'

'That was before last night,' Rebecca replied, completely ignoring Annabel's objections. 'Having spent a little time with him, I now happen to think he's perfect for you.'

'Perfect for me?' Annabel couldn't believe what she was hearing. She felt hijacked into a conversation she didn't want. 'Now listen to me, you two,' she said. 'I've already had the love of my life and I think you're both being very disrespectful.' She thought about what she and Tom had shared in their short time together. How she'd vowed to never replace him, before, and after, his death. 'And if *you're* being disrespectful, to even try and go there again with someone else, well what would that make me?'

Her friend looked to Rebecca and, despite not saying a single word, Annabel could see they were still in agreement.

Both women turned their eyes directly on her.

'Lucky!' they said, in unison.

***

Dan poured the freshly blended mix of vegetables, herbs, and stock from the mixer back in to the pan. 'Not bad,' he said. 'Even if I do say so myself.' He breathed in the soup's enticing aroma. No way would his mother be able to resist this.

He gave it a quick stir, and stopped to lean against the kitchen counter; he took his mobile from his pocket and, yet again, read the text from Annabel. Up until now, he'd been the only one to instigate contact outside of their usual appointment, so her message had come as a bit of a surprise. A nice surprise, he had to admit, especially when she'd expressed her gratitude already.

He smiled to himself, doubting she'd have shown any appreciation at all had she known he'd been half tempted to let her head off in search of Gavin herself. Considering her wardrobe, it would have been great entertainment value. Although she did look pretty cute in her PJs, he had to concede. Not quite as cute as when she opened the door in nothing but her dressing gown, of course. Now that was an image he'd never forget.

He almost laughed at how his mind actually went blank for a second, causing him to come out with some inane question about it not being a bad time. Obviously it wasn't a good time. The woman had had to answer the door half-naked. He continued to picture her though and couldn't help the words *tom-ay-to* and *tom-ah-to* springing to mind.

He snapped himself out of it, knowing it was exactly these kinds of thoughts that had gotten him into his current predicament.

What a mess, Dan thought to himself. Seeing her like that had left him unable to think straight, let alone remember why he was actually there. And by the time he'd pulled himself together it was too late to offer any explanation at all with regards to his impromptu visit, she was already on the phone to her sister. Why hadn't he just said what he had to say and then left them both to it, instead of playing the knight in shining armour? If he had, he wouldn't have heard about Rebecca's pregnancy. But hear he did and now it felt cruel to tell Annabel their arrangement was off. The mere mention of Rebecca having a baby had struck him, so he could only guess at how Annabel must feel. She might put on a brave face, but whether she admitted it or not, it had to hurt.

'Anyone I know?' asked his mum, entering the room.

As she peeked over his shoulder, Dan quickly tucked his phone into his jeans pocket. 'I shouldn't think so,' he said. He pushed anything and everything Annabel related to the back of his mind, it was something he'd have to deal with later.

He picked up the wooden spoon again and got back to his stirring. 'I hope you're hungry. This soup is to die for.' Dan cringed. There were so many innocuous statements that, under normal circumstances, would go unnoticed. Now, however, they seemed to take on a whole new dimension. He turned to his mother. 'Sorry. That came out wrong.'

Unusually quiet, she dismissed his comment with a wave of a hand. 'This looks nice,' she said, taking a seat.

He followed her gaze to the neatly laid table. His mum had always thought it important they eat together at least once a day. She viewed it as their time to catch up. Dan had to admit he hadn't always agreed and sometimes he had managed to get out of it, but not very often. He thought back to his youth, he could still recall his frustration at not being able to come in from school and head straight for his room. Unlike his friends, he wasn't allowed to shut himself away for hours on end. Instead, he'd have to sit and watch his mum prepare dinner, answering question after question about how his day had been, what he and his friends had been up to during break and did they have any plans for the weekend. Even after they'd eaten he still couldn't escape. Under his mother's watchful eye, he'd have to sit there doing his homework while she washed up and cleared everything away.

Now though, he understood why. The prospect of losing his mum had forced him to look at their relationship through fresh eyes. He'd come to realise their tea time routine, along with the incessant questions, had been her way of ascertaining what was going on in his head, rather than in his general day to day life. She'd simply been making sure she didn't lose him to all the badness out there in the world – crime, drugs, peer pressure, all the things that can drive a wedge between parent and child if left unnoticed. This was her way of keeping him on the straight and narrow. What he'd give to go back to those days.

'So what's on your agenda for this week?' asked his mum, interrupting his thoughts. 'Anything exciting?'

Dan smiled; he thought to himself that some things never changed. Not only did his mother still employ the same tactics, she was as protective of him now as she'd ever been. He just wished he had more time left with her to appreciate it.

'No plans to speak of,' he replied. He carried the pan of soup over to the table and began filling their bowls. 'What about you?'

His mum picked up her spoon. 'I'll be checking out the local hospice, but other than that nothing special.'

Dan stopped what he was doing. He knew that she hadn't intended to sound so blasé, but he still felt like he'd been slapped in the face. Hospices were where people went to die. They weren't something you casually dropped into a conversation.

'Don't look at me like that, Sweetie. We both know it's coming and, as hard as it is to accept, we have to be organised and ready. These things have to be done.' She paused as if thinking about the place in more detail. 'I'm most looking forward to seeing the gardens. Apparently they're gorgeous and, no matter the season, there's always something in bloom. I imagine it'll be quite comforting to be surrounded by beauty at the end.'

'But I …'

'What? Expected me to spend my last days here? I don't think so, Dan. That would be too much for the both of us.' She began to eat. 'And just because I had to bathe you and get you dressed once of a day, that doesn't mean I want you returning the favour. Surely you can see that?'

Dan didn't know what to say. On the rare occasion he had allowed himself to think about his mother's final days, she was right, he had automatically assumed they'd be spent here, with him, in their home. He'd assumed he'd be the one nursing her to the very end and not because of any sense of duty, but because he wanted to do it.

'After I'm gone,' his mum carried on. 'I need you to remember all the fun we've had over the years. Not when you had to carry me down the stairs to the sofa, or worse to the toilet. I couldn't bear it.'

No matter the explanation, Dan still felt hurt. 'So you'd rather be surrounded by strangers?'

She gave him one of her stern *don't even go there* looks and Dan realised there was no point arguing. The matter was in no way up for discussion. He shook his head and sighed. He might not like her decision, he might even want to return the favour as she put it, but he had to respect her wishes even if she couldn't respect his. 'Okay,' he said. 'We'll do things your way.'

'Thank you,' his mum replied. 'Now can we please talk about something positive? Tell me, how are things with Maeve?'

Dan fixed a smile on his face; he didn't feel like talking about anything. 'Fine,' he simply said. 'She's a lovely girl.'

'So things are progressing well then, are they?'

He shifted in his seat. Having stood her up last night, this was the one subject he especially didn't want to get into. 'As well as can be expected.'

While avoiding his mum's gaze, he picked up his spoon and dipped it in his bowl. He was beginning to wish that he'd made himself a salad instead. Unable to admit how he really felt about Maeve, he'd never been any good at lying to his mother and with every nervous tick and twitch on show, at least with a salad he could have stuffed his cutlery full of lettuce leaves to hide behind. As it was, he had nothing.

'I told you you'd like her, didn't I?' she said.

Dan suddenly got up from the table. 'Water?' he asked. His mum failed to answer, but he decided to get her a drink anyway and, after grabbing a couple of glasses from the cupboard, he headed for the sink.

'And last night's date?' she carried on. 'How did that go?'

Dan's hand faltered on the tap. She couldn't possibly know he'd stood Maeve up.

'Why do you ask?' he replied. He tried to sound equally as casual, but felt his body tense up as he waited for her answer.

'No reason.'

Relieved to hear this, Dan felt himself relax.

'It's just that Missy called this morning.'

Shit! *thought Dan*. Of course she did.

His mother always did have her ways and means of finding out what he'd been up to, sometimes before he'd even done it. However, rather than confront him on any of his wrong doings, she much preferred giving him the opportunity to own up first.

While standing there, he felt like a naughty schoolboy as opposed to the grown man he was meant to be, although he supposed on this occasion he only had himself to blame. Too busy playing the hero on Annabel's behalf, he should have realised his mum's friend would have been straight on the phone.

'She wondered if everything is alright,' she continued. 'I mean according to her, poor Maeve waited and waited for you to get there, but you didn't actually turn up.'

Dan could feel her eyes boring into him as she held out for some sort of explanation. And just like when he was a kid, he knew his deceit would be written all over his face, one of the reasons he never could get away with anything. He returned to the table and frantically tried to come up with a suitable excuse. Maybe he could say his car had broken down or that he'd ran out of petrol. Or that he'd bumped into an old friend en route and gotten waylaid catching up.

'So,' his mum continued. 'If you didn't spend the evening with Maeve, the only question is who did you spend it with?'

Dan let out a long, hard sigh. The time had come to tell the truth.

'Annabel,' he said. 'Her name's Annabel.'

TWENTY

'Higher! Higher!'

Annabel laughed. She couldn't deny the little one's bidding. Feeling such joy, she'd have stood there all day just to sense that smile and hear that giggle.

'Mummy, I'm flying. I'm flying.'

Push after push, Annabel could almost feel the tummy tickles as the swing to-ed and fro-ed, carrying her charge backwards and forwards – a sensation she remembered from her own childhood. As she felt the sun on her skin and the love in her heart, Annabel couldn't have been happier. She wanted the day to last forever and ever.

'Daddy! Daddy! Your turn! Your turn!'

With one last push, Annabel stepped back. More than content to share the excitement, she thought it only fair Daddy have his go too. Smiling, she turned; ready to give her husband a hug and a kiss before he took her place in front of the swing. Suddenly confused, she stared at the man before her.

'Dan,' she said. 'What are you doing here? Where's Tom?'

'Tom!' she called out. Annabel scanned her surroundings and looked for his face amongst the other dads. Starting to panic, she couldn't see him.

'Tom's gone,' said Dan.

He stepped forward, his arms out ready to reassure her, but Annabel recoiled. 'No,' she said. Her eyes still searching, he had to be here somewhere. 'He can't have gone.' Her heart began to race. He wouldn't leave her, not again.

She frantically tried to locate him, her voice got louder and louder. 'Tom! Tom!' Desperate tears welled in her eyes. 'Why isn't he answering?' she asked. 'Why isn't he here?'

She felt Dan's hand on her arm.

'Annabel,' he said. 'It's time to let go.'

Annabel bolted upright. Gasping for air, the darkness confused her and, in that moment, she couldn't work out where she was. Her heart raced, so fast that she could feel the blood pumping through her veins, every beat pounding in her ears. Tears streamed down her face, the fear of not being able to find Tom still with her.

She tried to control her breathing, forcing herself back to the here and now. 'It's not real,' she said. 'It's not real.'

Annabel managed to compose herself and switched on the bedside lamp, its brightness blinded her for a second. She reached for Tom's photo off the bedside cabinet and immediately hugged it close to her chest. Finally, her heart rate began to settle.

Feeling calmer, Annabel checked the clock. It was 4.30 a.m., she knew she should go back to sleep, but after throwing the covers off of herself, she felt too shaken to even try. She didn't want to risk falling back into the same dream. Except it wasn't a dream anymore, it was a nightmare.

After swinging her feet off the bed, Annabel wondered what it all meant. 'What's happening to me, Tom?' she asked. Waiting for an answer, she hoped against all hope that this time he would appear to answer her questions. She needed him to tell her everything was going to be fine. In the continuing silence, however, her anticipation turned to disappointment. As usual, she was going to have to figure things out for herself.

Annabel grabbed her dressing gown and headed for the bathroom. She turned on the cold tap and began slushing her face with the running water. She caught sight of her reflection in the mirror, she looked tired, something she supposed understandable at this time of the morning. While examining her features though, she knew it was more than that. It was as if she was losing her grip on the life she'd built for herself. Everything about her seemed to be changing and now she might not even have her dream for comfort. A dream that felt so real, it was the one tangible link she still had to her husband and it scared her to think that that could be gone too.

She made her way downstairs to the kitchen. After coming to the conclusion that a cup of tea might help, she clicked the kettle on, the sound of the water boiling cutting through the early morning stillness. She wondered how many others out there couldn't, or didn't want to sleep either, and stared out of the window, looking for signs of life. Out in the darkness, it didn't surprise her to find there weren't any. Everyone else was far too sensible.

Maybe that's the problem? thought Annabel. Perhaps in her heart of hearts she was sick of being sensible too. Ever since Tom's death, she'd kept both herself and her memories wrapped up in an invisible wadding of cotton wool. Over time, she acknowledged, a part of her was bound to want to break free. She sighed. If she gave in, where would that leave the part of her that didn't? Annabel felt a sudden urge to get out into the fresh air, and racing upstairs to get changed, she hastily swapped her night clothes for a pair of jeans and a sweater. She raced back down again, and grabbed her keys, phone, and a jacket, before heading outside. She took a deep breath and, after feeling the cool morning air fill her lungs, she set off down the street.

Without a clue as to where she was going, Annabel just walked and walked. After a while, she started to hear refuse collectors in the distance, the stopping and starting of the rubbish truck as it made its way along its route; a sign that soon everyone would be up and about ready to get on with their day. Annabel thought how nice it would be to simply click her fingers and bring everything to a halt, to freeze frame the moment; such thoughts suddenly reminded her of the run up to Tom's funeral when she really had wanted the world to just stop.

All those people milling around, she recalled, business as usual, when her life had come crashing down. They had to sense that the world had shifted, to realise something was wrong. They had to see it written all over her gaunt, expressionless face, and in the sadness of her eyes. Yet in reality no one seemed to notice anything, or care for that matter; a fact made more than clear when Rebecca dragged her out to buy a funeral outfit.

She remembered the numbness she felt, forced to go through the motions of checking dress sizes. They were both on automatic pilot, but rather than see their pain, the shop assistants merely followed them around as if they were a couple of would-be thieves. Of course, red-eyed and distracted, in Annabel's desperation to just pick something, anything, the two of them could easily have been mistaken for a couple of drug addicts looking to turn a quick buck for their next fix. However, as far as Annabel was concerned, that wasn't the point. The shop assistants didn't care beyond what they saw. No one did.

A dog barking somewhere interrupted her thoughts. She hadn't noticed the daylight creeping up on her, or realised how far she'd walked. 'Maybe you're listening to me after all,' she said to her deceased husband. She took in the familiar church spire, it felt nice to think he might have been guiding her.

While crossing the cark park, Annabel considered the number of times she'd hurried down this footpath. Today though, she felt in no rush. As she begun to leave the land of the living behind, she took the time to listen to the birds and their dawn chorus, to smell the scent of the wild flowers, and admire the hedges. Beginning to see the place in a new light, she soaked up the tranquillity, forced to give the caretakers their due. In her view, to bring such nature to what she'd always considered a very unnatural environment must've taken some doing. As Annabel looked around, she spotted a rabbit as it hopped behind a headstone. She could sense the serenity of her surroundings and yes, while it was still a cemetery, for the first time ever she grasped an element of real beauty.

While sauntering along, she noticed a glint in the grass just ahead and, leaning down for a closer look, picked up a shiny new penny. Annabel looked at it for a second, turning it over in her fingers before putting it in her jacket pocket. Despite not being superstitious, she smiled. It was about time she had her share of good fortune. Even if finding a penny didn't really bring much in the way of luck, she couldn't help but think she needed all the assistance she could get.

Finally, after approaching Tom's grave, Annabel sat down, cross legged in the dewy grass. As she tried to put her thoughts into some sort of order, she pulled out her mobile and dialled a number. She listened to the ring tone, waiting for the answerphone message to kick in.

'Hi, this is Tom,' *said her husband.* 'You've probably guessed I can't pick up the phone right now, so leave a message and I'll get back to you. Oh, and if this is you, Annabel, I love you, Sweetheart.'

She realised that people thought her mad for keeping his phone going all this time, but she was as scared of forgetting Tom's voice as she was his face. His voicemail recording made her feel like she had a direct line straight to him and on those times when her memories seemed to be fading, it offered proof that their life together really did exist. Sometimes she even left him a message, but that was her little secret. If anyone knew that, then they'd definitely see her as balmy.

Annabel clicked the phone off and tucked it away in her jacket. 'Even though I wish to God you were still here, Tom,' she said, while looking around. 'I suppose having a dead husband does have its advantages. I mean, how many other wives get to bend their other half's ear at this time of a morning.'

She pictured him chuckling at her attempt at humour, cheekily yawning as he nodded his head in agreement. In reality, when it came to one of them keeping the other awake they both knew it was usually the other way round. Tom had been the one to prevent her from sleeping.

The number of times that Annabel sat propped up in bed, bleary eyed, while Tom excitedly chattered on about something or other. He'd talk about the wedding, the perfect life they were going to build, and come the latter days, the success they would make of the shop. Annabel had felt daunted at their starting a business, concerned that if it failed they'd end up skint or worse still, homeless. If anything, it should have been her own worries keeping her awake at night, but they never got a look in thanks to her husband. She smiled, still able to hear him as if it was only yesterday. Oh yes, Tom's enthusiasm had been enough for both of them and she'd had the lack of sleep to prove it.

'I do miss you,' she said, still imagining his face. 'When I was with you everything felt right. Perfect, in fact.' She thought about their life together, about how happy they'd been. She thought about his death. 'Then you had to go and die and ruin it all,' she added.

'I'm still mad at you, you know. For leaving me,' she carried on. 'When it happened, I felt so angry I found it hard to breathe let alone function. And the pain, I wouldn't wish it on anyone. I don't know how I got through it.' She began to think about her darkest days. 'I remember standing at the roadside watching the traffic, thinking how easy it would be to just step out so we could be together again. It's ironic really. The only thing that stopped me from actually doing it was you. I realised how angry you'd be at me for not carrying on without you.'

She stared at Tom's headstone and wished it was him looking back at her instead of some cold, stone slab. Then again, she supposed talking to herself did make things easier; it enabled her to be more honest. A bit like in one of those counselling sessions, Annabel considered, where the patient laid on the couch, revealing their inner most thoughts. She'd often wondered why the doctor always seemed to scribble his notes from a chair just out of sight. It was obviously to give the patient the space to open up. She scanned her surroundings. Maybe that's what Tom was doing with her now?

She sighed, ready to get back to the matter at hand.

'Anyway, I did what I had to,' she continued. 'I got on with it. And I was alright in the end. I had my routine. Get up, go to work, come home, go to bed … . Not what most people would call fun, but I was happy plodding along in my own little world, I could cope with that.' She paused for a moment to contemplate how long it took to get to that point. 'Then it was my turn to go and change things. I decided I wanted a baby.'

'Oh I don't know, maybe things would be fine if I'd found a donor I didn't actually like. Some womanising, disrespectful oaf of a man, instead of Dan. Katy and Rebecca think I like him a bit too much and, the thing is, I'm scared, Tom. I'm scared they might be right.'

She began tidying his grave, pulling up the tufts in the grass that had sprouted since her last visit.

'I don't suppose it helps having to see the two of them so loved up. Rebecca's on cloud nine because Gavin isn't really having an affair, like I couldn't have told her that. And Katy's made the bold step of swapping house keys with this Oliver chap, who we still haven't met, by the way. I'm not jealous, as such. Seeing them just makes me realise what I'm missing out on. And if I'm honest, I'm not sure what I've been searching for has anything to do with babies like I thought it did. Not yet anyway.'

She paused to think about Dan. They may not have known each other for very long, but he'd begun to make her feel alive again. He'd stirred up feelings she's long since supressed.

'You'd like him, Tom. The two of you are very similar in many ways. And I know if I was to sit here and tell you I wanted to make a go of things with him you'd approve. You told me as much when you were still alive.'

Her mind drifted back to the day she gave him her word. Having not long moved into the house, they were giving the living room a spruce up with a fresh lick of paint. It took them weeks to decide on the right colour, but colour chart after colour chart and tester pot after tester pot, they finally settled on a gorgeous Dove Grey. Annabel chuckled as she pictured the scene. It was just like them to get as much on themselves as they managed to put on the walls.

'What would you do if anything ever happened to me?' asked Annabel, dipping her brush into the paint tin. 'Do you think you'd ever get married again?'

'I'd probably end up a merry widower,' Tom replied, finishing off the chimney breast. 'Living the high life on your life insurance.'

Annabel laughed. 'I'd never meet anyone else.'

'Rubbish,' said Tom. He stepped back to admire his handiwork. 'A good looking woman like you, men would be lining up to take my place.'

'But that's my point. No one out there ever could. I wouldn't let them.' She got back to her painting. 'I wouldn't want another relationship. I might not go down the Queen Victoria route and wear black for the rest of my days, but I certainly wouldn't start over. I can promise you that.'

'And I'm being serious too,' insisted Tom, turning his attention to the alcove. 'There's no way I'd want you giving up on happiness just because I wasn't around anymore.'

At the time, they seemed to be having one of those naïve conversations that Annabel assumed most newly weds had. She'd never forgotten it though and while looking back, she couldn't help but wonder if deep down, she'd known all along their happiness couldn't last; that they wouldn't be together forever.

Tom, however, clearly had no such concerns.

'I don't know why we're even talking about this,' he said. 'We're both stuck with each other, I'm afraid. Neither of us are going anywhere.'

Annabel took a deep breath and slowly exhaled. If only that had been the case.

She gathered together the loose bits of grass she'd pulled up. 'Please tell me what to do, Tom. I'm so confused, I can't think straight. I don't want to break my promise to you, but it feels like I've opened a door that I can't close again.' Hell, she didn't even know where the door led considering she and Dan had never talked about it.

She looked around as if waiting for some sort of sign, but all she felt was the cool breeze suddenly blowing around her. She shuddered, feeling chilled to the bone. It seemed the dew from the grass had seeped through her clothes onto her skin. Annabel tried to warm herself up and stuffed her hands into her jacket pockets, her fingers landed on the cold metal of the one penny piece she'd found.

She wondered if this was the answer she'd been waiting for. 'No,' she said. 'Surely not?'

While telling herself people had based their decisions on less, she pulled the penny out of her pocket and looked at it. 'What do you have to lose?' she asked herself. 'And let's face it, you've got to do something. You can't carry on like this.'

After turning it over in her fingers again, she wasn't sure she could be that brave. 'What do you think, Tom?' she asked. She looked up to the heavens. 'Shall I go for it?'

With no answer forthcoming, Annabel took a deep breath. She wrapped the coin up in the palm of her hand for a second and then placed it on her thumb. After a count of three, she flipped the penny high into the air, watching it spin as it first went up and then began coming down.

'Heads, I keep my promise,' she said. 'Tails I don't.'

***

Annabel flittered around the kitchen. None of these jobs were necessary, she just hoped that in keeping her hands occupied, her brain would be occupied too. After folding up the tea towel, she straightened up the coffee and sugar caddies, before moving on to wipe up around the sink. She knew she was killing time before Dan's arrival. She looked at the wall clock – his imminent arrival.

As if on cue, the doorbell suddenly rang and Annabel stopped still. She dropped the dishcloth in the washing up bowl and wiped her damp hands down the sides of her jeans to dry them. 'This is it,' she said, her pulse quickening.

As she made her way down the hall, she steeled herself ready. She put on a smile as she opened the door and gestured him inside. 'Go through,' she said, indicating towards the kitchen. 'Coffee?' she asked. Following him in, she struggled to look him in the eye and headed straight for the kettle. Her mind raced as she tried to organise her thoughts.

'Not for me, thanks,' said Dan. 'I told Mum I wouldn't be out long.'

Annabel put it on to boil regardless. 'How is she?' she asked.

'I must say I was surprised to get your call,' Dan carried on.

Annabel finally turned to face him. She signaled for him to take a seat.

His eyes narrowed in response. 'Is everything alright?'

'Please?' said Annabel, again she pointed to a chair.

She could see his confusion, but refused to be swayed, she had to see this through. Taking the seat opposite, she clasped her hands in front of her as she rested them on the table. 'We need to talk,' she said. 'About us.'

Dan automatically mirrored Annabel's posture as he straightened himself up in his seat. 'Okay,' he said. 'What is it you want to say.'

'I don't think we should see each other anymore,' she replied.

She watched him take a few seconds as if to absorb her words. 'Wow,' he said. 'I wasn't expecting that.'

Annabel took in his disappointment. She hadn't meant to just blurt it out and the last thing she wanted to do was hurt his feelings. But it needed saying. To continue in what they were doing was causing *her* too much pain, which in the long run affected both of them. 'I mean it's not exactly working, is it?' she said. She tried to sound light, hoping this might soothe the blow.

Dan regained his composure and finally looked her square in the face. 'I agree,' he said.

Annabel's chest all at once felt tight. His sudden coolness came as a surprise. 'You do?' she asked.

Dan nodded. 'Things are getting complicated.'

'They are?'

Now *he* appeared to gather his thoughts.

'I've been meaning to tell you.' He shifted in his seat. 'I just didn't know how.'

Annabel waited for him to continue.

'I've met someone,' he finally said.

TWENTY-ONE

Annabel continued to push her food around her plate; she knew Katy and Rebecca had meant well. She also knew they were right, ending her arrangement with Dan didn't mean she had to stop having fun with friends and family. However, turning up, intervention style, to drag her out into the big, wide world hadn't really been a good idea, no matter what their intention.

After realising she should have stood her ground more and simply point blank refused, Annabel wished she was back in the confines of home. At least there she didn't have to pretend she was having a good time, she could be as miserable as her heart desired.

She had to give them their due though. So far, Katy and Rebecca hadn't once mentioned the state of play with Dan. Up to now, topics had included anything but. They'd covered the weather, morning sickness, and the fantastic sales on the high street; their current conversation centred on the latest new movies, which ones to see and which to avoid. Not that Annabel had anything in particular to contribute. She hadn't watched a film on the telly recently, never mind taken herself off to the big screen.

She zoned out of Katy and Rebecca's chit-chat altogether and glanced around at her surroundings. Waiting staff, dressed in their all black uniforms, busily flittered about. Cheerful throughout, they delivered the restaurant's take on home cooked food to some tables, while clearing empty plates away from others. She took in the décor. With its open fires, wooden flooring, and cottage-like theme it looked pleasant enough. Warm and cosy even, thanks to the autumnal colour scheme. A quick peek out of the window, however, revealed its true colours. The adjacent cinema complex and ten pin bowling centre did nothing to counter the fact that a country pub without the countryside didn't work. The place was trying to be something it wasn't.

A bit like herself really, thought Annabel, as she sat there with an empty smile on her face while nodding and shaking her head in all the right places; she tried to give off the right vibe without an ounce of authenticity. Not that anyone else seemed to notice the façade, she acknowledged; neither her own nor the building's.

Annabel found herself thinking about Dan. She wondered if he was coping alright; after all, his mother's condition was bound to have worsened. She recalled his face the last time they talked. He seemed disappointed to hear her breaking off their arrangement, but at the same time had to acknowledge it was probably for the best. Apparently, he'd been coming to the same conclusion himself since meeting Maeve. Annabel didn't tell him that she'd seen them together, she didn't see the point. He'd accepted their arrangement had come to an end and she supposed, in the end, that was all that mattered. She took a deep breath and exhaled. Finally, she could put a name to the long legged, long haired blonde. Annabel pictured them together. They made a handsome couple and she hoped things worked out for the two of them. The proverbial *happy ever after* being the least Dan deserved.

'Are you going to eat that?' asked Rebecca. 'Or just keep playing with it?'

'Sorry?' said Annabel, her attention suddenly caught. She followed her sister's gaze to her plate. 'Apologies, I'm just not very hungry.' At last, she set her fork down.

'Why don't you just call him?' asked Katy.

'Call who?'

'You know who,' said Rebecca.

'Dan.' said her friend. Not that she really had to point out the obvious. 'That is who you're thinking about, isn't it?'

Annabel picked up her wine glass. It seemed she'd spoken too soon with regards to their silence on the subject. They both might not mean to go on, but as far as she was concerned, they were beginning to sound like a broken record. Why couldn't they just accept her dealings with Dan were a thing of the past, no matter how many times they suggested otherwise? 'Like I keep telling you, I've made my decision and there's no going back.'

Much to Annabel's annoyance, her sister rolled her eyes not even attempting to hide her frustration.

'Really?' said Katy. 'Because from where I'm sitting, going backwards is exactly what you are doing.'

'And I have to agree,' Rebecca joined in.

Annabel sighed. 'Now there's a surprise.'

'Oh come on, look at it from our point of view,' said her sister. 'It took a while, but after all the heartache, we finally get a chance to see the real you again. The Annabel that laughs and jokes and isn't afraid to show herself up. Then just as quickly as you reappear, *puff*!' She flicked her fingers out like some sort of magician. 'You, the woman we all know and love, are back to locking yourself away in that house of yours as if the outside world doesn't exist.'

Annabel didn't know what to say. She couldn't argue. She'd surprised herself at how quickly and easily she'd managed to fall back into her routine.

'And all in the toss of a coin,' said Katy.

Rebecca put her hand up in disdain. 'Don't remind me,' she said. 'Have you ever heard anything so ridiculous?'

It was clear the two of them were never going to give up and Annabel felt cornered, forced to question if this had been on tonight's agenda all along. To pretend all was well until they got her on neutral ground. Unlike at home, in public she'd have to listen to them and, with a bit of luck on their part, come to her senses. 'It might seem ridiculous to you,' she said. 'But it makes perfect sense to me.'

'Does it?' asked Katy. 'Because I don't believe you.'

As usual, it seemed Annabel was talking to herself.

'I think you're running scared. I think you started out on this journey with Dan thinking you wanted one thing and then you realised you wanted something else. Yes, a baby would give you someone to love and yes, that love would be reciprocated. I get that. But we both know a baby isn't enough anymore, why else would you call this pregnancy thing off? You want the whole package and that freaks you out.'

Annabel took a sip of her wine. The evening was going from bad to worse, and fast. The last thing she needed was another lecture. The last thing she needed was someone telling her how she felt. 'I almost had the whole package with Tom,' she said. 'And look where that got me. As for your scoffing, Rebecca, be it a penny or a couple of quid, people put their futures in the hands of the Money Gods all the time. You only have to look to the lottery to see that.'

'What? And now that these Money Gods have spoken, we're supposed to just accept it, are we? We're supposed to get on with our lives knowing you're sitting in front of the box night after night turning into some sort of amoeba? You'll be telling me you're going to get a cat next.'

'Funny you should say that,' said Annabel.

Desperate to change the subject, she knew she was just being mean, that she didn't really have any such plan. But her sister hated cats with a passion and Annabel knew that to even imply getting a feline friend would be enough to send the woman off on a tangent.

'Jesus,' said Rebecca, true to form. 'Mrs. Miggins down the street got a cat when her husband died.'

Annabel sat back, relieved to see her cunning plan play out.

'Granted she's a lot older than you, but one soon turned into two and then three and you know what cats are like. Before anyone knew it, she had a house full.' She pursed her lips, shuddering at the thought. 'Talk about a giant litter tray.'

'Look,' said her friend, keen to get their original discussion back on track. 'We all know how special Tom was.'

Bugger! thought Annabel. Trust her to bring things into line.

'Even though he's no longer here, how special he still is. And what happened, well it's beyond words. But that doesn't mean you can't find happiness again, Annabel.'

'For my sake as much as yours,' added Rebecca, obviously still pre-occupied with all things moggy.

Annabel almost laughed. Talk about a pair of hypocrites. It didn't seem too long ago that one of the women before her thought she was still grieving, while the other insisted she'd lost the plot. As for their dislike for Dan, they'd had him down as some sort of bad influence.

'What do you think Tom would say if he saw you like this?' asked Katy. 'Would he want you to just give up?'

'Because it doesn't stop at the cats, you know,' her sister carried on. 'Before long you'll be wearing floppy hats and hoarding pile after pile of newspapers.'

'To think, my own sister, a cat lady,' added Rebecca. 'I need a drink.'

Before she could protest, Annabel's glass was snatched from her hand. She watched on, wide eyed, as her pregnant sister began downing its contents.

'Thank you,' said Annabel. For the baby's benefit if not the mother's, she quickly re-claimed her now half-empty glass.

'Then you'll stop leaving the house altogether like some sort of hermit,' said Rebecca. 'And let's face it, when it comes to the life of a recluse, you're already half-way there.'

Annabel stared at her sister, unsure whether to laugh or feel offended. She supposed it was her own fault, a part of her even felt a bit guilty. In her desire to the change the subject she'd obviously pushed the poor woman over the edge. However, in her condition, it probably didn't help that her hormones were all over the place.

Annabel returned her attention to Katy and decided it best to ignore Rebecca and her cat complaints altogether. 'I know exactly what Tom would say,' she said. 'But we're not talking about him, are we? We're talking about me.'

***

Sitting in one of the armchairs in the lounge, Dan quietly watched over his mother as she slept on the sofa. She seemed so at peace when asleep, to the point that Dan wished sleep would come to her more often. It had to be a welcome relief from the increasing agitation she experienced when awake, a sure sign that her medication was losing its power over the pain. One of the reasons he wanted his mum to listen when he suggested she might be more comfortable upstairs. But as always, the very idea had been poo-pooed. *Taking to her bed*, as his mother put it, would be too much like giving in. Although Dan wasn't stupid, he knew her reluctance had more to do with the actual climbing of the staircase itself.

He continued to observe his mum and found himself insisting he'd give anything to take away her suffering. Offered the chance, he'd exchange places with her in an instant.

He took in the photo album lying on the coffee table, wondering which of her memories she'd been reminiscing about today. She'd taken to going through their many snapshots just before her naps, almost as if she wanted to impress each and every image to mind should she not wake up. He leaned forward and reached for the album to see for himself; his sudden movement causing his mother to stir. He stopped, holding his breath as he willed her to stay asleep and, much to his relief, she seemed to settle back down.

Dan picked up the album and, after getting himself comfortable in the armchair again, began slowly turning its pages. He couldn't help but smile as, photo after photo, his mum and dad stared back at him. In some of them they were goofing around, in others there was definitely a bit of posing going on. Throughout though, they were clearly at ease in front of the camera and no one could deny the feelings they had for each other, their togetherness leapt off of the pages. The family of two soon turned to three and Dan started to recognise himself in the photos. He'd been too young to remember when any of them were taken, but his parent's clearly adored him. In every shot, their love for him was as evident as their love for each other.

'What time is it?' his mum suddenly asked.

Surprised that his mother had awoken, Dan let the photo album rest on his lap. He checked the clock on the mantelpiece.

Disappointingly, she'd slept for less than an hour. 'Almost six-thirty,' he replied.

'Shouldn't you be getting ready by now?' she said. She gradually eased herself into a more upright position.

'There's no rush.'

'Still, it's a big night and you need to look your best.'

Dan didn't want to even think about the evening ahead. There was no getting out of it, of course, which did nothing to help his sense of foreboding. But at least he could delay the inevitable for a little while longer.

'I know,' he said. 'Don't worry. I will.'

He raised the album and continued to browse its pages.

'It's funny how the brain works,' said his mum. 'I can forget what I'm doing from one minute to the next, yet I remember each and every one of those photos being taken like it was only yesterday.'

'That's old age for you,' said Dan.

His mum laughed. 'I wouldn't mock,' she replied. 'It comes to us all eventually.'

She indicated for him to pass her the album, and Dan joined her on the sofa. Perching himself on the edge, he angled it so that they could both see the images without her having to move too much.

'Now this,' said his mum, pointing to one photograph in particular. 'Is one of my favourites. You were two years old and it was the first time we'd taken you to the beach. Boy, did you hate it.'

Dan stared at the young child in the picture. With his unruly blonde hair, big blues eyes, and great big smile, it was fair to say he'd been cute back in the day. Sitting in a deckchair, his shoeless, podgy feet just about hung over the edge of the seat and his arm was outstretched, as if pointing to something out of shot. Surrounded by blue skies and the orange sand typical of many UK beaches, it seemed your usual family outing. 'I look happy enough,' he said.

'That's because you're sitting down,' his mum replied. 'It was the sand you didn't like. Every time we put you on your feet, you froze for a second before bursting into tears. You were so funny. We put it down to you not liking the feel of the stuff. You were the same with grass for a while too.'

Dan smiled. He couldn't remember a second of it. 'Those were the days, eh?'

'They certainly were.'

They carried on browsing for a while; Dan listened intently as his mum animatedly filled in the details of this photograph and that photograph. She seemed in her element back then, and now. Dan smiled, able to understand why. The images proved just how good life had been. Perfect, in fact, the way his mother told it.

He began to wonder if he, himself, would be ever lucky enough to experience this. In years to come, would he sit on a sofa with his own children, looking back on a lifetime of memories filled with real love? At the moment, it was hard to imagine. He struggled to get his head around the possibility that he and Maeve could ever share the depth of feeling that his parents had shared. He just had to hope that, in time, things would change, that he'd start to think about Maeve in the same way he thought about Annabel. His heart sank. Funny how he could only admit his strength of feeling for the woman once they'd called things off.

'Are you okay?' asked his mum.

Dan fixed a smile on his face. 'I'm fine. Why do you ask?'

'You have that faraway look in your eyes again,' she replied. 'Anything you want to talk about.'

She'd accused him of that a lot these last couple of weeks, but Dan didn't see the point in talking. He'd made his decision, even before Annabel suggested they call it a day.

He pictured Annabel's face the last time they'd met. He could have sworn she'd been disappointed when he agreed it was probably for the best. He realised he'd imagined it, of course; foolish wishful thinking that she might feel for him what he felt for her. He took a deep breath, determined to dismiss all thoughts of the woman from his head.

'I'm just a bit nervous about tonight,' he said. 'Meeting Missy for the first time and all that.'

'Why don't I believe you?' asked his mum.

As she searched his face for the truth, Dan suddenly felt self-conscious. The truth was the last thing his mother needed to know and he quickly handed her the album ready to leave the room. 'I suppose I should go get a move on,' he said. 'Time to get ready.'

His mother suddenly appeared concerned and, gently placing a hand on his leg, she prevented him from going anywhere. 'I've been very silly, haven't I?' she asked.

'What are you talking about?' replied Dan. 'Silly about what?'

'About the whole caboodle, for thinking I know what's best. You don't really want a future with Maeve, do you? And I think we both know why.'

Sitting there, all pretence seemed to suddenly desert him. Dan felt as sick of lying to himself, as much as he did lying to his mother. But he still couldn't bring himself to answer the question. His mum was dying and the last thing he wanted was to add to her pain.

He stared at the floor and tears sprung in his eyes as he wished that everything could be different.

'I only wanted what I thought was best for you,' said his mum.

'I know,' he replied.

'I'm sorry, Dan.'

After wiping his eyes, he finally returned his mother's gaze. 'Me too,' he said. 'I did try.'

His mum smiled. She held her arms out for a hug, Dan could see she needed it as much as he did.

'That's settled then,' she said, eventually pulling away. 'We'll have no more of it.'

'But …'

'No buts. You're the person I care about here, no one else. Besides, if Missy is half the friend I think she is, she'll more than understand. And so will Maeve.'

The relief Dan felt was enormous. At last, he could breathe a bit easier again.

'Fancy looking at some more photos?' asked his mum. 'Before supper.'

Dan nodded as she re-opened the album and, proving herself true to her word, it seemed that was the end of the matter.

'Now this one,' said his mum 'is of me and your father on our wedding anniversary.'

Dan stared at the image; his mum and dad were raising a glass of bubbly for the camera. It was a cute picture. His mother, with her head thrown back, was laughing as his father whispered something in her ear. Dan sighed. Looking at how happy the two of them were, he couldn't help but think of Annabel.

TWENTY-TWO

With only half an hour before closing time, Annabel pawed through the TV guide she'd picked up at lunch. There was nothing like a good crime drama to make her forget her own problems and, with a couple of new shows starting this week, she wanted to know if they were worth tuning in for. The synopsis made the first one sound quite good. *At last*, she thought. *Something to look forward to*. Just as she was about to read the second synopsis, the shop doorbell sounded and Annabel looked up. She automatically put the magazine to one side and smiled at the young chap who, after a quick look around, seemed relieved to spot the bucket of red roses.

'Can I take a dozen of these, please,' he asked.

'Of course you can, sir,' Annabel replied.

As he handed her the container, she couldn't help but notice the man's nerves. The poor chap seemed so worked up that the whole thing shook in his hands. In Annabel's floristry experience, this could only mean one of two things. Either he'd been a very bad boy and was about to make a heartfelt apology, or he was being a good boy and about to do something romantic.

She hoped it was the latter and carefully selected twelve of the best blooms before laying them onto sheets of decorated paper. Annabel then began expertly wrapping them into a bouquet. She could see him anxiously fidgeting out of the corner of her eye and decided to let her curiosity get the better of her. 'Special occasion?' she asked.

'They're for my girlfriend,' the chap replied. 'I'm going to propose.'

Annabel felt glad to hear it. She much preferred to think of her flowers displayed in a vase somewhere, rather than simply dumped in the bin. Plus, the poor man appeared to need a good woman behind him, if only to show him how to use an iron. 'How exciting,' she said.

The doorbell sounded once more, signaling yet another customer and, after glancing over, Annabel gave a friendly nod to the older lady now making her way inside.

'Would you like to see the ring?' asked the young chap. He proceeded to take a box out of his inner jacket pocket and seemed to anticipate her response as he carefully opened its lid. 'I chose it myself.'

Annabel took in the simple gold band and beautiful solitaire diamond. Despite the man's appearance, he certainly had taste. 'She'll love it,' she said. 'It's gorgeous.'

Clearly relieved to hear this, the chap proudly tucked it away again.

'There you go,' said Annabel. 'Beautiful flowers for a very lucky lady.'

The man flushed red as he produced a couple of notes from his wallet and swapped them for his purchase. 'Keep the change,' he said.

'But won't you need it?' asked Annabel.

'Sorry?' said the man.

As she rang up the till, he seemed to suddenly panic and Annabel felt guilty for sending him into another tither. As these events go, it was as if she'd made him think he'd forgotten something important. 'For the champagne,' she calmly replied. 'When she says yes.'

The man visibly relaxed. 'Right, for the champagne,' he said. He still refused to take the money and simply waved a dismissive hand before heading for the door.

'Excuse me,' Annabel called out.

Before he could leave, she hastily raced from behind the counter and grabbed a couple more roses along the way. 'Here,' she said to the young chap. 'Twelve of these declare your ultimate love, whereas two show your commitment to the forthcoming marriage. Maybe you could give these to her tomorrow.'

The man looked at the roses in her hand. 'Thank you,' he said, appreciatively taking them. 'I will.'

'Good luck,' Annabel called after him, as he finally made his exit.

After re-taking her place behind the counter, she began cleaning up the odd bit of leaf left over from the dozen roses. Annabel glanced up at the older lady; she appeared to be looking for something in particular. 'Can I help you?' she asked.

'That was a lovely thing you just did there,' said the woman.

Annabel shook her head. 'Ah, it was nothing.'

The woman smiled before getting back to her search. 'Who doesn't love flowers?' she said. 'They're all so beautiful, so cheerful. Did you know each and every one of them has their own special meaning? That's what makes it so hard to choose.'

Annabel thought that it was nice to meet someone who appreciated all things floral as much as she did, she eyed her potential customer, who was wearing striking patterns and bold red statement jewellery; she obviously enjoyed the finer things in life, along with a sense of style. *Unlike me*, thought Annabel. After looking down at her own somewhat boring attire, even that young chap in his crumpled suit demonstrated more pizazz.

She suddenly remembered her conversation with Dan, about how his mother never saved anything for best. She pictured his face, just thinking about him made her heart pang and, in refusing to let herself go there, she tried to dismiss the memory as quickly as it had arrived.

She returned her attention to the customer. 'What is it you're looking for?' she asked.

'Oh, I'll know it when I see it,' said the woman. She continued her search. 'Here we are,' she all at once added. 'Perfect.'

Annabel watched her hastily reach down to pick up a bunch of her chosen flowers. In her excitement, however, she must have moved too quickly. It looked like she was about to faint and Annabel rushed over to help before the woman could injure herself.

After relieving her customer of her belongings, she gently took her by the arm and steered her towards the stool by the counter. 'Here,' she said. 'Take a seat.'

'Talk about a head rush,' said the woman, clearly thankful for the assistance. 'I don't know what came over me.'

'You do look a bit pale,' said Annabel. She placed the woman's handbag and flowers on the counter and helped her on to the stool. 'Let me get you some water.'

She quickly headed out back, grabbed a glass, and turned on the tap. 'Do you want me to call someone? A doctor maybe?' she shouted through. After returning to the woman, she set the glass down for her to drink from when she was ready.

'It's very kind of you to offer,' her customer replied. 'But I'll be alright in a minute.'

Annabel checked the time and decided it wouldn't hurt to close up a little earlier for a change. 'Then how about I give you a lift home?'

'Again, there's no need,' said the woman. 'I have a taxi waiting.'

She indicated outside and Annabel spotted the attending car. The driver, a cheerful looking, portly man, seemed to sense he was being watched and, gave them a wave. In return, the woman held up what looked like the victory sign and mouthed that she'd only be a couple of minutes. He smiled, sticking his thumb up in response.

'He seems a lovely chap,' said Annabel.

'Oh he is. He runs me about a lot these days. Honestly, anyone would think he was my own personal chauffeur. And he isn't one of those drivers who sits up front, all po-faced, refusing to say a single word. He tells me about his wife and his family, about what they're up to.'

The woman picked up the glass and began sipping on her water. Much to Annabel's relief, some semblance of colour finally began returning to her cheeks.

'Do you have children?' she asked.

Annabel felt thrown. After the last couple of months it was a subject she preferred not to discuss. 'I'm afraid not,' she said. She automatically placed a hand on her belly. 'I was hoping to, but, well you know.'

'It just hasn't happened yet?' said the woman. She nodded to Annabel's necklace. 'I noticed the wedding ring.'

Annabel put a hand up to the chain around her neck. 'No, it's not that,' she replied. 'My husband, he died.'

'I'm sorry to hear that,' said the woman.

Annabel recognised the sympathy in her eyes as she carried on drinking her water.

'My husband died young too,' she said. 'And although you've probably heard this a hundred times before, I can assure you, life does go on.'

Annabel smiled; she was trying to disguise the fact that, for her, it most certainly didn't. 'I take it you re-married,' she asked. She might not be able to move on herself, but that didn't stop her feeling pleased for those that could.

'Me?' replied the woman. 'No, I was too busy single-handedly raising a child to even think about meeting someone else. Of course, that's not to say I didn't have the odd admirer or two, I just kept them at arm's length. Nobody matched up to my husband, you see.'

'There's still time,' suggested Annabel. 'None of us know what, or who, is around the corner.'

The woman laughed. 'I think it's a bit late for me to start thinking like that. But you've got plenty of time.'

Annabel took in the woman before her. It felt good to meet someone who knew first-hand what she'd been through; what she was still going through. Family and friends meant well in their advice, but they had a tendency to come over as a tad judgemental when she didn't follow their guidance. This woman, well she understood.

'I thought I'd met someone,' she said. 'His name's Dan. But things didn't work out.'

'Oh,' said the woman. Her eyes widened, as if encouraging Annabel to continue.

'You'd like him. He's funny, smart, and in the short time we knew each other he helped me to start enjoying life again. And you know how hard *that* can be when it comes to us widows.'

The woman laughed. 'Tell me about it,' she said.

'It's not that I compared him to Tom. Tom's my husband, by the way. I just got scared.'

'Of what?'

'I don't know. Lots of things I suppose.'

'And did you tell this Dan how you felt?' asked the woman.

'No, I hardly dared admit it to myself and I haven't a clue how he feels about me. Anyway, falling for Dan seemed too much like a betrayal.' Annabel paused; she wondered if she was sharing too much information. 'You'll probably think I'm mad,' she said. 'But when my husband was alive I promised I'd stay faithful forever. Childish I know, but I gave my word.'

'Some promises are meant to be broken,' said the woman. 'Thanks to circumstance, sometimes we're left with no choice.' She too seemed to pause for a second, as if thinking about her own life. 'What would your husband want you to do?'

Annabel began wrapping the customer's flowers. 'He'd want me to be happy.'

'Even if that means starting over with someone else?' asked the woman.

Annabel nodded. 'Yep.'

'Well there you go then.'

Annabel sighed. 'It's not that easy though, is it?' she asked.

'The best decisions in life never are,' the woman replied. 'Look, I can't tell you what to do one way or the other, but what I can say is that you have a long road ahead of you. I know that makes me sound like a hypocrite, but I had a child to keep me going and even though he's all grown up now, I still do. But it isn't easy being on your own. No man is an island, as they say, and believe me, it can get very lonely. We need someone to share our lives with. We need to love and be loved.'

'You sound like my sister and best friend. They think I should just go with the flow and see where it takes me.'

'Wise words,' said the woman. 'Maybe you should listen to them?'

The woman carefully eased herself off of the stool and picked up her handbag. 'Time I should be going,' she said, as she headed for the door.

'Don't forget these.' Annabel called after her as she held up the flowers.

The woman turned with a knowing smile. 'They were never intended for me,' she said. 'They were always meant for you.'

Annabel watched her make her exit and felt confused. Why would a complete stranger want to gift her flowers?

'But …'

Before she could say anything else, the woman was already out of the door and half way into the taxi. Forced to watch it pull away, she looked down at the blooms in her hand.

'Daffodils.' Acknowledging their meaning, she couldn't help but smile to herself.

Annabel stared at the car as it drove off into the distance.

'New beginnings,' she said.

TWENTY-THREE

Music played in the background as Annabel flitted around the kitchen, tossing the last of the vegetable peelings into the bin and giving the work tops a final tidy up as she went. While humming along to the tune, she turned her attention to the mound of pots and pans on the draining board that were waiting to be dried and put away. Her humming stopped. Did she really use all that just to make a simple casserole?

As she grabbed a tea towel, she couldn't help but laugh at herself. Having never been what anyone could call an organised chef, she wondered why she'd never invested in a dishwasher. For most people, they came as standard and, looking at the pile before her, she could certainly see why. She thought back to when she and Tom had first moved into the house. Back then, such a purchase had seemed an unnecessary expenditure and, later on, she supposed there'd never been any point. After all, how hard was it to wash a single plate, a knife, and a fork?

She paused, and realised her solitary dining experiences could very well soon be a thing of the past. A prospect that felt both invigorating and scary at the same time. Forced to reign herself in, she tried not to think too far into the future. 'Now you're getting ahead of yourself,' she said. 'It's still early days. And as you well know, a lot can happen in the meantime.'

With the self-pep talk over and the last of the drying up put away, Annabel checked the kitchen clock. Never one to run ahead of schedule under any circumstances, it surprised her to find she still had plenty of time to spare. She smiled and looked up to the heavens. 'What do you think, Tom? Impressive, eh?'

Annabel refused to let herself think too much and took a deep breath. However, she knew it was a case of too little, too late; no amount of breathing exercises could stop her excitement creeping in. With her insides stirring, she couldn't work out if it was a host of butterflies now playing havoc in her tummy, or a little man in there using her intestines as a trampoline. Either way, she had to find a way to at least try and calm down.

'Maybe it's time for a well-earned glass of wine,' she said.

She made her way over to the fridge. Annabel took out a bottle of white and retrieved a glass out of the cupboard; she poured herself a small measure. 'That'll do,' she said. Although unable to resist, she decided to add just a tad more for prosperity's sake. She raised the glass into the air, in a self-congratulatory toast. 'Cheers!' she said.

'It's only us,' a voice suddenly called out.

Annabel paused mid sip. She hadn't even heard the front door go.

'The kids were playing up and I just had to get out.'

'And as I'm all on my lonesome,' shouted another. 'We thought we'd come and keep you company.'

Annabel's shoulders slumped. Katy and Rebecca, that's all she needed.

'Something smells good,' said her friend.

As she and Rebecca burst into the room, Annabel watched her sister stop in her tracks. Suddenly suspicious, Rebecca's eyes narrowed as she began surveying her surroundings. From the daffodils on the dining table to the casserole cooking in the oven, she took it all in, before walking over to the stereo and abruptly turning it off.

'What's going on?' she asked, the room at once silent. 'And before you try to even to deny there's something taking place here, remember, I know you too well.'

'As do I,' said Katy. 'So come on, reveal all.'

Annabel did her utmost to appear cool and collected. 'I haven't a clue what you're talking about,' she replied. 'You're both obviously imagining things.' Not that the lack of an admission did anything to allay her visitors' curiosity. If anything, it seemed to make it worse.

'I know what it is,' said her friend. She dumped her bag on the counter top, at the same time sighing as if something terrible had just dawned on her. 'You've gone and found yourself another sperm donor, haven't you?'

'Jesus, Annabel,' said Rebecca.

Their joint disappointment was more than evident.

Annabel laughed at the mere suggestion. The two of them couldn't be more off the mark if they'd tried. 'Of course I haven't,' she said. 'Why would I do that?'

'Doh!' replied Katy. 'Why did you do it the first time around?'

Annabel shook her head. Surely they knew that if anyone had well and truly learned their lesson on that score, it was her.

'Well you're up to something,' said her sister. As usual, she refused to give up. 'And it's only a matter of time before we find out what.'

'I assure you,' said Annabel. 'I am up to nothing.'

Looking at the two of them, it wasn't that Annabel didn't want to share her news. These were her closest confidents and she'd been dying to say something for days. In fact, she'd almost let recent events slip on more than one occasion and she knew full well how pleased for her they'd be were she to tell them what was going on.

But they'd also be equally devastated if something went wrong and Annabel knew first-hand how life could be perfect one minute, only to be turned on its head in the next. As far as she was concerned, why put them through that if she didn't have to? She didn't know how things were going to quite pan out herself just yet. Plus, there was the added bonus of having a little secret for a while. It seemed to make things more special somehow. However, despite standing firm, it seemed that her sister and best friend were as determined to uncover the truth as she was to hide it.

'Well if you're going to be like that,' said Rebecca. 'You leave us no choice.' Rebecca took her coat off and rolled her sleeves up, she turned to Katy. 'Let's look at the evidence shall we,' she said.

Annabel knew what was coming next. It was a game they'd been playing since childhood. As kids, one of them, usually Rebecca because she'd always been a *Little Miss Bossy Boots*, would set clues to a puzzle and taking on the persona of a couple of amateur sleuths, it was up to the others to try and solve it. Of course, as they grew older their game extended into real life situations. The mere whiff of a juicy secret in one and the other two would immediately come over all *Miss Marple* or *Hercule Poirot*. And this, it appeared, was one of those times.

After observing them get into character, Annabel decided to let them have their fun. She knew they'd find out soon enough anyway, even if she didn't plan on making it easy for them. She watched on as her sister began by wiping a finger across the kitchen counter and then inspecting it.

'Firstly,' said Rebecca. 'The place is spotless.' Her sister had adopted a rather posh and somewhat exaggerated English accent; she glanced around the room once more. 'Not a speck of dust in sight, no magazines lying around, and definitely no take-away boxes poking out of the bin.' She strode over to the cooker and, after picking up the oven glove, opened its door to check the pot inside. 'Secondly,' she continued. She took in the chunks of beef, carrots, and celery sticks, all sitting in a rich, simmering gravy. 'You're cooking.' Her sister calmly replaced the casserole dish lid and closed the oven door again, before swiftly turning to face Annabel. 'You never cook,' she added. 'A fried egg sandwich is more your thing.'

Katy stepped forward, more than happy to pick up the baton. 'Thirdly,' said her friend. 'The lady is looking pretty darn hot herself.' She raised her arm, ready to address Annabel's appearance from head to toe. 'Notice the French elegance of the *chignon du cou*,' she said to Rebecca. 'The way the hair wraps around itself, the odd wisp creating a sense of romance.'

While Rebecca sagely nodded her head in agreement, Annabel couldn't help but shake hers. The woman sounded more like a cheesy fashion show host than any insightful detective she'd ever read about.

'Then we have the little black wrap dress,' her friend carried on. 'Figure hugging in a sexy sort of way, yet, at the same time, casual enough so as to create the illusion of effortlessness. And, of course, moving on, we have the kitten heels.' She paused, looking Annabel directly in the eye. 'Need we continue?'

Annabel looked from her friend to her sister. As investigative double acts went, these two were no Sherlock Holmes and Doctor Watson.

What they were, however, was impossible and Annabel realised that if she didn't reveal all, they were likely to never give up; or more to the point, leave. 'Alright, alright,' she said. She steeled herself ready for the barrage of questions no doubt about to ensue. 'If you must know, Dan's coming round.'

Annabel took in their astonished faces.

'Really?' said Katy.

'Since when?' asked Rebecca.

Back to being themselves, the posh accents suddenly became a thing of the past.

'Since we've been talking,' Annabel replied.

The two of them looked at each other confused.

'Talking about what?' asked her sister.

'What do you mean, about what? What do you think?' replied Annabel.

'So this means the baby thing's back on again, does it?' asked her friend. 'Because first it is, then it isn't. Honestly, I can't keep up.'

Annabel felt herself blush. Surely she didn't have to spell it out. 'No, Katy, the baby thing is not back on.'

She waited for her friend to realise the significance of what she'd just said, finally, the penny seemed to drop.

'Oh, my, word,' said Katy. A great big smile immediately spread across her face. She turned to Rebecca. 'You know what this means don't you?'

Her sister frowned, seemingly trying to grasp what they were talking about. 'I haven't a clue,' she replied.

'Then let me help.' Katy cleared her throat as if ready to burst into song. 'Annabel and Dan are sitting in a tree. K.I.S.S.I.N.G.'

'No,' said Rebecca. She turned her attention to Annabel. 'Really?'

'That's not quite the way I'd have put it,' Annabel replied. 'But yes, really. Dan and I have decided to give things a go.'

There, she'd admitted it.

'I think we need to sit down,' suggested her friend. Katy headed for the table, her sister followed suit, both of them giggling as they went.

Annabel watched them take a seat and wondered if they knew what a pair of gossip merchants the two of them sounded. Not that they'd care anyway.

'I knew she'd see sense eventually,' said one, her excitement there for all to see. 'She just needed a bit of time to take on board everything we said.'

'Obviously,' said the other, full of relief. 'Although I have to admit, I was a bit worried for a while.'

Annabel couldn't help but smile as she listened to them, it came as no surprise to hear them taking full credit, even when it wasn't due. Yes, Katy and Rebecca had meant well in their advice, but they'd never been able to fully understand the fact that some things are easier said than done. Especially when it came to moving forward after the death of a loved one, Annabel considered; something she was grateful they'd never had to experience.

She pictured the kindly woman who'd called into the shop and thought it funny how it took a complete stranger, rather than family and friends, to make her see things differently. Goodness knew what they'd say once she told them about her well-meaning customer and the daffodils. Thanks to Katy and Rebecca, the poor woman's ears were, no doubt, about to burn.

'Well?' said Rebecca. 'We're waiting.'

'And start from the beginning,' said Katy. 'Don't leave anything out.'

Annabel stared at the pair of them. Arms on the table and hands clasped, they clearly anticipated a blow by blow update. It reminded her of way back when. As a trio of schoolgirls they often shared dating tips gleaned from magazines, advising each other on what to wear and how to behave when it came to meeting up with a boy. Afterwards, they'd animatedly spend hours dissecting every aspect of the evening, rejoicing when things went well and commiserating when they didn't.

Their eagerness seemed to be catching and suddenly feeling like a teenager again, Annabel giggled as she joined them at the table.

'Okay, okay,' she said. She looked at the clock. 'But we'll have to be quick. What do you want to know?'

***

With nothing but an empty wine bottle and half empty glass for company, Annabel sat at the kitchen table. She stared at the wall clock, the steady sound of its *tick-tock, tick-tock* seemed to scoff her as it broke through the silence.

'How could you have been so stupid?' she asked herself. 'How could you let someone do this to you?'

She tried to ignore the hopeful little voice in her head, as it continued to insist there was still time yet, there could be a knock at the door any minute now. But Annabel knew that was just wishful thinking. Dan had no intentions of turning up. He probably never did.

Sitting there in her finery, she felt humiliated beyond belief. And angry. He must have known how hard it was for her to call him in the first place; that just dialling his number had taken every ounce of courage she possessed. Her stomach sank as she recalled how she'd rambled and stuttered in her attempts to tell him how she felt. If it was embarrassing at the time, it felt even more so now. When he finally understood what she'd been trying to say, he must have been having a darned good laugh at her expense. Contending to be as keen as her that they should give things between them a go, he'd clearly been saying one thing while thinking another. Or maybe she'd misunderstood in some way? She'd simply heard what she wanted to hear. Whatever the case, Dan obviously wasn't the caring, trustworthy individual she'd thought. Usually so punctual, his no-show proved that.

A part of her couldn't blame him. She hadn't exactly made things easy for the both of them. Firstly, she wanted to kiss him and then she didn't. One minute she wanted his baby and then a few weeks down the line, she didn't want that either. And still too in love with her deceased husband to even contemplate a new relationship, suddenly she was on the phone telling Dan she's ready to give things a go. Who in their right mind would consider taking a screw ball like her on? Despite his apparent conviction, obviously not him.

To think only an hour or so ago, Katy and Rebecca had been celebrating with her; relishing in the fact that this was a new, exciting chapter for all of them. Katy was getting increasingly serious with Oliver, Rebecca was looking forward to having her baby, and Annabel was, at last, starting to engage with the outside world which, according to her friend and sister, was all thanks to Dan. They'd been right of course. As much as his influence had scared her, as much as she hadn't wanted to fall for him, Dan had been the one to coax her out of her over-protective shell. A place she now wanted nothing more than to retreat back into, something else this man could take credit for.

'Yes, cheers, Dan,' said Annabel. She held up her glass in a mock toast before taking a long, hard swig of wine. 'Cheers for nothing.'

She looked up at the ceiling. 'I should have listened to you and your coin, Tom. Not that bloody woman and her flowers.'

She began to feel nauseous and realised that she needed to eat; Annabel told herself that there was no point in letting good food go to waste. She got up from her seat and, after dragging herself over to the cooker, picked up the oven glove and took out the casserole. With a bit of luck it wouldn't be too spoiled. Annabel lifted the pot lid; sadly she'd spoken too soon. Her carefully prepared meal had all but dried out.

'Pizza for one, it is then,' she said.

She sighed. Having thought things were about to change for the better, *pizza for one* seemed to be the story of her life.

TWENTY-FOUR

Dan sat in his car, its engine was still running. He didn't know how long he'd been there, but it must have been a while. He'd noticed a few people parking up, disappearing and, after a time, making their return. He'd even garnered the odd strange look. Yet still, he just sat there.

Trying and failing to gather his thoughts, he realised he was being selfish, she had to be wondering where he'd got to by now. He also knew that he couldn't stay in his car forever. Whatever lay ahead, he had to face up to it at some point. However, with his mind all over the place, every time he tried to move his heart began beating so fast he thought he might throw up. If this roller coaster of a ride hadn't been scary enough already, it was nothing compared to how it felt now.

He took a deep breath and gripped the steering wheel so tight his knuckles turned white, but neither of these actions did anything to still his shaking hands. 'Come on, Dan,' he said. 'You can do this.'

Finally, he told himself he was ready and, after turning off the engine, got out of the vehicle. He stared at the building before him. *Dove Court Hospice* read the sign above the entrance; the word *Hospice* screamed out at him loud and clear. Dan almost froze again, he was forced to inhale and exhale in an attempt to get a grip. All he had to do, he insisted, was make it through the doors.

He reluctantly began putting one foot in front of the other, all the while praying this was an over-reaction on his part; that his mother's sudden admittance was simply a precaution. After all, as he thought about the increasing pain she'd endured lately, her medication clearly hadn't been doing its job. He crossed his fingers in the hope that the medical staff just wanted to keep an eye on his mum while they tested for a more suitable combination of drugs. 'Please, God,' he said. He, at last, entered the building. 'Please don't take her just yet.'

'I'm here about my mum,' said Dan. He tried to control the quiver in his voice as he made his way to the reception desk. 'I believe she's just been admitted.'

The receptionist gave him a gentle smile and while he knew there wasn't much else she could do under the circumstances, her sympathy only served to feed his fears.

'You must be Gerry's son,' she said.

'Yes, I am.' He tried to raise a smile of his own.

'Your mum said you'd be coming. Although she wasn't expecting you just yet.'

As the receptionist stepped from behind the desk ready to go and fetch someone, Dan gave her a quizzical look. He certainly wouldn't be anywhere else at a time like this and it surprised him to know others would think otherwise.

'Something about it being a big night tonight?'

Jesus, Mum, he thought to himself. His date with Annabel should be the last thing on her mind right now.

He suddenly felt a glimmer of hope. Surely her talking about his love life had to be a good sign?

The woman disappeared off down the hall leaving Dan to take in his surroundings. The hospice had a definite modern feel, but at the same time, didn't have that clinical air expected in a medical facility. He supposed places like this needed a relaxed atmosphere, that they prided themselves on the personal touch. All part of what was it they called it? Oh yes, palliative care.

As if to prove his point, he spotted a cork board hanging on one of the walls. Covered in photos, he leaned in for a closer look. Members of staff and former patients beamed back at him, although as he focused on their faces, Dan struggled to get his head around what any of them had to be so happy about. Seeing that most of them were dying, he couldn't help but wonder how many were still around to this day.

'Dan!' someone suddenly called out.

He hastily turned, eager to see who the voice belonged to. 'Jill,' he replied. As he raced to meet her, Dan had never felt so relieved to see a familiar face. 'How is she?' he asked. 'Why are we here? What's happening?'

The nurse indicated they should sit down and guided him over to a couple of seats. 'The doctor's with her now. We'll know more once he's finished.'

'I don't understand,' said Dan. 'She said she was fine.'

He pictured his mother only a while earlier, he felt guilty for leaving her. He hadn't wanted to; they'd even had a bit of an argument about it. But she'd insisted he had nothing to worry about as per usual; that his date with Annabel took priority over him babysitting her. Why couldn't he have been just as adamant as his mum and flat out refused?

'I should have put my foot down more,' he said.

'If there's one thing I've learned about your mother these last couple of months,' said Jill. 'It's that she has one hell of an independent streak.'

Dan felt himself relax a little. 'Tell me about it. You should have heard the message she left. Anyone would think that she was checking into a hotel not a hospice.' He paused to recall her exact words, his frustrations returned to the fore. 'But to think I wouldn't turn the car around and come straight here. What kind of son does she have me down as?'

'Tonight was as important for her as it was you, you know.'

'I know,' Dan replied. 'And every step of the way I've tried to do things her way. But come on. Look at where we are, Jill. Even Mum must see that things with Annabel aren't exactly important right now.'

He steeled himself ready for the worst, while desperately hoping for the best. 'So,' he said. 'Tell me.'

Jill placed a reassuring hand on his and, knowing this was never a good sign, Dan felt his heart skip a beat.

'She has lymphedema, Dan. She did her best to try and hide it from me, of course. But as soon as I realised what was happening I knew it was time to come in.'

Convinced he'd read about lymphedema somewhere, Dan tried and failed to recollect the details. He'd read so much about his mother's condition lately that everything seemed to have merged into a mass of undecipherable information. Confused, he looked to Jill for an explanation.

'Lymphedema refers to the swelling that generally occurs in a patient's arms or legs,' she said. 'It results from a blockage in the lymphatic system, which, in turn, is part of the immune system. The blockage prevents lymph fluid from draining properly, hence, its buildup in the limbs.'

Dan still didn't fully understand, however, he could tell by the nurse's face that it was serious. 'And what caused it?' he asked. 'You're going to treat it, right?'

'The cancer could be blocking your mum's lymph nodes or vessels, or it could be a side effect of treatment. Either way, there's nothing we can do.' She paused, as if trying to come up with the right words.

Dan knew that his fears were being realised; he just sat there. He wanted her to both continue and not continue at the same time.

'It's a sign that her organs are failing, Dan. That's why she's here.'

As Jill's words slowly began to sink in, Dan suddenly felt numb. He'd known all along that this day was coming. He just hadn't anticipated it being so soon. Fear and fury began to well as he leaned forward and after placing his elbows on his knees, ran his hands through his hair.

'So this is it?' he said. He straightened himself back up. 'She's dying?' He scoffed at his own statement. 'Of course she is. We wouldn't be in a hospice if she wasn't.'

Jill smiled softly. 'She's always been dying, Dan.'

'You think I don't know that?' exploded Dan, as he jumped to his feet and began pacing up and down.

'Sorry,' he said. Dan made an effort to control his voice. 'I didn't mean to snap. I know none of this is your fault, it's just …'

'That you're angry?' said the nurse. 'That's understandable. I'd be angry too.'

She fell quiet and Dan felt glad of the emotional space the silence gave him.

'I sometimes wish I could just run away and hide from all this,' he eventually said, his voice shaky. 'I want to curl up and go to sleep so that when I wake up I'll find none of this is real. It's all just a bad dream, a cruel nightmare.'

Dan started to pace again, it all felt too much and he rubbed his forehead as he attempted to grasp the inevitable. He stopped in his tracks. 'How long does she have?'

'Let's not get ahead of ourselves,' Jill replied. 'Let's speak to the doctor. He'll be able to tell us more.'

'Can I see her?'

'Soon. Things shouldn't take too long now.'

When he heard another set of voices down the hall, Dan immediately looked over to where they came from. A doctor stepped out of a side room and after spotting Dan, smiled as he began walking towards him.

'She's quite a character is that one,' he said. 'And in very good spirits considering.' He held out his hand, ready to greet Dan as he approached. 'You must be Gerry's son. She's just been telling me all about you. And about your big night tonight.'

Dan sighed. Was there anyone whom she hadn't told? 'If we could get to the important stuff,' he said.

'Sure. Of course.' The doctor took a seat and signaled for Dan to do the same.

'So what are we talking about?' he asked.

'It could be a couple of days or a couple of weeks.'

Dan took a deep breath, his cheeks filled with air before he let out a long, hard sigh. Grappling with the reality of the situation, tears sprang in his eyes; however, he quickly wiped them away. 'Okay,' he said, trying to sound stronger than he felt.

'In the meantime, it's our job to make sure your mum's as comfortable and pain free as possible.' The doctor turned to the nurse. 'We've already fitted a syringe driver.'

'A syringe driver?' said Dan. His mum had kept him in the dark for so long on the medical front, he needed to know exactly what was going on and why. 'What's that?'

'It's like a battery pack,' explained Jill. 'It's a rectangular box that houses all your mum's drugs in one side and a battery in the other. The battery's used to pump the medication through a tube and straight into her abdomen.'

Dan cringed; he felt his own stomach lurch on behalf of his mother's.

'Don't worry,' she said. 'It sounds a lot scarier than it is.'

'And what?' he asked. 'We just wait?'

'I'm afraid that's all we can do,' said the doctor.

'Fuck!' said Dan. He rose to his feet again. Fear enveloped his whole body, it all felt too much to cope with. 'I thought we had more time. She can't die. Not yet.'

The doctor stood up, meeting him at his level 'She's in the best possible place,' he said. 'And we're doing everything we can.'

'To make her more comfortable?' Dan replied. He knew he sounded harsh, but he couldn't seem to help himself. 'Yes, you said.'

No doubt having gone through this numerous times, with God knows how many other patients and their families, Dan could see in his expression that the man understood his pain. He felt guilty; he told himself that he had no right to take his feelings out on anyone else. But no amount of understanding helped any. He still felt overwhelmed.

'We have everything she needs both physically and emotionally,' the doctor continued. 'Spiritually too, if she chooses.' He put a hand on Dan's arm. 'As do you. We're not just here for your mum, you know. We have a fantastic support system in place for family members.'

Dan shrugged off the doctor's words. He didn't care about himself. As far as he was concerned, it was his mother's wellbeing that mattered, not his own. 'I don't know what to say to her,' he said. His voice caught in his throat. 'I don't know what to do to help.'

'Just being at your mum's side is enough,' said Jill. 'We'll do the rest.'

Dan nodded. He took another deep breath and reminded himself that he had to be strong for his mother's sake, if not his own.

'Would you like to see her now?'

'Please.'

He turned to the doctor and shook his hand once more. 'Thank you,' he said.

'No problem. And if you have any questions at all, just give me a shout. I'll be around here somewhere.'

'I will,' Dan replied.

As he watched him head off towards another part of the building, Dan doubted he'd be seeking him out any time soon. In his view, the man had already answered the biggest question of all.

Jill indicated that they head down the hall and he followed her towards his mother's room before pausing at the door to try and pull himself together.

'You ready?' Jill asked.

'No,' said Dan. 'Not really.'

He watched her tap on the door regardless, before opening it and popping her head inside. 'You have a visitor, Gerry,' she said. She gave him an encouraging smile as she made way for Dan to enter.

'Dan,' said his mum, as if surprised to see him. 'What are you doing here?'

'What kind of questions is that?' he asked. As hard as it felt, he did his best to sound equally as cheery.

After making his way over to her bedside, Dan looked around as he pulled up a chair. The room appeared typical of those found in any hospital facility, except the floor was carpeted instead of being laid with industrial type vinyl. He spotted the door to an en-suite bathroom and there was a television on a cabinet at the foot of her bed, remote control included. She had one of those tables on wheels so she could even have her meals in bed if she wanted to.

Finally, his eyes fell on the syringe driver lying next to her and, despite it scaring the hell out of him, he did his best not to react. A job easier said than done and he knew by the way his mother quickly hid it under her blanket that fear had automatically registered on his face.

'This could have waited, you know,' she said. 'I don't plan on going anywhere tonight.'

Leant against her pillows, she looked so small and frail, nothing like the strong individual she'd always been. Dan felt his heart go out to her, but while he continued to wish, more than anything, that he could trade places, he knew he had to keep his emotions in check.

'I should hope not,' he replied.

She smiled, but underneath the façade, Dan could see in her eyes that she was hurting emotionally as well as physically; that she knew as much as he did that time had never been more precious.

'I don't suppose you rang to cancel either?' she said.

Dan shook his head. 'Let's just say I had more important things on my mind.'

'Oh, Dan.' His mum took his hand in hers, at the same time giving it a squeeze. 'What are we going to do with you?'

'Enough about me,' he replied. 'Let's talk about you. How are you feeling? How's the pain?'

'I feel like I should be at home,' she said. 'I told the nurse this could hang on until tomorrow, but she insisted I come in now. Still, I suppose the poor woman's only doing what she thinks is best.'

As much as Dan wanted to keep up his mother's pretence, something inside seemed to break and the last of his denial suddenly drained from his body. Neither of them knew exactly how long his mother had left and from what the doctor had said, this could be his last chance to tell her how much he loved her. He needed his mum to know how thankful he was for everything she'd done for him and how she'd been the best mother a son could ever wish for. All things that had to be said before it was too late.

Regardless of any acceptance, Dan couldn't stop the lump suddenly forming in his throat. He swallowed hard, but he still couldn't manage to speak and, not wanting to break down completely in front of his mum, he hastily got up from his seat and headed for the window, determined to compose himself. Looking out, he realised she'd been right when she'd said how beautiful the gardens were. The hyacinths, tulips and primroses brought new life to a place dealing in death.

'I know about the lymphedema, Mum,' he said, at last, getting the words out.

Awaiting a response, none was forthcoming and he turned to look at her.

As if feeling his gaze, she began straightening the fold in her blanket and refused to look at him while she processed his admission.

'Jill told you then?' she eventually said.

Dan re-took his seat at his mother's bedside. 'Yes.' He took hold of her hand. 'She did.'

Finally, his mum faced him head on. 'And you know what that means?' she asked. There was no disguising the upset in her voice.

'I do.'

In a single breath, the last of his mother's fighting spirit seemed to vanish. Tears suddenly rolled down her cheeks as she, at last, succumbed to the reality that this was the end. Before Dan knew it, she all at once threw her arms around him and, welcoming her embrace, he hugged her tight in return.

'Oh Dan, we've always been a team,' she said. 'And I love you so much, it hurts. What am I going to do without you? What will you do without me?'

Dan began to cry too. 'I don't know, Mum,' he replied. Finally, he let his own tears flow. 'I honestly don't know.'

TWENTY-FIVE

Annabel, book in hand and feet up on sofa, stared at the page before her. Having read and re-read the same passage twice now, the words wouldn't seem to go in. She let the book drop and didn't see the point in trying for a third time. Not really in the right frame of mind, reading took too much concentration.

'Anyone home?' Rebecca called out.

Despite not being in the mood for yet another welfare check, she decided her sister's company was better than just sitting there doing nothing. Even if she didn't understand why she and Katy kept popping in to make sure all was well. In her view, their visits were completely unnecessary. She might have been stood up, however, Annabel had no intentions of sinking back into a dark abyss of despair. If there was one thing the other night's fiasco with Dan had taught her, it was that men simply weren't worth it. She pictured her husband. *Yes I'm including you in that, Tom,* she silently told him. As far as she was concerned, she was better off on her own. Men either died or simply buggered off never to be seen again.

'There you are,' said Rebecca, appearing in the doorway.

'Yep,' Annabel replied. 'As you can see, I'm still here.'

'There's no need to be like that,' said her sister. She entered the room and plonked herself down in the nearest armchair. 'So have you heard from him?'

Wow, thought Annabel. Her sister was certainly quick off the mark today. The woman usually partook in at least five minutes of general chit-chat before going in for the kill. Then there was another five checking on her mental health.

'Well?' asked Rebecca.

'No, I haven't heard from him.'

'Not even a phone call?'

'Nope.'

Rebecca sighed.

'And before you start telling me all over again that there's probably a simple explanation,' said Annabel. The last thing she needed was more sisterly advice. 'Let me save you the trouble. Whatever the explanation is, I don't care.'

'That's a bit harsh. What if … ?'

Annabel refused to let her mind go there.

'No *what ifs*, Rebecca. The man's as unreliable as the rest of them. I mean, would it have really been such an inconvenience to pick up his mobile and let me know he wasn't coming? Under any circumstance?'

The doorbell rang, interrupting Annabel's rant.

'That'll be Katy,' said Rebecca. She rose to her feet again. 'She said she might pop round. You put the kettle on and I'll go and let her in.'

Annabel hauled herself up off the sofa and, doing as she was told, headed out into the hall and towards the kitchen. After entering the room, she went straight for the kettle and filled it with water before clicking it on to boil. She grabbed a trio of mugs and a teaspoon. 'Coffee for three it is,' she said.

While wondering what words of wisdom Katy and Rebecca would be offering today, she heard a cough from behind. Turning, her sister stood in the doorway, suddenly looking a little sheepish.

'You have a visitor,' she said.

As she signaled for the unknown caller to come forward, Dan stepped into view. Just the sight of him left Annabel lost for words. Not only did he have some nerve, he looked awful. His clothes were all disheveled and he definitely needed a shave. Her heart sank. The last time she'd seen him in this state it had been because of his mother.

She knew Rebecca was right, that she was being harsh. But for her own well-being, she also knew she couldn't allow herself to be swayed. Instead, she maintained her resolve that nothing and nobody excused him for not contacting her. He had to know that even a few seconds of phone call would have been better than nothing.

'I'll just grab my things and leave you both to it,' said Rebecca.

'No need,' said Annabel. 'He's not staying.' She looked Dan directly in the eye. 'We have nothing to say to each other.'

'Well, I think you do.'

Annabel willed her sister to stay put, however, she continued to tip-toe out of the room regardless. Suddenly, finding herself alone with Dan, Annabel fumed and insisted that Rebecca would pay for this.

She felt her anxiety levels begin to rise. Being in Dan's presence felt way too uncomfortable and a part of her wanted to make a run for it too. She'd said all along that his mum's dying was too close for comfort and now she had the scary prospect of being forced to deal with it head on. Why couldn't Rebecca understand that it was easier to view Dan as an ignorant bastard? To believe that he had played a cute game and didn't give a damn about anyone but himself? Her sister had to see that was better than the alternative. Especially when coping with his loss would undoubtedly stir up feelings about her own. Why else would she have chosen to stay angry with him?

Annabel just stood there waiting for him to speak, the silence continued well after the front door opened and closed again.

'Sorry about turning up like this,' Dan eventually said. 'I didn't know where else to go.'

Oh God, thought Annabel. Her heart immediately went out to him, but news about his mother was exactly what she'd been afraid of. She steeled herself.

'Is she … ?'

Dan shook his head. 'No,' he replied.

Relieved, Annabel felt herself relax slightly.

'But she is in the hospice. She ordered me home for a shower and a change but when I got there, I couldn't bring myself to go in.'

'I can understand that,' said Annabel.

He attempted a smile. 'I can't seem to face being on my own. Stupid, eh?'

Annabel knew that feeling all too well. She recalled the sheer loneliness she experienced after Tom's death; how empty and soulless the house felt without him as she wandered from room to room. His things were still there. His smell was still there. But Tom had gone and he was never coming back. Even with Rebecca to console her, nothing filled the gaping hole he left behind.

She felt her defences beginning to crumble, as she realised Dan's mum probably wouldn't be going home again either. At least she had her sister and best friend for support. If she turned this man away, he'd have nobody.

'I can understand that too,' she said.

Their eyes locked and a sense of anticipation suddenly filled the air. Confused, she knew she should say something, however, words again seemed to fail her. She watched him silently take a step forward and nervously realised that the kitchen counter prevented her from taking a step back. He took another step and then another. Annabel knew she was in dangerous waters. But it didn't seem to matter how much her head wanted to tell him to just go and never come back, her heart began to scream something else.

She felt her stomach flip as he reached within touching distance and her heart raced even faster as he looked into her eyes. He cupped her face and leaned in to kiss her; without even thinking about what she was doing Annabel couldn't help but respond. One gentle kiss turned into two and then three, each one lasting a little longer and tasting that much sweeter. With her arms suddenly around him, her body ached as tentativeness turned to passion. She felt his hands grip the back of her thighs as he lifted her onto the counter and while keeping her lips on his, she began frantically unbuttoning his shirt.

'Are you sure you want to do this?' whispered Dan, through their desperate kisses.

Annabel pulled back to look at him, his concerned expression only made her want him more. 'I'm sure,' she said.

She released him of his shirt altogether and drew him close once again.

***

As they drove along and passed street after street, Annabel couldn't deny her sense of elation. At last, she'd allowed herself to move beyond her fears and confusion. She didn't just feel happy in letting go, she seemed whole again. For the first time in a long time, she truly felt that life was meant to be lived and not just endured.

Almost hugging herself, Annabel smiled. It seemed her new chapter had finally begun.

She snuck a look at the man beside her. Still able to feel his skin against hers, it was strange to think that only an hour ago they had been in the throes of passion. Even stranger was the fact that they'd finally admitted their feelings for each other. They had been honest and used the 'L' word, a word Annabel never thought she would use again. She felt a warm glow burning inside as she realised that Katy and Rebecca had been right. She was lucky to experience this kind of connection for a second time.

As if feeling her gaze, Dan turned his head. 'Everything okay?' he asked.

Annabel took in his gentle, yet masculine features, his kind eyes, and unruly hair, still damp from his post-sex shower. 'Everything's fine,' she said.

He raised his hand and touched her face for a second, before returning his attention back to the road ahead. Like her, he seemed happy to just sit out the rest of the ride in content silence.

As they neared their destination, Annabel couldn't help the sense of trepidation kicking in. About to meet the woman she'd heard all about, a part of her wanted to tell Dan she'd changed her mind and to just keep driving. *What if his mother didn't approve?* she asked herself. *What if she died thinking Dan was making a big mistake getting mixed up with a screwball like her?* Suddenly feeling the pressure, as far as Annabel was concerned, the answers didn't bear thinking about.

Dan pulled the car into the car park and, manoeuvring into a space, he turned off the engine. 'You ready?' he asked.

Annabel tried to mask her fears with a reassuring smile. She nodded. 'As ready as I'll ever be.'

Dan leaned forward and kissed her. 'Thank you,' he said. 'For being here.' He unclipped his seatbelt, ready to go. 'And believe me, she's going to love you.'

Annabel followed his lead and got out of the car. As if meeting his mother for the first time wasn't bad enough, she had to do it in a place like this.

Dan gave her a wink, but despite the bravado, she could see his concern. Not necessarily in relation to her and his mother, she acknowledged. He'd always maintained that the two of them would get on. His worry undoubtedly revolved around the building itself and, as they made their way towards the entrance, she could tell each step took all the emotional strength that Dan could muster. *Understandably so*, thought Annabel. Having never been to a hospice before, the prospect of being met with bad news scared the hell out of her, let alone him. As did the old wounds a place like this could open up.

She took his hand as they approached the building and trying to put all thoughts of Tom's death to one side, for the first time since his passing she refused to let her past interfere with the present. The big glass doors automatically slid open and she gave Dan's palm a gentle squeeze, letting him know that come what may, they'd face it together; a gesture he seemed to appreciate as he gave her hand a squeeze in return.

'Good afternoon, Dan', said the receptionist, upon clocking their arrival. 'And looking a lot less worse for wear, I see.' She turned her attention to Annabel. 'Now I don't need to ask who you are. Isn't it nice when you can finally put a face to a name?'

Annabel wondered what the woman was talking about and looked to Dan for an explanation. He seemed to blush.

'I'll tell you later,' he whispered, before getting back to the matter at hand.

'How is she?' he asked.

Annabel noticed the receptionist's smile weaken. As she looked from her to Dan, she could see things were bad.

'She's okay,' the woman replied. 'The nurses have been keeping a close eye on her.' She paused. 'Let's just say she'll be all the better for seeing you.'

'Can we?' he asked. Dan indicated down the hall.

'Of course,' said the receptionist. 'Go on ahead.'

Annabel felt her nerves come to the fore as Dan led the way down the corridor. She wished that she could have met his mother under different circumstances and she wondered what to expect. Having listened to Dan's colourful descriptions, she'd allowed herself to imagine a glamourous woman, donning perfect hair and make-up as she casually leaned against her pillows. Thanks to the receptionist, however, that image was now shattered. She felt stupid and silently scolded herself. This was real life not an American soap opera. How could she have been so naïve?

Dan came to a standstill outside one particular room and Annabel took a deep breath, realising this was it. She was seconds away from meeting his mum.

Dan hesitated before knocking. 'Do want me to go in first,' he asked. 'To let her know that you're here?'

Annabel hastily nodded. Her apprehension insisted the longer she could delay this, the better.

Dan almost laughed. 'She doesn't bite, you know,' he said. He gave her an encouraging smile. 'Just be yourself.'

'That's easy for you to say,' she replied.

While Dan tapped on his mother's door and let himself in, Annabel straightened her attire in readiness. Hearing muffled voices, she crossed her fingers in the hope that she'd be met with a sense of approval rather than disapproval and for Dan's benefit as much as her own. She continued to feel all of a tither and began to wonder what was wrong with her. She certainly couldn't remember being quite so jittery when introduced to Tom's mum for the first time. Then again, she reminded herself, Tom's mum hadn't been dying, there didn't seem to be quite so much at stake. Plus, Annabel had been a bit younger during that meeting and, to be fair to herself, a lot more carefree.

The door suddenly opened, which made Annabel jump. 'Bloody hell, Dan,' she said. 'Don't do that.' She put a hand up to her chest. 'Are you trying to give me a heart attack?'

Clearly trying to hide his amusement, Dan made way for her to enter and Annabel took a final deep breath as she stepped inside. While hovering by the doorway, she glanced around the room, relieved to find it void of any distracting medical machinery. In her mind, coming face-to-face with Dan's mum felt nerve wracking enough, without having to contend with scary equipment like monitors, drips, and respirators.

'You can say hello,' said Dan.

She felt his hand in hers as he guided her towards his mother's bedside.

'Mum, I'd like you to meet Annabel,' he said. 'Annabel, this is my mum.'

As she looked at Dan's mother, Annabel's heart immediately skipped a beat. Maybe her befuddled brain and over-emotional temperament these last couple of months were to blame, but after everything she'd learned about the woman, she knew she should have realised. Whatever the reason though, she'd managed to miss all the clues – the fabulous clothing, the funny turn, and the daffodils, not to mention their meaning. Only now did everything make sense. Of course, her well-intentioned customer and Dan's mum were one and the same person. How could they not have been?

His mother beckoned for her to take a seat. 'Lovely to see you again,' she said.

Annabel felt saddened. Her voice sounded a lot weaker than she remembered. However, with her nerves suddenly vanishing, she readily welcomed the invitation. After pulling up a chair, she sat down and took the sick woman's hand. 'And it's lovely to see you too,' she replied. 'The flowers are still going strong, by the way.'

'You've met before?' asked Dan.

After deciding Dan's curiosity could wait, Annabel chose instead to keep her attention on his mother. She could see a slight twinkle in the woman's eyes, probably because the two of them knew something that Dan didn't. At the same time, she appeared a shadow of the lady Annabel had previously spoken to. She thought back to the day in the shop when she'd helped her over to the stool, her hand felt bonier than before and her breathing hadn't just quickened since then, it now seemed dangerously shallow. No wonder she found it hard to speak. As she looked at her, it was clear she didn't have long in this world and Annabel couldn't help but question how so much could change in such a short time.

'Don't feel sad,' said Dan's mother. 'You and I both know I'm lucky to make it this far. Not everyone gets that chance.'

'I know,' Annabel replied.

'Excuse me,' said Dan. He gave a cheeky wave in an attempt to catch their attention. 'I might not know when or how you two ladies met, but in case you've forgotten, I am still here.'

His mother signaled he come and join them.

'You'll have to excuse my son, Annabel,' she said.

Dan drew up another chair.

'Being an only child, he's not used to sharing.'

Annabel smiled. She doubted that she could keep her own sense of humour up throughout a difficult journey like this and had to admire the both of them for keeping theirs.

'So,' said his mum. 'Was I right to interfere?'

Annabel turned her head to look at Dan. With his confusion over what they were talking about there for all to see, she couldn't help but let out a laugh. 'Yes,' she said. 'Definitely.'

'And you'll look after him once I'm gone?'

'Of course, I will,' Annabel replied.

She gripped Dan's mum's hand even tighter and felt tears in her eyes as she wished she'd had more time to get to know this wonderful woman.

'Thank you,' said Dan's mum.

TWENTY-SIX

Annabel stood at the window. Her hands wrapped around a cup of coffee, she stared out into the garden. The sun shone down making the pink, cup-like blossom of Gerry's magnolia tree even more vivid; especially when set against the bluest of skies. *So beautiful*, thought Annabel. She acknowledged how, to the Victorians, this tree meant dignity and nobility. With the magnolia flower representing both decorum and pride, she couldn't think of a more apt bloom for this mother and son.

She took in the solitary figure stood amidst its branches. *Poor Dan.* He missed his mum so much that Annabel thought her heart would break. She wished she could do more to ease his pain, but she knew from experience that she just had to be patient, only time could heal his wounds.

She admired his bravery. For the most part, he'd managed to cope, putting on a strong front whenever the telephone rang or people stopped by to give him their condolences. He'd even been able to keep a calm head when dealing with the funeral director. Then again, thought Annabel, being so organised his mother had made all things official pretty straight forward. Be it in relation to her burial, her will, and her insurances, she seemed to have thought of everything. And, no doubt, to ensure Dan had less to concern himself with during this difficult period.

Then there'd been times like now, when he just wanted to be alone for a while.

While respecting his wishes, sometimes Annabel would hear his sobs as he hid himself away in another room. On other occasions, there would be silence as he simply sat in quiet contemplation. In both these cases, Annabel felt powerless and she'd had to stop herself from rushing to his side. Thankfully though, he had shared some of his grief with her too, as if he'd instinctively known not to shut her out altogether.

She wondered if she should go out and join him now. But as he began to pace up and down, he seemed to be talking to someone. Annabel smiled gently. If the neighbours saw him, they'd probably think his mother's death had tipped him over the edge. But she knew from experience that he was chatting to his mother, talking about the day ahead and, no doubt, saying his last goodbye.

She looked at the clock and realised his mother would be here soon. She dreaded seeing the hearse. Not sure how she'd react, this was the first funeral she'd attended since burying Tom. For a moment, she allowed herself to recall the long slow procession as she, her family, and friends made their way to the church – the hardest journey she'd made in her entire life and here she was, about to do it again. The tears that flowed at having to say goodbye and the many kind and heartfelt eulogies spoken that day were unforgettable. And she remembered how she silently pleaded that she, too, could die as her husband's coffin was carried to its final resting place. Even more so when it was gently lowered into the ground.

She looked up to the heavens, in a bid to ask for help. 'If you can hear me, Tom,' she said. 'I could really do with some support right now.'

Annabel realised that she had tears in her eyes and wiped them away. She told herself she couldn't dwell. Today wasn't the day to be thinking about herself or what she had been through. Today was about being there for Dan.

The doorbell rang and suddenly diverted her attention. Not sure what to do, she glanced out into the garden again and wondered if she should call Dan inside. After deciding to leave him a little while longer, she took one deep breath after another, in an attempt to get herself together. If the coffin had arrived, she needed be in control.

Annabel headed out into the hall, it felt strange to be taking charge in someone else's home. But just like his mum, she wanted to take care of as many details as possible so that Dan didn't have to. Deep down though, she knew his mother would approve. Annabel might not have known the woman for very long, however, they'd still managed to grow close thanks to their joint love for Dan. She thought about those last days, at how she witnessed the precious bond between mother and son. Such a sad experience, yet at the same time so beautiful and Annabel felt both honoured, and privileged, to have been included.

She took one last deep breath, ready to greet the funeral director and, after fixing a smile on her face, she opened the door. Annabel suddenly felt her whole body relax, relieved to see Katy and Rebecca standing there instead. 'Thank goodness,' she said. 'I was expecting you to be the Men in Black.'

More than pleased to see them, she couldn't help but wonder if Tom had had a hand in this. Despite having expected to meet her friend and sister at the church, she realised that she should have known they would turn up. After all, they both had form for stepping in when needed.

Grateful for the support, she gave them each an appreciative hug. 'Thanks for coming,' she said.

'How is he?' asked Rebecca.

'And how are you bearing up?' asked Katy.

Annabel stood aside to let them in. 'I've had a couple of wobbly moments and I'm sure he has too. But I think we're both doing okay considering.'

They both returned her gaze, their sympathy evident.

'Well you concentrate on making sure Dan's alright,' said Rebecca. 'And we'll do what we can when it comes to the rest.'

After leading them through to the kitchen, Annabel gave Dan a wave through the window, letting him know they had visitors. She smiled affectionately, as he signaled his acknowledgement, telling her he would be in shortly.

'Tea? Coffee?' asked Annabel, heading for the kettle.

'Tea for me,' said Rebecca. She dumped her handbag and jacket next to a chair. 'By the way, this looks very nice.'

Glad of the approval, Annabel watched on as her sister inspected the food that she'd already prepared for the after-service get together. 'I thought it better to get as much done as I could beforehand,' she said. 'I can make the sandwiches once we get back.'

'Don't worry,' said Rebecca. 'I can get on with that.'

'And what about wine and beer?' asked Katy. After opening the fridge, she began counting the bottles and tins. 'Do you need me to go to the off-licence?'

Annabel rolled her eyes and laughed. *Trust her.*

'What?' asked her friend. 'Everyone knows a wake isn't a wake without alcohol.'

The back door opened and Dan made his entrance. Annabel watched him immediately look at the clock; like her, no doubt counting down the minutes until his mother's arrival. He turned his attention to Katy and Rebecca, he didn't just have a sadness about him, Annabel could sense an air of agitation. For some reason, he appeared unnerved by her sister and friend's presence and she could tell from their expressions that this wasn't her imagination, the two of them had clearly noticed Dan's awkwardness too.

'They're here just to make sure we're okay,' said Annabel, however, no sooner had she spoken and she could have kicked herself. While attempting to alleviate his discomfort, even she knew how feeble her statement sounded. Of course, they weren't okay. They were about to bury his mother.

'Could you excuse me a minute?' he said.

Dan quickly left the room and, hearing his footsteps on the stairs, Annabel began to feel at a loss. 'I'm sorry,' she said. 'He isn't really being rude.'

'Of course, he's not,' said Rebecca.

'Don't worry about it,' said Katy. 'We all know how difficult this is. For the both of you.'

Annabel took a seat at the table; she felt her eyes getting watery again. 'Sometimes I don't know what to do or say for the best.'

Rebecca reached down and wrapped an arm around Annabel's shoulders. 'There's nothing you can say or do,' she said. 'But he will get through this. You'll see.'

Footsteps sounded once more and, as Dan began making his descent, Annabel tried to compose herself and attempted another smile as he re-entered the room.

Rebecca began gathering up her things. 'I suppose we should be getting off,' she said. 'You'll probably be wanting a bit of time to yourselves before … well, you know.'

'We'll see you at the church, yeah,' said Katy, following Rebecca's lead.

Annabel nodded, appreciative of their understanding as they moved to exit the room.

'No,' Dan suddenly said. 'Please. Don't leave.'

The two women stopped in their tracks. They looked from him to her, Annabel could see they didn't know what to do for the best.

'You being here means a lot,' said Dan. 'To Annabel and to me.'

Glad to see Katy and Rebecca relax, Annabel wished she could say the same for Dan, who understandably wasn't quite himself. She watched his chest rise and fall as if for some reason he was trying to collect his thoughts.

'There's something I want to say,' he continued. Again, he addressed her friend and sister. 'And if you don't mind, I'd like you to hear it too.'

'Okay,' said Rebecca. Obviously curious, she put her handbag down once more.

'No problem,' said Katy.

They looked to Annabel, wondering what this could be about, but feeling equally as in the dark, she wished she knew and shrugged in response.

'You know how mum said today is all about celebrating her life?' Dan began.

Annabel nodded, unable to help but recall the twinkle in his mother's eyes as she insisted her send-off include lots of reminiscing, cheering, and dancing. Because that's what she and Dan's father would be doing as they looked down on everyone, she'd said. There was to be none of this morbid rubbish, as she put it.

'Well she wanted it to be more than that,' Dan continued. 'She wanted it to be a celebration of the future too.' He paused. 'Not just for me, but for us, Annabel.'

'You're all probably going to think this is a bit weird on a day like this,' he carried on, now glancing round at the three of them. 'But Mum had such a unique way of looking at the world compared to most. And no matter what, she could always turn a negative into a positive.'

Annabel had to agree. In the short time she had known his mother, this was certainly a quality she'd come to recognise.

'And she was right to think like that,' said Dan. 'Like she always said, life's too short for anything else.'

'Here, here,' said Rebecca.

'Anyway, I know that if I don't do this now, today will forever be marked with sadness, something Mum definitely wouldn't want.'

He turned to Annabel, her heart suddenly leaping thanks to the way he now looked at her. His gaze had become so intense and his face so full of love, she began to blush. 'What's going on?' she asked.

She took in his shaking hands as he reached into his pocket, her pulse racing even faster as she watched him get down on one knee.

Surely not. He can't be.

'Annabel,' he said. 'Will you marry me?'

Dan produced a ring from his pocket; Annabel stared at the diamond before her. Such was her surprise, she couldn't bring herself to speak.

'It was mum's,' said Dan. 'She wanted you to have it.'

A tear rolled down her face as she looked from the ring, to Dan, and then to her sister and friend. Much to her surprise, tears rolled down their faces too as they willed her to say something.

Annabel couldn't help but smile as she imagined his mother and father looking down on them, excitedly awaiting her response. But she knew they weren't the only ones. Tom was with them, readily giving his blessing too.

She took in Dan's hopeful expression. The love she felt for this man suddenly making her heart fit to burst.

'Yes,' she said.

Her sister and friend gasped, the delight written all over Dan's face said more than words ever could.

'I'd be honoured to marry you.'

THE END

A NOTE FROM BOMBSHELL BOOKS

Thanks for reading The Trouble With Words We hope you enjoyed it as much as we did. Please consider leaving a review on Amazon or Goodreads to help others find and enjoy this book too.

We make every effort to ensure that books are carefully edited and proofread, however occasionally mistakes do slip through. If you spot something, please do send details to info@ bombshellbooks.com and we can amend it.

Bombshell Books specialise in women's fiction. We regularly have special offers including free and discounted eBooks. To be the first to hear about these special offers, why not join our mailing list here? We won't send you more than two emails per month and we'll never pass your details on to anybody else.

Readers who enjoyed The Trouble With Words will also enjoy

The Queen of Blogging by Therese Loreskar

Holding Myself by Victoria.

ACKNOWLEDGEMENTS

A big thank you goes to Jeannette Prescott, a lovely lady who willingly relived her story to help me write mine. I'd also like to thank Linda Balis for advising me when it came to all things flora and fauna. If I didn't know anything about flowers before, I do now.

A massive thank you goes to everyone at Bombshell Books. It's been an absolute pleasure working with you all.

A very special thank you goes to Robert, my husband, whose unwavering support has made my writing journey possible. And to Adam and Ben, my reasons for writing to begin with.

Lastly, I'd like to say thank you to all you readers out there. When the going gets tough, you are the ones who keep me going.